"*Suddenly Forever* is a heart-achingly poignant story filled with lyrical prose and enchanting imagery. It's a beautifully written tale of friendship, love, and hope that conquers the deepest grief. This long-awaited return to Laurel Cove will immediately pull the reader into a delightful community populated with lively characters and descriptions so vivid, you'll long to visit in real life."

Jaycee Weaver, author of *Whatever Happens Next*

"Teresa Tysinger takes the reader on a heart-tugging journey of grief and the beauty of hope in *Suddenly Forever*. Luke and Cora's story will have you reaching for the tissues, praying as if they're real, and praising the balm new love brings."

Toni Shiloh, author of the *Faith and Fortune Series*

SUDDENLY Forever

Happy Reading!

Teresa Tysinger

Teresa Tysinger

© 2020 Teresa Tysinger

Published by Good Day Publishing
Fort Worth, Texas 76109
http://teresatysinger.com

All rights reserved.

ISBN: 978-0-9990209-2-0

Non-commercial uses may reproduce portions of this book (not to exceed 250 words) without the express written consent of Good Day Publishing.

Commercial Uses: No part of this book may be reproduced in any form, stored in a retrieval system, or transmitted in any form by any means—electronic, photocopy, recording, or otherwise—without prior written permission of the publisher. The only exception is brief quotations in printed reviews.

This is a work of fiction. Any name, characters, and incidents are all products of the author's imagination or are used for fictional purposes. Any mentioned brands, places, and trade marks remain property of their respective owners, have no association with the author or publisher, and are used strictly for fictional purposes.

Scripture quotations are taken from the New Revised Standard Version – NRSV Standard Version, Copyright 2011. Used by permission by HarperCollins Publishers. All rights reserved.

Cover design by Teresa Tysinger
Images from Unsplash.com

FOR ERIC

How do I not dedicate this book to
the person who enthusiastically
brainstormed for countless hours
to help make it the best
it can be? Thanks for being so
invested in me. I love you.

When we lose someone we love
we must learn
not to live without them,
but to live
with the love they left behind.

Anonymous

CHAPTER One

*G*rief was like a shipwreck, surrounding you with a chaos of debris on unrelenting waves. Sometimes shards hit you square on, inflicting fresh pain as you worked tirelessly to tread water. Other times, bits floated by as a reminder of the beautiful vessel that once was. Eventually, the wreckage would settle in its resting place on the calm, dark ocean floor. It became unseen, but never forgotten and never really gone—leaving you at the merciless surface to drown or fight to survive.

Cora Bradford gulped for air, arms flailing in the dark abyss of her A-frame bedroom. Beads of sweat cooled her skin as she rushed to the window and fought with the latch. Just as suffocation threatened, her lungs filled with the crisp autumn air.

Not again.

Once her breath returned to a natural cadence, she sat on the window seat and gazed out over the black water. A faint yellow glow outlined the mountains to the east. Her eyes followed the rise and fall of the peaks, inhaling on the climb and exhaling on the descent. She'd do it as many times as it took for her mind to give up the visions from her dream.

The cabin's wooden floors creaked underfoot as she collected her worn flannel robe and headed down the stairs. She moved around the kitchen in a sequence of slow choreographed moves.

Place full kettle on stove. Turn knob on. Place tea bag in mug. Wait.

The only light came from a dim bulb over the stove. Leaning against the counter, she stared through the darkness of the adjoining dining area, past the sprawling deck, and again to the mountains. Her heart longed for the light of day, ached for it. The darkness often brought nightmares, inhabited by ghosts Cora both feared to see *and* to forget.

A low whistle sounded, and she turned to finish her pre-dawn dance.

Turn knob off. Pour water over tea bag. Stir in sugar, tap spoon three times, and place on spoon rest. These small routines saved her.

Cora stepped out onto the deck and let the brisk early-October air welcome her. Another week and she'd have to pull out her long wool sweater. Leaves and pebbles crunched under her feet as she made her way down the path to the lakeshore. She tipped a low-seated chair, letting dried leaves scatter to the ground.

The sound of the geese overhead pulled her eyes skyward as she sat. A line of them came into view, silhouetted against the faint glow of the coming dawn. It was her therapy to catalog the details of life around her. The gentle lapping of the lake water against the shore. The spired tops of pine trees enveloping her from every other side. The damp earthiness of already-fallen leaves working their way into the rich soil. Each detail filled her mind and inched out the tortured visions.

She lifted the mug, steam warming her nose as she watched the golden glow at the horizon increase its victory over the expiring night.

Then, uninvited, the deafening sound of steel scraping against steel returned. Cora's eyes slammed shut. Her head spun as weightlessness followed by the harsh return of gravity racked her body. The metallic taste of blood. The screams. The eventual silence.

She jumped to wobbly legs as hot tea rained on her lap, mug teetering precariously in trembling hands.

God, make it stop.

Open your eyes, Cora.

Panting, she willed her eyes to open and find the horizon. Inhale on the climb...exhale on the descent. She returned again and again to the left of the mountains as if returning her old typewriter carriage for a new line. By the time her heartrate and breath returned to normal rhythms, various shades of blue joined the tapestry in the sky. Faint lines, now visible on the lake's surface, revealed gentle ripples.

A small shadow materialized in the middle of the lake. Squinting, Cora tried to make out its shape. After a moment, it morphed into what almost looked like a person rowing a kayak. Her eyes darted left then right, as though searching for someone to confirm what she was seeing. But no one had been on the lake in more than three years, and even then, never before sunrise. She scanned the water again, sweeping twice before finding the shape as it disappeared into the still-dark cove at the left side of the lake.

Cora looked to her mug and found the tea bag sitting in a puddle of remaining water. She turned, glancing over her shoulder toward the cove before making the gradual climb up back to the cabin for a refill. She stepped up onto the deck and turned once again to face the lake, its reflection matching the brightening sky. A breeze whipped through her hair and threadbare robe, prickling her skin.

The unexpected kayaker, if that's what the shape had been, meant someone was nearby. Her stomach knotted. Who would be out here at this time of day? These parts of Laurel Cove, North Carolina, on the far outskirts of town, had few residents. The woods on her right drew her gaze. In fact, Ina McLean's cottage, a half mile down the road in that direction, was the only other home on the lake road. Except for...

She faced the tight bundle of spruce pines at her left. Through those woods, down the road about a quarter mile, another cabin nestled on the shore of the cove. It had sat empty since Ellie Bassett passed away a few years ago. Even though she was a seasonal resident only for the summer and fall months, Ellie had been a friendly addition to the lake's tiny community.

Cora tilted her head, tracing the wisps of pink cloud now visible. She'd seen no For Sale sign posted at the hidden driveway of Ellie's property. Ina hadn't said anything, and if someone would have news of a new neighbor it would be her. There had been no unfamiliar cars driving down the road, no trash set out—nothing.

But would she have noticed if there had been? She wasn't the most observant, except when a moment of panic dictated it.

Cora shuddered against another brisk wind and retreated inside to the warmth. After a quick change into dry pants, she refilled her mug, bobbing the tea bag before discarding it into the sink, then sat down at the small desk tucked under the staircase. As the white glow of the laptop filled the small space, her eyes were drawn yet again to the lake. The sun finally crested over the horizon and announced the arrival of day. Night was over.

A shallow sigh escaped. She entered her password and navigated to her email—the main contact she had with the outside world. Her eyes scanned the bolded new messages, landing on two at the bottom of the short list.

FROM: HARRY BRADFORD
SUBJECT: THINKING OF YOU

FROM: GAIL FREIDMAN
SUBJECT: CONTRACT OFFER (AGAIN)

She closed the laptop and stood, the legs of the chair scratching along the wooden floor. Those emails had sat in her inbox for over a week, *unopened*. Maybe today, she'd read them. Maybe not. She reached for her mug and noticed the calendar hanging on the paneled wall of the staircase. Next to three boxes marked with X was October 4.

Cora buckled under an intense weight, her breath suspended. She braced herself with both hands on the edge of the desk for a long moment. *There's more than a month to go. It's too early to give in to it. Breathe.*

Her hands felt blindly along the wall, atop the curved cap of the banister, and up the smooth handrail of the staircase to the doorway of her room. She crawled under the rumpled covers and begged sleep to take her away. But all she found was the wreckage of her life pulsing like sonar from the dark depths. So, as she had learned to do, she'd hold on—for dear life—to whatever debris she could find until this storm passed.

"All right, let's see what we got." Luke Bassett ruffled the head of Toby, the black Labrador next to him on the couch. Staring at the small viewfinder on his DSLR camera, Luke scrolled through the dozens of shots he'd taken that morning and studied the balance of composition, contrast, and exposure.

He turned the screen toward his attentive companion. "What about this one? The outline of the mountains really pops against that faint line of yellow."

The dog cocked his head sharply to the right.

"You're a tough critic."

Toby's head tilted to the left.

Luke sighed and set the camera down on the cushion, rising to his feet. With a thud and jingle of his shiny new tags, Toby followed him into the kitchen. Only four days together and the dog had learned quickly where his food was kept. Luke filled a bowl on the floor next to the fridge with kibble.

"Sit."

Toby blinked, tail wagging furiously.

"Toby, sit!"

The dog lowered his head and stepped backward a few paces.

Luke crouched and reached out a hand. The guy at the rescue had said a firm voice helped with training, but when Toby gave him those puppy dog eyes, all bets on best practices were off. "Aw, boy. We're just a pair of gun-shy fellas, aren't we?"

He picked up and shook the bowl, smiling at Toby before returning it to its spot next to a matching bowl of water. Toby's tail resumed its back-and-forth rhythm. Maybe Luke's furry companion was like him and needed time to come to terms with a new situation. Let it sink in.

Luke stood and turned to the chrome espresso machine on the counter next to the small sink. It barely fit. He pulled a mug with hand-painted blue flowers on the side from the high cabinet and readied the machine. As it whirred to life, he took in his new surroundings.

It was a good thing that the espresso machine was one of the few things he'd decided to have shipped from his apartment in Boston. It was hard to imagine his modern art and sleek furniture inside the log cabin's natural aesthetic. And judging by the few times he'd been into town, he probably could have left behind the Brooks Brothers suit and silk ties hanging in the bedroom closet.

The machine hissed as it finished. Luke poured the espresso into the mug and topped it with frothy milk. He'd definitely missed his daily latte while on the road this past year. He stepped out onto the deck and leaned on the wooden rail with both arms. The early morning sun, now fully risen over the mountains on the far side of the lake, warmed his face.

His mom had only brought him and his sister, Rachel, to the cabin in North Carolina during the summer. The beauty of the place in the fall was alarmingly gorgeous, and that was saying something. At one time or another in the last twenty years, he'd travelled to just about every continent during every season. But there was something uniquely mesmerizing about the vibrant confetti of golds, reds, and oranges scattered among the reliable evergreens.

He looked down into the creamy mug, a weight settling deep inside. He should have come a few falls ago when his mom had first invited him. But the life of a photojournalist was not suited for taking a week off on a whim.

She'd died a month later.

Heaviness filled his heart. Scratches sounded behind him, and Luke turned to find Toby squeezing his belly through the small crack in the sliding glass door.

"Maybe we should both work on patience next." Toby's tongue left cold slobber on Luke's hand. The dog then froze at attention, focused on a squirrel rooting around in the leaf-covered yard just several feet away. "Don't even think—"

Before Luke had the chance to utter the entire command, Toby shot off the deck, crunchy leaves flying in his wake as he chased the squirrel toward the lakeshore. Luke hung his head for a brief moment before running after them. Saving wildlife from the jaws of his new best friend wasn't his idea of idyllic pet ownership. The chase ended with Toby barking up a tree on the righthand side of the yard just before the short bank dropped off into the dark water.

Luke grabbed ahold of Toby's collar and pulled. "That's enough, killer. Squirrels are our friends, not food."

After several pulls, the dog finally gave up and came back down to all fours. He now seemed content with sniffing the damp ground. Luke released his grip and gazed out over the water, past the cove to the A-frame cabin several hundred yards down the shore. He'd been in town just several days, but from what he remembered of Laurel Cove, it seemed the type of town where neighbors knew one another. Each night he'd seen lights on, so maybe he'd head over later and say hello.

What else was there to do? The fallout from last year's fast-paced campaign trail still burned. It's what had ultimately led him here, desperate for a change. *Be patient, man. You've not even been here a week.* He'd come for peace and something else maybe. He wasn't sure yet. It eluded him like a taunting whisper through a maze. So far, he'd just found boredom.

Rap. Rap. Rap.

Cora flinched, then drifted back to sleep.

Rap. Rap. Rap.

She startled, sat straight up in bed, and fixed her eyes on the open door of her bedroom. Was someone knocking? Ina always called if she needed something. There was even a note next to her door asking for deliveries to simply be left behind the wooden porch column.

Rap. Rap. Rap.

Cora's heart quickened. She stood, gathered the robe she already had on with its dangling belt, and started slowly down the stairs. Part way down, she stopped and bent until the windowpane in the top half of the front door came into view. Sharp light flooded through the wavy glass, revealing only a shadowy figure. How long had she slept? If the front of the house was sunny, that meant it was well into the afternoon.

Rap. Rap. Rap.

Good grief. She stomped down the remaining steps, turned the dead bolt, and yanked the door open.

"What is it?" she barked.

The shadowed figure stilled then stepped back. She winked an eye shut and raised a hand to shield the sun.

"I'm, uh...sorry if I disturbed you." A man's voice spoke.

There was something familiar about it. Cora feverishly blinked, her eyes unable to adjust with the bright light behind the mysterious man. She stepped out onto the porch and pulled the door shut behind her. As she moved to the side to find the shade of one of the thick columns, she bumped into him. He grabbed her shoulders firmly to steady them both, and her face pressed against his chest. He must be well over six feet tall.

Her throat snarled out a grunt, and she pushed against him with flat palms, setting a good five feet between them. "What exactly *are* you doing?"

He threw up his hands. "Listen, I'm so sorry. I just wanted to stop by and introduce myself."

"Why?" Even to her, it sounded like a snarl.

Her eyes finally focused. His face was serious, emphasized by a chiseled jawline and square chin covered in light scruff. But he was otherwise clean cut, with what looked like freshly trimmed and styled hair, dark except for where it grayed at the temples.

His thin lips pressed together as he gestured behind her. "I just moved in down the road."

She crossed her arms, fingernails pressing tightly into her skin through her robe and pajama shirt. She'd been right. There *had* been someone on the lake this morning. She shifted her bare feet on the cold stone. "Okay."

He studied her longer than felt necessary. "Okay. Well, I don't want to keep you."

"Great." She stepped back into the amber sunlight, twisted the doorknob, and started inside.

His steps creaked on the wooden boards of the steps off the porch. "Oh, by the way, my name's..."

The door slammed shut behind her, and she leaned against it letting out a moan. Her head rolled to one side, and she found her reflection in a small mirror on the wall of the entryway. She didn't even recognize the woman staring back at her with stringy hair and dark circles under lifeless eyes.

Cora looked around the cabin, particles floating in the rays of light coming through the door. The clock under the television read 6:38. Again, as had happened so many days in the weeks that immediately followed the accident, the sun had made an entire trip from east to west without her knowing it. This time, more than six months had passed since she'd had to escape her grief in this way. But she'd felt its slow crescendo the last few weeks. She always did when the anniversary neared.

Two years, ten months, two weeks, three days, one hour, and four minutes ago her life changed forever. When it was mercilessly split into *before* and *after*.

Luke craned over his shoulder at the cabin as he neared the end of the driveway. He shook his head and broke into a jog as he turned to the right toward his place. That had gone quite different than he'd expected when he'd decided to stop by toward the end of his evening run. Maybe things here weren't much different than in the city, where people liked to be left alone. But it was as though he'd woken her. Maybe she was a night-shift nurse or something. Still, something told him that wasn't the case.

Despite his neighbor's disheveled appearance, he could tell she was naturally beautiful. Porcelain skin, full pink lips, astonishing eyes the color of the waters of the reefs in the South Pacific, and an unusual scar that ran from the corner of her left eye down to the center of her cheek.

He'd made a career of quickly noting details worth documenting. And yet, her wavy blond hair fell in uncombed, wild strands around her face. Her clothing, even her robe, was wrinkled. He hadn't caught her at her best—bad luck for him.

Luke moved to the narrow shoulder as a car approached behind him. A 1990s white Cadillac rolled to stop at his side. An elderly woman barely tall enough to see over the steering wheel rolled down the passenger window.

She pushed her rather large glasses up on the bridge of her nose and looked him up and down. "Are you Lucas Bassett?"

He walked to the car, leaning forward to peer in the window. "I am. Just moved in down the road a few days ago."

Her wild, bushy white eyebrows rose into high arches. "I'm not sure how you got past me. I usually know everything that's going on around these parts."

"Well, I guess I'm pretty good at keeping a low profile." He chuckled.

Her eyes narrowed, full round cheeks falling in a frown. "I don't like that. Can't trust a man who feels the need to hide."

"Well, that's not what I meant, Ms....?"

"It's *Mrs.* Ina McLean. I live down past Mrs. Bradford." She poked a thumb over her shoulder.

Hmm. His closest neighbor was married, too. He'd only seen one car, and no one else had seemed to be home.

Mrs. McLean cleared her throat. "We've been the only ones on this lake for years. You best mind your manners."

"I intend to." Luke stood as the car began creeping forward inch by inch. "By the way, how did you know my name?"

The car lurched to a full stop, and the tip of a white envelope appeared out of the window. "Our postman is lousy and mixes up mail all the time. This was in my box."

Luke took it, glancing at the return address. His jaw tensed. Before he could thank her, she sped off. He watched her quickly maneuver the car onto his driveway, reverse it, then turn back for the direction from which she'd come. He waved and smiled as she passed, but she didn't even look his way.

What a day for bad first impressions.

He tucked the envelope into his jacket and trotted the last hundred feet before turning onto the long drive up to his cabin, leaves crunching with each step. Speaking of first impressions, Luke had loved this place at first sight. As a kid, on the first day of every trip he'd tell his mom that it looked just like his Lincoln Logs. He'd spend all summer building and rebuilding a replica on the deck.

He came to a stop next to his truck, hands on his hips. Yeah, it had definitely seen better days. Weeds made it hard to know exactly where parking was intended. Along the front porch, he couldn't tell where one shrub stopped and another began. Tentacles of a greedy vine covered one window and had begun to creep over the ledge of the roof.

How was he supposed to fix the yard? He'd never even mown a lawn. His father had always paid someone to do the landscaping. Luke could certainly afford to pay someone from town to come and clean up the place. But it could also be a great project to occupy his time and mind.

The envelope. He pulled it out from his pocket and read over the sender's address again. He drew in a deep breath and fixed his eyes on the tips of tall trees behind the cabin. They glowed a fiery red in the late evening sun. If recent experience told him anything, nothing good came from his lawyers.

CHAPTER Two

Cora woke the next morning to sunlight streaming through her bedroom window. A full night of restful sleep brought energy and clarity. She knew, though, the two things were likely making cameo appearances, not here to stay as supporting roles. Still, she welcomed the better day and would ride the calm waves while they lasted.

Showered and dressed, she took a seat at the desk. She opened her email and studied the two messages she'd been avoiding. Chewing on a nail, she rolled the mouse with the other hand to hover over the one from Harry. Her hand trembled. No, she wasn't ready. Instead, she clicked on the email from Gail, her agent of more than a decade, and scanned the lines.

Cora:

I hope this note finds you well. As your friend, I know this time of year can be tough for you. All of us here think of you often. As your agent, I'm passing along two bits of business that really need your attention:
1. An updated offer from the studio for the movie option is attached. They apparently took your putting them off as a negotiation tactic. It's more than an excellent offer. They want an answer by the end of October. Review it and let me know if you have any questions.
2. Random House called. They're talking about revisiting your contract if you don't have any projects in the works. We need to discuss this sooner than later.

Let's schedule a call for October 5. I'll give you a ring late in the morning.

All my best,
G.F.

Cora darted her eyes to the calendar on the wall behind the desk. That was today. The clock in the upper right corner of her laptop read 9:50AM. She bounded up the stairs to grab her phone from her bedside table. No missed calls.

It really was ridiculous how Cora avoided even the people who'd been the most supportive, both before and after. Gail was one of those people. She'd negotiated the sale of Cora's very first novel to Random House thirteen years ago, when Cora was a determined twenty-three-year-old fresh out of

Harvard. Following the wild success of that first book, Gail had orchestrated a multi-title deal. Today, Cora had twelve best-sellers and was a household name among mystery writers—thanks, in no small part, to Gail and her team. Now, Cora avoided her emails. She shoved the phone in the back pocket of her jeans.

Downstairs, Cora ran her hand over the spines of her books, lined up on the floor-to-ceiling shelf in the living room. She tipped the black spine of *Stranger Times*, her latest release, and turned the book over in her hands. She'd returned the final edits to her editor, putting the book to bed, just two days before the accident. It had released the following year. Cora had cancelled all of her appearances and interviews to help promote it, but even so, the book went on to become her biggest seller and was the novel the studio was shopping to turn into a movie.

The buzz of her phone startled her, and she dropped the book then fumbled to answer. "Yes, hello?"

"Hello, Cora dear."

Cora flopped onto the couch, sighing. "Oh, good morning, Ina."

"You usually call me before running into town on Sundays. Something come up yesterday, or did you forget about this poor old woman?"

Cora felt a small smile pull at one corner of her mouth as she envisioned the impish grin creeping across her neighbor's wrinkled face. "I didn't go. It was one of those days."

"Oh." The woman's voice softened. "I'm terribly sorry, dear. In bed all day or mad and worked up?"

Cora winced at her predictability. Ina had endured more with her in the last few years than anyone else. "Slept."

A soft, understanding moan flowed through the receiver. "Anything I can do?"

Cora ached for motherly, or grandmotherly, arms to envelop her. She only had bandwidth, however, to grieve one lost family at a time. She stiffened, sitting up to the edge of the couch. "Thank you, but today's better. I plan to make a quick trip later on. What did you need?"

"Just milk, bread, and bananas. And since it's Monday, would you mind running by the pharmacy too?" Ina took no fewer than half a dozen prescriptions, double the amount since before Charles died two months ago.

"Sure, no problem." Cora scribbled the list of items on the bottom of a pad lying on the coffee table. A tone alerted her to another incoming call: Gail Friedman. "Ina, my agent is calling. I've got to run. I'll be by no later than five."

"Thank you, dear. We've got some catching up to do. Bye now."

Cora took a deep breath and pressed the button on the screen to swap calls. "Hi, Gail."

"Cora. It's good to hear your voice. How are you?" Gail's voice was refined, slow and methodical as if she considered every word carefully before speaking it.

"I'm okay." Cora crossed the room to her desk. "How are things in New York?"

"Work is extremely busy, actually, but going well. In fact, I've only got about ten minutes before running out for a big pitch. Do you mind if I cut to the chase?" Gail was unfailing in her efficiency.

Cora's stomach twisted. Her unreliable communication these past three years must have driven Gail crazy. She grabbed for the papers coming from her printer. "Yes, of course, please do."

Gail cleared her throat. "First, I'm going to trust you to review the offer from the studio. The pressing matter is about your contract with Random House."

The knots in Cora's stomach tightened.

Gail continued. "It's been almost three years since *Stranger Times* published. No one questioned granting an extension for the next title following the accident. They even did an unprecedented favor by publishing new editions of your early works. At this point, however, they need to know what's next."

Cora swallowed hard and licked her lips. "Okay."

"They're proposing two options. First, they're willing to revise your current contract to include two new titles, with the next manuscript due in no more than nine months."

Her current contract included five as-yet-unwritten novels. She leaned back in her chair, eyes falling to the book she'd dropped. It still lay upside down on the woven carpet. "Or?"

"Or..." Gail paused uncharacteristically. "Or they cancel the contract."

Cora stood, walked to the back door, and stared out over the sparkling lake. She'd known this was coming at some point, in some form. But knowing didn't stop it from hurting. "When do they need to know?"

"This Friday."

Leaves danced in a line all the way across the yard. Cora sighed as she watched the same wind travel across the lake in snaking ripples. "Let me give it some thought, and I'll call you by Thursday."

"Good. Just know that if you sign a revised contract next week, they'll want a synopsis by mid-November."

The women exchanged brief pleasantries before hanging up. Alone again in the quiet cabin, Cora rubbed both hands up and down her face. It struck her how there were so many double-edged swords with grief. Remembering always restored wounds to as fresh as the day they were inflicted, but forgetting was scarier than remembering. In this case, the frivolity of writing mysteries felt irreverent to her grief. Yet, if she didn't, it felt like turning her back on the one thing God had put her on earth to do. She was pulled in two directions—between devotion to the past and longing for what could be.

"I signed a non-disclosure agreement at the beginning of the campaign. I haven't made one single comment. He's the one who can't keep his mouth shut about this." Luke paced the length of the creaking deck, Toby a shadow behind every step.

His lawyer, Paul Holman, sighed through the receiver. "Listen, once Dennison's original statement on the photos was published in the New York Times, he did no fewer than two dozen interviews. His people know you've been extended the same invitations. They're just making sure you won't find a way around this and add fuel to the firestorm."

Luke stopped and Toby ran into the back of his knee. He turned for the unfolded letter on top of the deck railing and picked it up, shaking the paper in the air as if gesturing to a jury. "Believe me, if I had a hose long enough, I'd put out this ridiculous fire myself. I'm not signing anything else—the First Amendment still stands, last I checked—but feel free to also tell them I've moved to a rural town where reporters won't find me."

Paul's laugh was hearty and long. "Well, you don't need my counsel. Consider it done. How is it up there in the sticks anyways?"

Luke's posture relaxed as he took in the scenic autumn day. The glassy lake reflected the multi-colored forest surrounding it. Somewhere nearby, maybe at one of his neighbors' homes, a woodfire burned. "It's actually exactly what I needed, Paul. Really serene."

"Serenity is definitely a far cry from the Dennison for President campaign. What do you do all day long?"

Luke wrinkled his nose at the rusty rake and shears that he'd found in the shed, leaning against the side of the cabin. "If you'll believe it, I'm heading into town in just a bit to get some yard tools. The place needs a good clean up."

"I can see the headline now: *Pulitzer Prize-winning Photojournalist Luke Bassett Finally Domesticated.*" Paul snickered.

"Laugh all you want." Luke patted Toby's head and watched a hawk glide high over the water. "There's something peaceful about this place. Maybe the work will keep my mind off of everything."

"I get needing some anonymity after what you've been through. But moving to some cabin in the woods still seems extreme. Thoreau lived alone in nature for two years, two months, and two days. Promise me you won't be gone that long."

Luke smiled and glanced over his shoulder to the cabin, imagining the copy of *Walden* sitting on the coffee table inside. "I'm not looking to devise any dissertations on ethics out here. There's just got to be more to life than chasing the next story or the next award. I've seen it in people's expressions and reactions through the lens for years. I want..." Luke's heart knocked hard against his chest. "I *need* to figure out what that looks like, and could mean, when there's no camera between me and the world."

The ringing of a landline telephone sounded in the background of Paul's office. "That's another client. Listen, I'll get word back to Dennison's people and be in touch. Oh, and add gloves to your list. Got to protect those baby-soft hands."

"Very funny. Bye."

Luke disconnected the call then opened his list app and scrolled through the things he needed to get from town. Rake and shears, of course. Lawnmower, trimmer, shovel, contractor bags, wheelbarrow. At the end of the list he entered gloves. Paul might have been teasing him, but it was an item Luke hadn't thought to add.

Another whiff of burning wood traveled past on the breeze, sending Toby's nose to the sky twitching. He couldn't imagine old Mrs. McLean throwing logs on a fire. Though gruff and spunky, her frame was small and frail. And when she'd extended the letter to him, it'd visibly shaken in her unsteady hand. Was the fire coming from Mrs. Bradford's home then? Maybe that meant she was having a better day, up and about during the daytime hours. He hoped so.

You hope so? Luke shook his head and slid his phone into his back pocket.

Meeting his neighbors had been unpleasant, for him and them. Yet here he was wondering about them both—their habits, limitations and abilities, moods. He'd wondered about many people after he'd photographed them over the years. The malnourished children in Africa. The prisoner of war with empty eyes who'd just returned to the States. Still, it surprised him that these relative strangers stirred such curiosity.

Luke retreated into the house and picked up *Walden*, flipping through its worn and dogeared pages for a particular passage. After searching a few moments, he found it and read aloud:

"But man's capacities have never been measured; nor are we to judge of what he can do by any precedents, so little have been tried."

He closed the book and looked down at Toby by his side, eyes attentive. Had he come to Laurel Cove to change? To be tried? To grow? Or could capacities he already possessed, such as empathy, be more awakened in this serene place?

Cora was the only person walking through the open-air farmers market, except for a young man in a dark green apron stocking pears a few rows over. She may consider making Mondays her day to come into town if it meant encountering fewer folks like today.

"Finding everything you need, Ms. Bradford?"

The basket fell from Cora's hands, sending apples rolling in every direction. "Oh, I'm sorry. You startled me."

Handy Peterson, the gray-haired owner of the market, bent to retrieve the basket and rogue produce. His smile was kind as he wiped an apple across the front of his apron. "Didn't mean to spook ya. This one got bruised. Let's get you a new one."

Cora just wanted to get in and get out. She crossed her arms and followed him back to where the apples lay in neat rows. He placed three fresh ones in the wire basket and handed it back to her.

"There you go. Threw in a few extra." He winked, then looked past her to the check-out counter and hollered, "Hey, Marie! Just charge this little lady for a half-dozen apples. The others are on the house."

"That's not necessary, but thank you." Cora took the basket and forced a smile before she started for the bananas at the end of the next row.

"Uh, excuse me."

The voice from a woman standing somewhere behind Cora was familiarly tentative. *Just great.* Cora tightened her grip on the bunch of bananas she'd just reached for before turning around.

"You're not Paige Price, are you?" The young woman's eyes were bright with expectancy and excitement.

Cora pressed her lips into a tight smile. "Yes, I am."

"Oh, my gosh. Me and my best friend just love your books, Ms. Price. She's not going to believe this. I mean, I knew you lived somewhere around here, but I never thought I'd be lucky enough to run into you. I live over in Boone and was just passing through. Man, I sure wish I had my copy of *Stranger Times* with me for you to sign."

Cora nodded, noticing the chatty woman clutching her cell phone. "Maybe next time."

Then the inevitable happened.

"Could I maybe get a picture with you?"

No way, not today. "I'm actually in a rush to get somewhere. But thanks for saying hi." Cora dropped the bananas in her basket and rushed toward the check-out counter, swallowing past a lump in her throat.

Running into fans was the one thing Cora dreaded most about coming into town. It hadn't always been that way, though. She used to thrive in the spotlight, coming alive at book readings, launch parties, talk shows, awards dinners, and even when fans approached her on the street. Since the accident, though, Cora just couldn't muster the energy to match the excitement of a fan.

Cora set her basket down at the checkout counter and glanced over her shoulder at the woman now browsing shelves of bread packaged in plastic wrap. Before, disappointing a fan would nag at her insides. Now she gladly rode a wave of relief back to comfortable isolation.

"It's been a while since someone recognized you, honey. You okay?" Marie, Handy's wife, didn't look up as she cataloged the contents of Cora's basket and punched buttons on an old register.

"Oh, I'm fine." That persistent lump in her throat said otherwise.

"That'll be seven dollars even." Marie's chubby fingers were warm around Cora's when she handed the woman a few bills. "I know it's hard. We sure do miss seeing you out with your fella."

Cora let her hand linger in Marie's for a moment before pulling back. "Thanks, Marie. But I'm really fine." The words were strained as her throat ached to hold back tears.

Right after the accident, people she didn't even know would sometimes hug her and cry. She did *not* need grieving to be a community effort. Before long, Cora stopped going out except when absolutely necessary. Ina had once encouraged her to see the townspeople's displays of sympathy as respect for someone many of them knew and loved too. Cora would keep trying to see it that way instead of an intrusion on her private grieving.

With the bag of produce in her arms, she headed for the gravel parking lot just as a black pickup rolled to a stop alongside her SUV. She kept her head down, fishing for her keys in the small purse she wore across her.

"Mrs. Bradford?"

Again, Cora prickled. *What now?* She looked up to find her new neighbor standing between her and the cars. How did he know her name? He was dressed in jeans and a gray sweatshirt with Boston University in red across the chest. That explained why his voice had sounded familiar. He was from her hometown.

"Oh, hello." She shifted the brown paper bag holding her produce to her hip and focused on the group of kids on the school playground across the street.

"Hey, I'm sorry again if I caught you at a bad time yesterday."

Cora reluctantly met his gaze and found kind, caramel-brown eyes. She hadn't noticed their color before. Why was he sorry? She was the one who had been so rude. "It's fine. Don't worry about it."

"I'm Luke Bassett, by the way." He extended a hand.

His hand was large and warm around hers. "Cora Bradford."

He nodded softly. "Yes, Mrs. McLean mentioned your name yesterday when she brought me a piece of mail. It's nice to formally meet you."

She started for her car, the headlights blinking as she pressed the fob.

"I'm pretty sure I made a bad first impression on Ina, too," he called after her.

He'd sure made the rounds. Cora set the bag in the passenger seat then walked over to the driver's side. "Ina's tough on the outside, but harmless. See you later."

"Yeah, see you around."

Luke's mouth turned up on one side, and he waved as she bent to get in the car. She lifted the strap of her purse over her head, setting it next to the grocery bag, and pushed the key into the ignition. When she looked up, he was still watching her. She gave a quick wave and put the car in reverse. Gravel crunched under her tires as she pulled out onto the road.

There was something about the way her new neighbor studied her that made Cora's pulse quicken. It was different than the anxiety she'd grown so accustomed to—not so frightening. But it was familiar and *almost* intriguing.

Luke watched Cora's navy-blue SUV until it turned left at the traffic light. He wouldn't say their second meeting was a smash hit, but it was a far cry from yesterday's disaster.

She'd looked so different from the day before that he'd had to take a second glance before addressing her. The woman he'd met today was dressed smartly in a white collared shirt under a snug-fitting black sweater, and jeans. Her long, honey-colored hair was still wavy but gathered neatly behind her with a black ribbon.

He made his way toward the produce stand, replaying one part of their brief conversation. She'd said that Ina was tough on the outside but harmless. He couldn't help but wonder if the same could be said about Cora. Yesterday, she'd been downright gruff. Today, while not exactly cheery, she had been less combative, a bit softer. If he had to put a word to it, he'd say that she'd seemed guarded. It wasn't a stretch to see how someone wary, for whatever reason, could be pushed to aggression.

Luke stepped under the corrugated steel roof of the farmers market and let his eyes adjust to the shade.

"Welcome to Handy's Market. I'm Handy. Looking for anything in particular?" A man with thinning gray hair smiled at him, holding a produce box full of yellow squash.

Luke scanned the rows of wooden tables holding everything from pumpkins and gourds of all shapes and sizes, to apples, greens, onions, and potatoes. "I was just driving by and thought I'd stop in to see what you have, but thanks."

"You passing through on a drive up the Parkway? We get lots of visitors wanting to catch a peep of the leaves this time of year." Handy set the box down and started stacking the squash on a table nearby.

"Actually, I just moved into a place up at the lake east of town," Luke said.

Handy's eyebrows arched and he nodded. "Did you now? I know it's pretty secluded up there. You must have bought Ellie's place."

Luke's mouth dropped open. "Uh, yeah. Ellie was my mom. You knew her?"

The man perked and slapped Luke on the shoulder as if welcoming a friend. "Well, I declare! If that don't just beat all. Ellie was a faithful customer. Came by all the time. In fact, she and Marie got to be friends over the years of her visiting." He turned and called to a rather large woman sitting behind a counter on the far side of the market. "Marie, this is Ellie's boy!"

Luke and Handy walked to meet the woman who labored on swollen legs toward the center of the place. Her rosy cheeks nearly pushed her eyes shut when she smiled at Luke. "Your mama talked about you and your sister all the time. We sure were sad to lose her." Marie grabbed for one of Luke's hands and held it in both of hers, patting the top with cool, pudgy fingers.

Luke sighed and smiled. "It's sure nice to know she had some good friends here in Laurel Cove. She loved this place."

Handy reached an arm around Marie's broad shoulders, clicking his tongue and shaking his head. "Strange, really. I saw you chatting with your neighbor before you came in. It's sort of odd that the only three people living up at the lake have all lost loved ones."

Luke stiffened, a sinking feeling taking over.

Marie, continuing her gentle pats, held Luke's gaze. "Not odd at all. The Lord always knows what He's doing. The Bible says, 'Blessed are those who mourn, for they will be comforted.' God uses us all as his tools for comfort. Who better to comfort a mourner but another mourner?" She smiled encouragingly, her head bobbing in short nods before she released Luke's hand. She then turned and slowly made her way back to her seat behind the counter.

Handy reached out and shook Luke's hand. "You be sure and let us know if you need anything, son."

"I will. Thank you, sir." Luke went about shopping for a few fruits and vegetables, though his mind was muddled with what he'd just heard.

He wandered over to shelves stocked with jams, jellies, and other canned goods. A memory sprang to mind of the jelly his mother used to buy every summer they were in town. Strawberry and jalapeño was such a unique combination, but even as a kid he'd loved it. A quick scan of the jars' labels revealed nothing like it, so Luke moved on.

The brief conversation with Handy and his wife nagged him. It had begun to shed light on the complex lives of his neighbors. Who had they each lost? Luke assumed elderly Mrs. McLean had likely lost her husband. It explained why she was adamant he address her as *Mrs*. Had Cora lost a husband, too? At her age, which he guessed to be in the mid-30s, the loss would be tragic. Even more tragic was the other possibility—a child. Luke's jaw tightened.

The idea of discovering new things about himself here in Laurel Cove didn't bother him. But he wasn't sure how he felt about God using him to bring others comfort. Talk about the blind leading the blind. Not to mention that Luke didn't remember the last time he'd set foot inside a church for worship. In fact, the last time he'd entered a church at all was for Dennison's town hall meeting in Iowa last year. All business.

Still, he had to agree with Handy. It was an odd coincidence that three neighbors living around one remote lake had something like this in common. But the old saying was that *misery* loves company, not grief.

CHAPTER Three

"I wish you'd let me pay you for the groceries." Ina waved a ten-dollar bill in front of Cora from where she sat at her kitchen table.

"You only needed a few things. It's nothing." Cora placed the milk carton in the fridge and let the coolness kiss her face several seconds before closing the door. Why Ina kept her thermostat at a stifling 79 degrees, Cora would never know.

With the rest of the groceries put away and Ina's pill bottles lined up on the counter, ready for her to dispense into a daily pill caddy, Cora folded the brown paper sack and tucked it under her arm. "Anything else I can do before I go?"

Ina pushed her glasses up on her nose and tapped a crooked finger against the table. After a long pause she whispered, "Did you know we have a new resident among us?"

Luke's face, and the way he'd studied her, filled Cora's mind. "Yes, I've met him. Twice, actually."

The old woman struggled to stand, reaching for the three-legged cane next to her. "A piece of his mail was delivered here yesterday. A letter from some law office. Last night after *Jeopardy!* I got on the computer and used that Google place you told me about to look him up. Come with me."

Ina was always on some wild goose chase for dirt on people. Cora should have the woman help her write one of her mystery plots. That was, if she ever wrote again. She followed Ina into the wood-paneled den. A laugh track of some sitcom filled the room as Ina lowered herself into her recliner and reached for an envelope scribbled all over with her fancy penmanship.

Ina gestured for Cora to take the matching chair on the other side of an end table that held a lamp, magnifying glass, two remote controls, several pens, and a half-eaten bowl of oatmeal. From the congealed look of the stuff, it had probably been there since the morning.

"Now, this is one interesting fella." Ina tilted her nose up so that she could read the envelope out of the bottom of her bifocals. She turned to Cora and with a pointed finger said, "For starters, you have Boston in common. He's a Boston University graduate."

"Yes, he was wearing a BU sweatshirt when I ran into him today at the market."

She scanned her notes, tapping the envelope on her knee. "This is good. Yes, very impressive. Earlier this year, he won a Pulitzer Prize for Feature Photography." She peered over her wire frames at Cora.

Cora leaned forward in the recliner, eyes wide. She had to admit, that was indeed impressive. What was a Pulitzer Prize-winning photographer doing in Laurel Cove? "What else did you find out?"

"Ah, you're ready for the interesting stuff." Ina smiled and set the envelope down between them on the table. "I found an article in the New York Times, printed just a few months ago. Apparently, Mr. Bassett won the prize for a series of photographs showing small-town America on the campaign trail of Scott Dennison, the presidential candidate. Mr. Dennison had some less than nice things to say about one of the photographs, saying it slanderously implied things that could hurt his political aspirations. To date, Mr. Bassett has had no comment. In fact..." Ina gave a long pause.

Cora hung on for the conclusion, her knee bouncing.

"...he's said to have disappeared altogether."

Cora sat back with a sigh. The woman sure knew how to deliver a gripping story. "Wow, that's something. Why do you suppose he's come to Laurel Cove? It's an awfully random place to hide."

Ina rested both hands on top of her cane and glanced at the television for a moment. "When I took him the letter yesterday, he did say something about keeping a low profile. But the thing is, he didn't strike me as someone hiding. And I know how to read people."

"How did he strike you, then?" Cora was growing more curious by the moment.

"He struck me as a nice man but a bit lost. I'd say Laurel Cove is a pretty good place to get lost, though."

Cora could attest to that.

Ina pushed up on the cane just as a rumble of thunder sounded outside. She darted her eyes to Cora. "You best be getting on before the rain starts. Will you be okay?"

Cora's insides twisted as she stood, gazing past Ina and out the kitchen window. She knew all too well how quickly storms came up in the mountains. "Yes, I'll be fine. And thanks for the debriefing on Luke. That's pretty interesting stuff."

After quickly getting Ina's fire started, Cora drove under ominous clouds back to her place, knuckles white the whole way. Just as she stepped inside the front door, a crack of thunder sent her jumping in the air. She worked with trembling hands to get the logs lit in her own fireplace before starting the kettle on the stove. Out back, the storm clouds loomed over the lake, casting a sprawling black shadow. Small whitecaps danced along the surface. Just as the tea kettle began singing, big fat raindrops pounded the roof. She watched the ceiling as the pounding moved over the house then across the deck and into the yard, creating a white curtain between her and the lake.

Get mug down from cabinet. Place tea bag in mug. Listen for whistle of kettle.

Even beneath her sweater, the hair stood at attention up and down her arms. Like so many things in her life affected by the *before* and *after*, she wondered if she'd ever love storms again after that one fateful night.

"That's really nice of you, Jack." Luke gripped the hand of Jack Bowdon, the owner of Bowdon's Supplies.

Located on Main Street, apparently the place had been owned and operated by several generations and was basically a Laurel Cove landmark. Several folks Luke spoke to around town that day all enthusiastically suggested he stop by Bowdon's for the supplies he needed. Luke glanced at the pile of yard tools they'd just tied down with bungee cords in the bed of his truck.

"Well, I can imagine how much work the place needs. Happy to help if I can. I'll give you a call soon when I've got a free day coming up." Jack scanned the westward sky and let out a low whistle. "Hope you don't have any other stops to make before heading back. Smells like rain."

"No, you were my last stop." Luke took in the same sky, shielding his eyes from the sun that was still shining. Just a few light-gray clouds lingered in the distance. "My weather app didn't mention any rain this morning."

Jack chuckled, his hand firm on Luke's shoulder. "If you're going to be around here awhile, you'll learn how to read the skies. Better than any weather app. These storms come up quick, so you best get going."

Luke climbed in his truck and headed east out of town, the sun warming his neck through the back window of the cab. He shook his head and smirked. He could count the number of times his weather app had let him down on one hand.

Not fifteen minutes later, Luke shook tingling hands one at a time, his heart pounding in his ears. His truck had just floated along the road, losing traction for a brief moment for the third time since he'd started for home. He'd never seen a storm come up so fast. Slowly pumping his brakes, he came to an easy roll near the stop sign for the lake road. Loose bits of gravel pinged the undercarriage as he turned. He released a sigh, grateful for something to keep the truck good and grounded, but also for almost being home.

Home.

A slight smile punctuated a short sigh, despite a menacing rumble of thunder that shook Luke's truck. How long had it been since he'd thought of a place as home? Whatever had drawn him back to the cabin in the first place probably had something to do with it. Or everything. Even his apartment in the city was more of a place to squat between assignments. He'd molded the nomadic road life into some version of home that not many others recognized. It was more centered around the routineness of the irregular. Irregular schedules, time zones, languages, and meals.

The cabin came into view, a shadow of itself behind the veil of precipitation. Luke parked and glanced back, cringing at the pile of wet tools. Maybe the storm would pass as quickly as it had come, and he'd be able to unload them to the shed before bed. With a few deep breaths to ready himself for the deluge, he bolted for the door.

By the time he made it to the porch, he was drenched. Shivering, he went inside, greeted by warmth. But no dog. Toby always greeted him. He scanned the living room, breath quickening. "Toby?"

Drips of water trailed through the house as he made quick work of checking each room, calling the dog's name repeatedly. He stepped inside his bedroom, kneeling to check under the bed. Nothing. He sighed, sitting back on his heels. "Aw, Toby. Where'd you go, boy?"

He jerked at the sound of thumping coming from one corner. Huddled on the far side of the dresser was the dog, tail slapping the side of the wall. Luke's eyes went heavenward, and he slumped onto the floor next to Toby, rubbing him behind both ears. "You don't like storms, huh? I'll have to remember that."

What would he have done if Toby had gone missing in weather like this? Just a short time together and the dog was like family.

First home, now family?

Luke stood and started to peel off his sopping clothes, trading them for his robe. Sure, Luke had family. An emotionally stoic father who made millions as a stock trader. A sister who taught at Oxford and mostly called on holidays. And a deceased mother whom Luke himself had been too busy to see before she died. He ran his fingers through his hair several times. What did he know about family?

Luke yanked at the tie on the robe and exhaled sharply, heading for the living room. He started a few logs on the fireplace and headed for the shower. Toby stuck as close to Luke's side as he could, even poking his black nose past the shower curtain a few times.

By the time Luke showered and the wood started to crackle in the fireplace, the storm had passed, leaving fiery streaks of pink and orange across the evening sky. He started a pot of pasta boiling on the stove then stepped out onto the deck to catch the last few minutes of the brilliant sky. Patches of evening color shone like stained glass through black silhouettes of branches. The same wind that had blown the storm in must have stripped more autumn leaves. Through the thinned forest, several windows of Cora's cabin glowed.

Luke stared at the square boxes of light, just far enough away to reveal nothing else. Thanks to the way her cabin sat on the tip of the cove his was tucked into, there were only a few hundred yards between them across the water instead of the quarter-mile down the road. In the light of day, he was able to make out many more details of the charming A-frame and yard leading to the water and her dock.

A window went black.

Luke turned, lightning flashing in a now-distant storm cloud far past the darkened mountain ridge.

Was she all alone after losing her someone? Her outburst from yesterday replayed in his mind, and his heart twisted. Melancholy eyes, clouded like the stormy skies, remained even today outside the market. Loss like hers, probably tragic, must be fueled by intense love and devotion. Surely, her experience of family was much different from his.

CHAPTER *Four*

The nightmares are too much, Lord. Every one sharpens my memory. I don't want to forget them, but I need to forget that night. Please. I'm tired.

Cora relaxed her pen and looked up from her journal, the fringes of the blanket draped across her legs blowing in the breeze. Yesterday's storm had brought with it flashbacks—crueler than her nightmares because she was awake and lucid. Snapshots of flashing red lights. The ache of fighting against the strong arms of a stranger holding her back as she kicked and screamed. Drifting into artificial sleep as tears dripped from her face in an operating room.

The flashbacks came and went throughout the evening, like nods that kept one from drifting off. She avoided sleep as long as possible, but when she did finally succumb, the nightmares picked up where the flashbacks left off. Only this time, a new genre. One less violent but equally harmful. Visions of happiness that once was. Of laughing, touching, and planning for a future that wasn't to be.

She basked in the glow of the morning sun as it warmed her face through the crisp air. The morning, once again, a reprieve. Pen to paper, Cora scribbled and said aloud the words to the verse echoing in her heart. "Weeping may last through the night, but joy comes in the morning."

Though she obeyed her pastor's suggestion to claim verses of truth in faithfulness, they often didn't yet feel true. She hated the night and yearned for the light of day, yes. But joy still eluded her.

I trust you will restore joy in me. Let me receive it.

Leaves rustled around her as she wrote the line before closing the small leather-bound book and placing it on the table next to her chair. She inhaled deeply, holding the breath for a long moment. Now, she really must think on the publishing contract. She pulled her knees up to her chest, resting her feet on the slanted chair seat as she scanned the lake shimmering with threads of gold light. She stilled when she spotted a red kayak gliding out of the cove.

Luke Bassett, the Bostonian Pulitzer Prize-winner, hiding in their small town. She squinted to make out a dark form seated in front of him but pulled the blanket up to her nose as he neared the open water at the mouth of the small cove. Why was her instinct to hide? Not to mention from where she sat, tucked away from the shore, there was surely no chance he could see her.

Then his arm flew up, waving in a slow, wide arc over his head in Cora's direction. Her heart jumped, feet pulling in to fold herself tighter. She swallowed hard then released an arm from under the protection of the blanket and waved her arm just once. For a city dweller he sure was embracing this whole neighborly thing.

Slowly, the tip of the kayak turned until it was pointing right for her dock. *Oh, come on.* Cora stood and rolled her eyes to no one but the squirrels digging for acorns nearby. With the blanket wrapped tight around her shoulders, she reached the dock just as the kayak glided up alongside it. In one leap, a black Labrador wearing a life vest bounded onto the deck and ran for her at full gallop.

"Woah!" Luke's hands grabbed the sides of the kayak as it swayed back and forth.

Cora knelt to one knee, catching the large dog in a full embrace. Through its warm, wet licks, she managed, "Well, hey there."

"Toby! Down!" Luke bellowed, heavy steps thundering on the dock.

"He's okay." Cora scratched behind his ears, and the dog quickly calmed, eyes narrowing and tail thumping against the wood.

Luke reached them, panting, with hands on his hips. "I am so sorry. I just got him. I guess you could say we're still learning each other."

Cora kept her eyes on the dog, who appeared to smile at her with his tongue hanging out of his mouth. She chuckled, the amusement almost foreign. "It's really all right. He's super sweet." As if encouraged by the compliment, the dog pounced with both front paws resting on her shoulders. She fell back onto the cold dock, a full belly laugh escaping.

"Toby, no!" Luke lunged at them, grabbing the dog.

With the weight of Toby off her, Cora considered Luke's offered hand, squinting against the sunlight at his back. He sure was tall. Her cheeks warmed and she waved him off, pushing to her feet and brushing off the back of her black yoga pants. "I'm okay."

"I don't exactly have the best track record with you, do I?" He kept hold of the handle along the back of the dog's life vest.

The back of Cora's throat stung with the cold air she drew in sharply. The way he said it sounded so personal. "Uh, I guess. It's fine."

She picked up the blanket lying on the dock and shook it out before folding it over her arm. Her weight shifted back and forth from one hip to the other. She locked eyes with the dog, sending his tail wagging. The number of times she'd spoken with a man other than her doctor and her pastor in the last year could probably be counted on one hand. Now, in less than three full days, she'd been thrown into three conversations with the same man. None of which she'd initiated. Would it be rude to just turn for the cabin? *Yes, Cora. It would be.*

"You, uh, have a great place here." Luke's voice cracked. He cleared his throat and gestured behind her.

"Thanks." She chewed on her lip and looked toward his place in the cove, about to return the comment when something else caught her eye.

She pointed just past him. "Your kayak."

Luke spun on his heels and ran for the end of the dock. The kayak floated aimlessly a good fifty feet back toward the cove. Freed from Luke's grip, Toby stayed by Cora's side. *Just great.*

Shrugging his shoulders, Luke started back toward her. "If you're not too busy, want to help me get it back? I've got a canoe we can use."

Cora willed the flips in her stomach to cease. Why would she spend part of her day helping a strange man who kept showing up unannounced and uninvited? Not to mention one she couldn't even keep eye contact with.

She hugged the blanket to herself, nails digging into her arm. "Sure. Why not?"

So much for man's *best friend.* Luke smirked to himself and followed Cora up the sloped yard to her cabin, watching Toby prance as close as he could get without tripping her. The dog hadn't left her side since the second he'd jumped out of the kayak. But if Toby could keep her laughing the way she had when he knocked her over, Luke could get used to sharing the dog's attention. When she laughed, she was radiant, coming alive for the first time since Luke had met her. It had a dizzying effect on him.

At the first step up to the deck, Cora stopped with her back to Luke. He waited on the graveled path a few feet away. After a long pause, her chin reached her shoulder. "Wait here. I'll be right out."

Luke's brows furrowed as he watched her walk through the back door. Toby waited a few moments, nose pressed to the seam of the door, before turning to explore the new smells her deck offered. It wasn't so much that she hadn't invited him in that piqued his curiosity—they barely knew each other after all. It was more her long pause. Had she been considering whether to let him in? Sizing him up for trustworthiness? Or had she been questioning coming to help him altogether?

More curiously, why did Luke even care?

He shoved his hands into the pockets of his hooded sweatshirt and turned to check the status of the kayak. Now out of the cove, it floated a few hundred feet toward the center of the lake. He'd never once not secured it properly. Toby wandered down the steps and stopped to sniff Luke's sneakers. "It's all your fault, you know."

Toby looked up at Luke before carelessly going about sniffing until the back door creaked open. The dog then straightened to attention and ran to Cora when she stepped out and turned to lock the door. Luke rubbed both hands together, the sight of her heading toward him stirring something inside him. Over the leggings and flannel button-up she'd had on before, she wore a black athletic jacket that looked to be waterproof. Long wavy strands of hair pulled back behind her flowed out from under a crimson Harvard baseball hat. He perked.

"Did you go to Harvard?" he asked as she slid her hands into a pair of gloves.

Focusing on her task, she gave a short nod. "Yes."

"I graduated from Boston University. But I bet I was in the city a few years ahead of you." He watched for a reaction, but with her head bent, the hat blocked her eyes. He leaned down to connect a leash around Toby's collar and followed her as she started for the side of the cabin in silence. "What year did you graduate?"

"Two thousand and five." She waited while Luke stopped to coax Toby onward when he got distracted by some scent.

"I was right. I was class of two thousand. We missed each other." He offered her a smile. *Missed each other, in the metropolis of Boston? Geez, how lame.* He fidgeted with the loop at the end of the leash, his jaw clenching tight.

She kept her eyes down as they crossed her front yard in silence except for the clinking of Toby's tags and the crunching of leaves. Luke pressed his lips together. Clearly she wasn't interested in small talk.

At the road, she didn't even check for oncoming cars, which Luke was still in the habit of doing, before turning right toward his place. She readjusted the hat on her head then said, "I actually grew up in Boston."

Luke let out a breath he hadn't realized he was holding in and chuckled. "No kidding. Me too. What neighborhood?" He looked down at her, but her eyes stayed on either Toby or the ground in front of them.

Finally, she cut her eyes over and up. Their brightness pierced him. "Beacon Hill. You?"

Woah. Even after his dad became so successful, they never bought in the prestigious Beacon Hill area. How in the world had she made it all the way to Laurel Cove? Then again, how had he? The corners of Luke's lips turned up. "Roxbury, so not too far."

"I thought your voice sounded familiar when you stopped by the other day. That explains it." She reached down and patted Toby's head when he trotted between them.

"I wasn't sure you'd remember much about that except for how much your new persistent neighbor annoyed you with incessant knocking." He smiled thinly and shrugged his shoulders at her.

Though she didn't return his gaze, he noticed her cheeks plump with a soft smile from under the bill of her hat. With every step farther away from her cabin, she seemed to relax a bit more. He changed the leash to his other hand to keep them from getting tangled up as Toby darted back and forth. After another moment of silence passed, he continued. "I haven't noticed any accent in your voice. You must have been gone a long time. But I don't hear the local drawl either."

"Yeah." They passed by a large tree with branches covered in bright orange leaves. She reached out to a low-hanging branch, plucked a leaf off, and sniffed it. "I left Boston for New York right after I graduated. After a short time there, I bounced around a lot just because I could. Then..." Her voice trailed off. Her feet crunched louder as she suddenly picked up her pace.

Luke increased his stride, which he'd shortened to avoid outpacing her with his considerably longer legs. Even Toby noticed, adjusting to a trot.

"Then I moved here several years ago." Her arms swung at her sides as they clipped along for several seconds.

Those last words from her were spoken fast and barely above a whisper, drained of life but pregnant with meaning Luke could only attribute to loss. He rubbed the back of his neck. She had such a depth and intensity about her. It made him both want to retreat and to dive in headlong.

Neither of them spoke another word the rest of the way to Luke's place. If she was comfortable with the silence, maybe he could learn to be, too.

She wasn't sure if it was from the chilly air or from holding tight fists, but Cora's hands ached by the time she and Luke reached his place. And was she enjoying herself or ready to run at a full gallop back to the safety of her cabin?

Nothing he asked was prying. It's casual small talk. Just be friendly.

Cora sprawled her gloved fingers apart at her sides. This walk was asking her to flex muscles long ago atrophied. Her only regular conversations were with Ina, and she already knew everything. The good and the bad. What if Luke asked another question that threatened to pick a wound? His simple, benign curiosity about how she'd come to reside in Laurel Cove ended with her clamming up, thinking about what, or who, had drawn her here.

Her eyes darted to the details around her. *Overgrown shrubs. Crow perched on a low-hanging branch. The dark, shiny enamel paint of Luke's truck.*

A brisk gust of wind pricked at her cheeks as Luke bounded up the few steps of his front porch, Toby right behind him. From the yard, she folded her arms and studied her sneakers.

He held the door open and tilted his head toward the inside. "I'm just going to get Toby settled. We can walk through the house and warm up a bit on the way to the lake."

Cora clenched her hands, tucked under her arms, and focused on a sand-colored female cardinal perched on top of Luke's parked truck. "That's okay. I'll meet you around back."

Several seconds later, the door clicked shut. She sighed, her fingers tingling as she released her grip. Just as she rounded the back of the house, he stepped onto the deck holding two life vests and two long-handled oars. He handed her a thin, bright orange vest. "I've learned the hard way how challenging it is to swim in frigid water. You can have mine. I'll take this stylish retro one."

He danced a faded neon-yellow Styrofoam vest in front of her, its dirty straps dangling toward the ground. She hid a smile behind her hand as they started down to the lakeshore.

"The canoe is on a stand down by the water. It came with the cabin, but don't worry. I've already taken it out once, and there's no leaks." His elbow gently touched her shoulder.

Cora reached up and rubbed her neck, widening the gap between them by a foot or so.

At the shore, he made quick work of getting the canoe halfway in the water. With one foot on the shore and one foot in the boat, he reached out a hand. "Ready?"

There really was no way to avoid taking it, so Cora pulled in a deep breath and reached out. She let go as quickly as her feet steadied and took a seat at the front. He handed her an oar before giving the canoe a push and jumping in, taking a seat behind her. She pulled the zipper on her jacket up higher on her neck, the breeze chillier already.

When he didn't say anything for several strokes, she licked her lips. *Say something. You can do this.* "So, uh...you really like being out on the water."

She felt some drag on the left side of the canoe and pulled her oar out for a moment as Luke guided them slightly to the right for the mouth of the cove.

"Yeah, I've always been drawn to water. I even rowed for BU all four years."

Wat-ah. She grinned to the lake as his accent showed itself. The first few years away from home she wouldn't have even noticed, but there was something comforting about hearing it now.

"Did you do any sports?" he asked as they paddled in rhythm.

She laughed, surprising herself. "Absolutely none. I like to get a walk or short run in every day, if I can, but that's about the extent of my athletic ability."

A chuckle floated past her. "I run every evening, too. Well, except for nights like last night. That storm was crazy."

Cora's stomach knotted. She gripped the oar tightly, letting it graze the surface of the water. "Yeah, it was," she said over her shoulder, then let out a long slow breath through pursed lips. As her lungs emptied, her grip loosened too. *It's okay. Just change the subject. Anything.* "What do you have planned the rest of the day?"

They glided past the mouth of the cove and onto open water. Cora felt the canoe lurch forward with more momentum and glanced behind her. Luke had pushed up the sleeves on his sweatshirt, forearms bulging as he sliced the oar through the water.

"Well, I'm sure you noticed how much work my yard needs. I need to get working on that. Other than that, I'm looking forward to cooking a decent meal tonight. I picked up some squash and apples at the market yesterday for a risotto."

Cora raised her eyebrows. That was probably one of the last things she'd expected him to say. "I'm not sure I would have pegged you as the cooking type."

His laugh was hearty. "I've traveled all over the world and enjoyed lots of great food that was hard to find when I was home, so I learned to make a lot for myself. It turned into a hobby, I guess."

She recalled Ina's investigative report. He must have some great stories to tell from his assignments. She opened her mouth to ask him, then stopped, realizing he didn't know she knew what he did. Or used to do. Had he given it all up when he moved here?

"What about you? Any hobbies?" he asked.

"I really like to bake. I used to do it all the time." Tingles shot from her fingertips to her arms, and her eyes pinched shut. *Used to?* She held her breath, waiting for him to ask why she'd given it up.

Suddenly, he let out a wild groan. "Are you kidding me?"

Cora spun around to find his nose wrinkled, a white blob slowly oozing from his hair down the middle of his forehead. Her eyes shot to the sky, catching the underside of a bird flying away. She laid her oar at her feet and twisted to face him, biting her lip to hide a smile. Reaching inside her jacket, she pulled out a tissue from a travel pack and waved it at him. "I'm so sorry. Here."

"Thank goodness one of us came prepared." He wiped his face with the tissue then splashed a little lake water on his hair, shaking it off over the side. He looked a bit younger with his wet hair spiking up. Then he darted his eyes across the sky.

"Let's go get the kayak before that guy decides to come back for you." He winked.

Her cheeks flushed. She pressed her lips thin, righted herself to face forward, and picked up her oar. Soon they were back into a rhythm, gliding forward. In a matter of minutes, they reached the rogue kayak. Luke quickly attached the front nose of the kayak to the back of the canoe with a bungee, and they started back for shore.

Between trading more casual questions with Luke, realization began to dawn in Cora. She felt relaxed. What's more, she couldn't recall the last time she'd been distracted enough to go a few hours without thinking about the accident. After nearly three years of constant, consuming grief, she was so tired. She closed her eyes and slowly inhaled the crisp autumn air.

Here on the lake with a virtual stranger, she'd started to let her guard down and had actually had...*fun*.

As soon as the word sounded in her mind, guilt bubbled up. A familiar weight settled, though less debilitating than usual, and she held the oar across her lap. Could grief, which Cora had turned into a suffocating shrine, survive next to her living? Up until now, she'd been convinced it could not.

She opened her eyes to find geese flying in a V-formation approaching from over Luke's cabin. She eased her oar back into the water and looked over her shoulder. He'd stopped paddling a moment, too, and was watching the same birds as they flew over the canoe. Their eyes met and he smiled warmly. She turned back around, her heart making a little space for gratefulness. She'd prayed for joy just this morning, and while this might not quite be it, it was close.

CHAPTER *Five*

Cora stood at the side of the kitchen table, hands on her hips. She pulled her mouth to one side and tapped a foot. *Where to start?* Three yellow legal pads lay side by side, each with notes on a different topic scribbled in a different colored ink. She'd made the lists yesterday afternoon after getting back from the kayak-rescuing expedition with Luke. The slight pep in her step still remained this morning.

Glancing at her watch, she smiled and stood a bit straighter. It wasn't even lunch time, and she'd already cooked herself a fresh breakfast, showered and dressed, swept leaves off the deck and front porch, washed laundry, and dusted. She couldn't recall the last time those tasks hadn't collectively taken her several days.

She picked up the pad on the left scribbled with "Baking Stuff" across the top in blue. After mentioning baking to Luke when he asked about her hobbies, she'd come home with the urge to make cookies. As she scanned the list of ingredients needed for simple chocolate chip cookies, her hands moved from her hips to fidgeting in front of her. What was the worst thing that could happen if she actually did something that reminded her of Christopher? Thinking about him would happen throughout the day no matter what, so why not get cookies out of it, right? She gnawed on her bottom lip. *You could have a panic attack.*

She sighed and picked up the center pad titled "Pros/Cons of Writing" in green ink. Gail was expecting her answer for Random House tomorrow. The longest of the three lists—and arguably the most important—Cora read over each line. She walked to the back door and looked out over the yard carpeted in brown and orange leaves. Resolve rallied. She took a deep breath and read the first few entries on the pro side aloud.

"More income. Recommitment to a career you worked hard to build. Renewed purpose. Make yourself (and C) proud." Her voice cracked as the last few words left her. She gazed out the window and swallowed hard. He'd been such a champion of her writing.

She cleared her throat and shifted her eyes to the cons penned on the right side of the lined paper. "Pressure to perform. Expectation to be the same as before. What if I can't do it?"

You worried about all those things before, too. Cora drew in a sharp breath and cocked her head. It was true. So often, as was true for many artists, she needed a great deal of reassurance from day one. Never one to get too comfortable with success, the process of edits and reviews was painstaking with every one of her books. If most of the reasons she'd given for not writing again were things she'd already proven she could endure, then what was the problem?

Her eyes darted to the desk. She tossed the pad onto the kitchen table and sat down at her laptop. A few clicks of her mouse and she typed out an email to her agent.

Gail,

It's been long enough. And the fact of the matter is, there is no amount of time that will make this easy. The time is now.

Please tell RH to send on the new contract when you've reviewed it. I'll work on a pitch.

CB
PS: Thank you for your patience.

Cora didn't even read over the email before clicking Send. She bounced against the back of the chair, her chest rising and falling rhythmically. With a deep breath, she stood and picked up the third and final legal pad from the table. It shook in her hand.

In black letters, the top read "Story Ideas."

The rest of the page was blank.

You know what you need. Her eyes landed on the door of the coat closet to the right of the living room near the base of the stairs. She laid the pad down and slowly walked over to the closet. One hand folded into the crease of her elbow as her other hand wrapped around her mouth and chin. She stared at the knob a long moment then reached out, only to recoil as if it were on fire.

A high-pitched ringing sounded in her ears, setting her heart racing. She slammed her eyes shut.

This is crazy, Cora. You. Are. Fine.

The knob was cool against her palm as she reached out again and turned it. The door creaked loudly. She pulled on the cord hanging from the ceiling, and the small closet illuminated. Sitting on the floor, under coats Cora hadn't laid eyes on in almost three years, was *the box*.

Crouching down to the dusty floor, she reached out. Before she'd even touched it, she pulled back her hands and shook off electrifying pinpricks. Her eyes closed as she rested back on her heels. What was she scared of, exactly? The memories that were burned into her mind could not be made any more vivid by seeing the contents. Could they?

Cora clenched her fists a few times and opened her eyes. With shaking fingers tucked into the handles of the cardboard lid, she stood and carried the box over to the coffee table. She took a seat on the couch and stared at the words written across the top with thick black marker: "Recovered at Scene: C. Bradford."

Familiar trembling from her core began to physically shake her. She again found brief refuge behind closed eyes, hands rubbing up and down her thighs.

You're fine.

She drew in a long, full breath then exhaled slowly. "You're fine."

When Cora opened her eyes, the room seemed brighter. She eased the lid off the box from the Laurel Cove police station. It had been left in the care of her in-laws until she was discharged from the hospital, then she'd insisted they put it in the closet. Not once had she summoned the nerve to go through it. Until today.

Her fingers quivered, pressing against her lips. She reached for the brown knit sweater lying folded on top and pulled the garment close to her face, but it smelled musty. She set it across her lap and returned to the box. Shuffling through a few papers, Cora found a pack of cinnamon-flavored breath mints and other odds and ends. She picked up a blue scarf in one corner, revealing the thing she needed underneath.

She picked it up and blinked fast. There was a long scratch across the black leather, and some pages were crinkled, having gotten wet. Otherwise, her writing notebook was intact. She used to carry the thing with her everywhere. *You never know when an idea will strike.* Her thumb flipped through several pages, landing on a bright scribble of red ink that stood out among her sole use of a black pen. She ran her fingers across the numbers 1437.

Cora choked back hot, stinging tears. Their code.

1 – I

4 – Love

3 – You

7 – Forever

Like surveying a shipwreck for artifacts, grief sometimes offered mementos that cataloged a life lived. Cora replaced the lid on the box and stood, tucking the sweater and notebook under her arm.

Christopher's life had been well lived. He'd loved her so well, too. And he deserved to be remembered as more than just a lost soul. The time was now.

Cora stepped onto the deck, pulled her arms into the knit sweater, and took a seat at the wooden table they'd once shared meals at together. Black pen in hand, she opened the notebook to a blank page and started writing. Maybe she'd try weaving some romance into the mystery this time.

Luke lifted a torn piece of mesh on the screen door of Mrs. McLean's porch and tried to tuck it back into the split wood frame. Shielding his eyes, he peeked in. She was hunched over a walker, scooting at a pace that'd give the tortoise a leg up on the race.

He tucked his hands into his jeans pockets, turned, and surveyed the porch. It was a disaster. A rust-covered iron chair sitting underneath the porch light held a large terra-cotta pot filled with a dead fern. Next to the chair, two eyeless gnomes lay on their sides, one with a wide crack along its blue pointy hat. The house's white siding, though shielded by the overhang of the porch's tin roof, was covered in patches of green mildew.

A rattle of the knob turned his attention back to the door. It creaked open and Ina puttered into view behind the screen.

"What are you doing here, Mr. Bassett?"

Luke had really set his expectations way too high for small town neighborliness. "Hi, Mrs. McLean. How are you doing today?"

"Well, it took me longer to answer the door than to plant a bean crop. How do you think I'm doing?" She shifted her weight back and forth on unsteady feet, knuckles white atop her walker.

Luke reached for the handle of the screen door. "Would you let me help you to a more comfortable spot inside? We don't have to talk out here."

She scoffed but took his arm when he stepped inside to offer it. "Why in heaven's name did you come to talk to me?"

"I actually just came to bring some of your mail that was left in my box today." He showed her the few envelopes before placing them on the kitchen table they passed.

A plate with a half-eaten sandwich and applesauce sat on one end. Luke took in the rest of the kitchen. A trashcan overflowed. Several dirty dishes stacked in the sink. And a jumble of multi-colored pills sat scattered in front of a line of prescription bottles and one of those plastic pill organizers. It appeared to be empty.

He frowned, turning back to guide the old woman into the living room. The television showed a man spinning a large colorful wheel with various dollar amounts on it. With his hand on her frail elbow, Luke helped her into a recliner. "There, that's better."

"Thank you for the mail. Frank really is useless. I'll have to call down to the post office again, I suppose." She picked up a remote control and the television quieted. Staring up at him from behind her thin wire-rimmed glasses, she scrunched her nose. "Sit down. You're making me nervous."

Luke chuckled and took the matching chair next to her. He hadn't spent any time around older people before, but she was something else. A strange mix of pint-size stature and larger-than-life attitude, like a chihuahua.

He glanced around the small living room. It was tidier than the kitchen, but held signs of what life was like for her here. A three-footed cane sat within arm's reach next to her recliner. Several newspapers, still in their thin yellow wrapper, lay on the floor next to a sliding glass door that looked to lead to the back side of the wrap-around porch. A thin layer of dust covered just about every surface.

He turned back to find her holding an envelope, waving it at him, eyes narrowed. It appeared to be covered in writing. "I know all about you, son."

Luke couldn't stop a laugh from escaping. "I'm sorry?"

"I know that everyone is talking about what you did."

At that, his breath caught. What could she possibly know about what he'd been through in the months before coming here? He rubbed a hand across his stubbly cheek and jaw. "I'm not sure what you're referring to, but..."

She threw her head back, sending her white curls bouncing, and cackled. "You young people underestimate us old folk. Think we've got one foot in the grave and aren't paying any attention to the world. I know how to use the Google as much as you do, son. And I can read, probably better than you." She shook a bony finger at him.

For a long moment, Luke held her steady gaze. What was he supposed to say? There certainly wasn't anything to be ashamed of in what he'd done. If anything...

"I've got just one question." Her voice was much softer as she lowered her finger and rested her hands in her lap. "Are you all right?"

Luke drew back, mouth open. "Uh, I'm not sure what you mean, Mrs. McLean."

She rested her head back against the recliner's cushion. "I imagine having your name dragged through the mud for simply doing your job is difficult." She turned, her eyes piercing him. "A single, successful man doesn't up and move to the quiet, albeit beautiful, western mountains of our great state for the fun of it. Are you all right, son?"

He sighed, shoulders slumping as he leaned his forearms on his legs and stared at his feet. Had anyone asked him that since the feature published, followed by the interpretive article that kickstarted the whole firestorm? He turned his head to consider the old woman.

"It has been a tough year. But I'm okay."

She nodded. "Why Laurel Cove? Why our lake?"

He studied his feet again, weighing how to answer. "My mother rented the cabin almost every summer when my sister and I were kids. When my life started to feel too noisy and complicated, I needed peace. Our summers here were the only times I've felt real peace. My mother bought the cabin several years ago, and she started to spend a lot of time up here. Then she got sick." His stomach knotted. He should have come. Should have helped her.

"Anyway, the house still belongs to my family. So, here I am." He sighed and looked up.

Somehow, she'd managed to stand with her cane without making a peep. He watched as she closed the short distance between them then straightened when she stood directly in front of him. They were eye-level, despite their great height difference. She reached a cool wrinkled hand to his cheek. He leaned into it slightly and looked into her light eyes.

She spoke in a hushed tone, words that were both a salve to his soul and a reminder of a long-ago disconnected faith. "There is nothing you can't endure with God as your rock."

He nodded, tension melting off his shoulders that he hadn't even realized was there.

She patted his cheek before shuffling back to her chair. "You're also not the only one searching for peace on this lake. You, me, and Cora. We're peace seekers, all of us."

The words of Handy and his wife at the market echoed in his mind. Could there really be a divinely orchestrated reason that the three of them were here at the same moment in time, each needing similar healing though for different reasons? Who had Cora lost and how? And was Mrs. McLean suffering a broken heart, too?

He turned to ask her about the peace she sought, but found her eyes closed and chest calmly rising and falling. Smiling, he left her resting and washed the dishes before heading back to his place. On the way out the door, he glanced at the pills again. Maybe he'd stop by Cora's and ask her what she knew about Mrs. McLean's health. It seemed the neighborly thing to do.

CHAPTER Six

Cora dipped her pinkie finger into the glass bowl and licked it. "Mmm."

She'd forgotten how good whipped butter, sugar, and vanilla tasted. The beaters of her hand mixer clanked against the sides of the bowl for several more seconds. Just as she flicked off the switch, her ears perked. She stilled and waited for the sound to repeat, then picked up another egg just as the rapping came again. She returned the egg to the open carton on the counter and grabbed a kitchen towel on the way to the front door.

Through the windowpanes, she spied Luke's tall figure. She ran her fingers through her hair, and smoothed her hands down her apron. *What are you doing?* With a glance in the mirror in the entry way, she rolled her eyes and twisted the knob.

"Hi, Luke."

He flung his hands up as if she'd greeted him with a gun drawn. "I mean no harm. Just here to chat a minute." His playful smile revealed a subtle dimple on his left cheek.

She lifted the towel to her upturned mouth, pretending to wipe at something, then glanced over her shoulder back at the kitchen. "I'm, uh, in the middle of something..."

His smile faded. With a wave of a hand he reached into his back pocket and pulled out his wallet. "Oh, sure. I just wanted to ask you about Mrs. McLean. But here's my number. Let me know when would be a better time."

Cora took the business card he offered. That was about the last thing she'd expected him to say. Her brow furrowed and she tapped a finger along the card's edge. She turned to look again at the bowl and mixer in the kitchen, then back to him. It wouldn't do any good to put him off just to have to get up the nerve to call him later. "If you don't mind watching me make cookies, we can talk in the kitchen. Come on in."

She eased the door farther open and tilted her head toward the inside.

His eyes brightened, smile returning. "My timing is improving!"

He waited for her a few steps into the living room. She darted her eyes up at his as she moved past him. *He is so tall.* Somehow, his stature was more impressive standing inside the house. "How tall are you, exactly?"

"Just shy of six feet, five inches."

Cora's eyes widened. They reached the small dining area that opened up into the kitchen. "That puts my five feet, four inches to shame. You can sit at the table if you'd like. These won't take too long to get into the oven."

Instead, he followed her and leaned up against the counter adjacent to the stove. With his arms crossed, he considered the items sprawled out in front of her. "That's okay. I'm more of a participant when it comes to cooking. Anything I can do?"

Cora's breath caught in her throat as she reached for the egg and cracked it on the side of the bowl. So much for easing into having someone in her home for the first time in ages. She leaned over the cookbook sprawled out in front of her. "Um, you can stir one teaspoon of baking soda into that bowl of flour I've already measured out. The spoons are right..."

Before she could finish, he'd stepped up next to her and picked up the set of small copper spoons next to the flour bowl. A musky aroma, like the woods outside but crisper, took over the sweetness of sugar and vanilla. She gripped the handle of the mixer tightly and focused on starting to stir another egg into her bowl. Having a man, and the smell of a man, in the house was distracting.

She took a measured breath. "You said you wanted to talk about Ina?" Cora peeked up at him.

His finger traced down the cookbook page, then he measured out a little bit of salt and added it to his bowl. "Oh, right. The prospect of cookies took over." He smiled, then whisked through the dry ingredients and set the bowl closer to Cora before resuming his place against the counter. He crossed his arms, stretching the black fabric of his sweater on his biceps, and a few wrinkles formed above his nose.

Cora bit at the inside of her lip, not liking the way he grew serious at the mention of Ina. After dumping the flour mix into her bowl, she folded the ingredients together with her mother's old wooden spoon.

"I was just up at her place delivering some of her mail that was in my box. How long has she lived alone?"

"Not long. Her husband, Charles, died just two months ago." Cora watched Luke nod as she reached for the chocolate chips. She poured them in and stirred. "He'd been sick a long time. Ina was his caretaker until just a few weeks before he died, when hospice came in to help."

Luke shifted his weight, crossing one ankle over the other. "Her mind seems as sharp as a tack. But physically, I can't imagine her being capable of caring for someone with too many special needs."

Cora shook her head and started spooning small mounds of dough onto the cookie sheet. "She's started to change since he passed. Two weeks after the funeral, I came to bring her a few groceries and found her on the kitchen floor. Nothing was broken, but she couldn't manage to get herself up. Thank God she'd only been there about an hour. Ever since, she's been more and more unsteady on her feet."

Luke's head bobbed as he rubbed the side of his face. "No family?"

Heat from the oven sent a wave of goosebumps up Cora's arm as she slid the cookie sheet inside. She set the timer and turned to face Luke. "No one. It was just her and Charles. No children. Neither of them had siblings. Other than a few church friends who are as old or older than she is, there's no one. Just me."

Cora walked over to the sink to wash her hands, sighing. *Just me.* She was by no means Ina's family. Just a friendly neighbor who checked in on her every now and then and picked up groceries and prescriptions. But the ninety-three-year-old woman really did not have anyone else. She wiped her hands on the kitchen towel and turned to Luke, who was watching her.

"There's another thing I noticed today. The big reason I wanted to come by." His eyes turned down to his feet, and he shifted his weight again. "There was a pile of pills scattered all over the kitchen counter. I'm no doctor, but I assume that at her age getting off schedule with taking meds can be a big deal."

A weight dropped in Cora's stomach. She'd left the pills out two days ago for Ina to sort. That's how they'd always done it. Why hadn't Ina called to ask for help? "I'll head over there this afternoon and help her sort it out. Thanks for letting me know."

Though the oven was closed, she fanned at her neck. She hung the damp towel on a hook next to the sink and motioned for Luke to follow her as she walked to the back door and stepped out onto the deck. The chilly air hit her face and filled her lungs like a refreshing dip in the lake on a hot summer's day.

They both leaned on the ledge of the deck railing, gazing out over the shimmering water. After a few moments, Luke straightened and turned to face her.

"Do you know what broken heart syndrome is?"

Cora's body surged with a current of pinpricks from her head to her toes. What *didn't* she know about a broken heart? Her eyes closed and she breathed deeply, the exhale slow and controlled. "Yes. The idea that a person is more likely to die soon after their spouse passes away."

Cora dizzied with memories of those weeks after the accident, so lost and suddenly alone. Death indeed felt closer and less frightening when it already held those you loved.

When she finally looked up, Luke was studying her. His eyes were kind but searching. A few seconds later, he rested his arms on the railing again and turned back to the yard.

"I'm not saying that's what's going on with Mrs. McLean, but I am a little concerned about her. I know I'm the new guy around here, and you've got no reason to trust me. But I'm more than happy to help where I can. Check in on her. Maybe clean up the yard, even. I just got all those new tools." He poked a thumb over his shoulder in the direction of his cabin.

From somewhere nearby, a crow cawed, pulling Cora's attention into the trees. Several moments of comfortable silence passed between them. She should have read more into Ina's recent decline, but now it was time to step up. It said a lot that in just a few short days Luke seemed to feel the same. What an unexpected and strange trio they were turning out to be.

Luke and Cora stood just a foot or two apart on her deck, but she seemed to wander miles away for brief moments. He suspected the talk of Ina losing Charles hit close to home and pulled her off somewhere else. It seemed best to let her return in her own time.

The quiet was filled with the orchestration of autumn around them. Fallen leaves crackling across the ground harmonized with the low, constant rustling of soft leaves still holding on to strong branches. The cooing of an unseen dove paired with the sharp, staccato call of a crow. Luke drew in a deep breath of crisp air, finding hints of sweet cookies.

As if on cue, the oven timer sounded faintly from inside, and Cora returned, regarding him with a faint smile. They walked inside and Luke watched her pull out the sheet of perfectly golden cookies. "Not bad for my first batch in ages."

"I'd say so." Luke wanted desperately to ask her why she hadn't baked in such a long time. And why today was the day she finally did again. But something told him to tread lightly and let her lead the way.

Cora moved the cookies to a cooling rack and set it on the kitchen table. She tucked a few strands of hair behind her ear and placed her hands on her hips, a pleased smile breaking through. "I think I'll take some with me to Ina's when I go later on. I hope you'll take some, too. Since you helped and all."

"Don't we get to try one now? I've never been good at waiting where cookies are concerned." Luke bent over the rack and took a dramatic whiff, shooting Cora his most pathetic pleading eyes.

She chuckled and shook her head. "You're worse than a kid."

He held his hands up. "Okay, okay. I'm willing to wait exactly three minutes for the molten chocolate to cool to a more palatable temperature. But then it's fair game, and I dare you to try and stop me."

Her smile widened and she rolled her eyes before turning to the kitchen. As she cleaned up the mixing bowls and returned ingredients to their rightful places in cabinets, Luke examined the small dining space that opened to the cozy living room. He ran his hand along the smooth top of a wooden desk then moved to a floor-to-ceiling shelf. It was filled with a few plants, little decorative items, and lots of books. He fingered the coordinating spines of a large set.

Over his shoulder he said, "Looks like you've got the whole Paige Price collection."

"Yeah." Cora stepped up next to him holding out a cookie on a napkin.

"Here we go," he said, taking it from her. The bite he took was warm and full of melted chocolaty goodness. With eyes closed, he moaned. "Oh, yeah."

When he looked at her, she was chewing and nodding, a smile pulling at the corners of her plump lips. Luke found himself wishing she'd turn those icy blue eyes his way. Instead, she just turned back toward the kitchen, pulling at the strings of her apron. She laid it over the back of a kitchen chair and said, "The recipe is one my mom used my whole life. It never fails."

Luke sighed, took another bite, and returned to the bookshelf. He picked up one of the books and studied the cover. "I've still got a few of hers to read, but I know she hasn't come out with any new lately. You mind if I borrow one?"

Her voice light, Cora said, "Uh, sure. Take whatever you want."

He turned the book over in his hands to peruse the synopsis on the back. His eyes grew wide as he found the photo of the author in the bottom corner. Staring back at him was a woman with the same wavy blond hair, though it was cropped to her shoulders, freckles across her nose, and those icy blue eyes. *Wait a minute.*

Luke spun around, mouth gaping, to find Cora resting against the arm of the couch. "Is this you?"

She crossed her arms, pressed her lips into a thin smile, and nodded.

Luke glanced again at the square photo then closed the distance between himself and Cora. His head spun with this unexpected new development. His neighbor grew increasingly complicated and interesting by the day. "You're *the* Paige Price? I had no idea it was a pen name. This is wild."

He joined her when she moved to sit on the couch. She turned sideways, crisscrossing her legs in front of her casually. "My dad was extremely smart. He wisely suggested a pen name early on when I first started having small things published in college. I think he believed in me wholeheartedly even back then and knew some level of anonymity would be necessary. I used to do a lot of interviews and whatnot, but it's come in handy over the years. Actually, when we moved here with a different name, it helped me keep a low profile."

Luke noted her use of *used to* and *we*, but he could only process one newly revealed layer at a time. And this was a big one. All this time he'd been living next to one of America's most celebrated and top-selling authors of the last decade. *Too wild*. He chuckled as he set the book on the coffee table and sat back against the cushion.

"Working on anything?"

"Well..." She drummed her fingers across her mouth and glanced to the left in the direction of her desk. After a long pause, she looked back at him with her nose crinkled and sighed as she sank back into the couch. "I just agreed to write a new book. It'll be the first attempt in a few years."

Why would such a successful author, considered to be one of the best at her craft, seem so tortured by the prospect of writing again? Surely some of the many details about Cora Luke still had to uncover were at the center of it all. "That's great, right?"

"I guess it's complicated."

She ran her fingers through her hair, gathering it in a twist and pulling the wavy strands over one shoulder, exposing her neck on the other side. Luke's eyes trailed the gentle slope to where her cream-colored sweater began at her collar bone. Light freckles danced across her chest, fading into the shadows of her curves.

This wasn't the first time he'd noticed her beauty, but as heat rose up his neck, a sudden attraction dawned. Mixed with a growing urge to protect her, though from what he wasn't sure, it was an almost intoxicating combination. What was it about these two women on the lake that awakened in him a strong empathy? And, where Cora was concerned, something else entirely foreign to him.

Her sigh pulled Luke back. "I feel pretty rusty. And I've got to get a pitch ready for the publishers pretty soon."

"I know it's nothing like helping to make cookies, but if you need someone to bounce ideas off or whatever, just let me know," he said, trying to stay focused on her eyes.

She tilted her head to one side and studied him with narrowed eyes. Luke's insides twisted. Had he given himself away? Was he staring again? He held his breath, waiting.

"I might just do that. Thanks."

He smiled and let his chest deflate. "Of course."

Sitting up to the edge of the couch, he leaned his elbows on his knees. The book on the coffee table in front of him suddenly represented her past, present, and future. He wasn't creating anything of his own these days, which he had to admit was leaving a bit of a hole. Between the book and Mrs. McLean, if it gave him more chances to spend time with Cora, he'd take it.

CHAPTER

Seven

"I didn't say that, Ina." Cora snapped the lids shut on the plastic pill organizer and placed each orange prescription bottle in the cabinet above the counter.

Ina sat at the kitchen table in a light-pink house coat, shaky finger tracing the flowers on the vinyl placemat. "What else would you call it? He tattled on me like a nosy schoolboy running to the teacher about a fight on the playground. I'm not a child."

Cora took the seat next to her, pulling at the top of her sweater to create a cooling breeze. "I'm glad Luke noticed the pills. You need those. And wasn't it nice that he cleaned up for you, too?"

"I suppose it was nice to wake up to an empty sink." Ina pursed her lips and pushed her glasses up on her nose. "I confronted him about those articles, by the way."

Flipping through a few pieces of mail lying on the table, Cora arched her eyebrows. It dawned on her just then that after all that talk about her books, she hadn't asked Luke once about his career before sending him off with a bag of cookies. For so long now, she'd been consumed with her own life, loss, and grief. It was time to start making room for other things. Other people.

"And?" Cora asked as the envelope at the bottom of the stack caught her eye. The pale-yellow envelope read Laughlin & Gregory Mortgage Company in the upper left corner. She set the rest of the letters aside and looked up at Ina.

The woman patted her white hair, fluffing lazy curls. "He didn't say much. But I think he got the raw end of a pretty sour deal. Needed to get away from it all. And that cabin…" She motioned in the direction of the road to Luke's place. "He used to come here as a child in the summers. Loved the place. And get this, Ellie was his mama."

Cora perked. "What? You're kidding."

Ina shook her head slowly as she grimaced and rubbed her knobby fingers. "Oh, this weather does a number on my rheumatism."

"Ellie mentioned having two kids, but I don't remember either of them visiting. Do you?" Cora frowned and felt her posture stiffen. What kind of son didn't visit his mother when she became ill?

"No one ever came." Ina turned to gaze out the window above the sink, hands now folded in her lap.

Ellie had been a sweet, quiet woman. Cora and Christopher had had her over a few times for dinner and enjoyed her company. Several months after the accident, with Cora self-confined to the house, Ellie had come by looking very thin and pale. The doctors had found cancer. Subtle regret washed over Cora, pricking at her heart. She'd been in no place to offer support to a suffering Ellie. Weeks later, Ina had told Cora of Ellie moving away for treatment. Word got back of her passing not long after she'd left. The cabin had sat empty ever since.

That was, until Luke had shown up out of the blue. Cora sometimes felt chained to her cabin by the memories, nightmares, and even long-given-up dreams. Luke had retreated to his cabin willingly, despite the memories of a mother now gone. How strange were the ways in which grief and family ties could be so different.

Cora watched Ina. When not doling out opinions and interrogations, it was easier to see her smallness. It couldn't be denied. Without Charles and a purpose to rise for each morning, Ina was fading. Cora reached out and placed a hand on Ina's frail shoulder.

"I'd like to bring you dinner. Would that be all right?"

Ina placed a trembling hand atop Cora's and patted it. "That sounds lovely, dear. But on two conditions."

"Name them."

"First, you let me take my afternoon nap. I'm dreadfully tired." She sighed.

"And the second?"

"You invite Mr. Bassett, too. I've decided he's nice to look at." With a twinkle in her eye, the old woman's shoulders shook with a chuckle.

Cora sat back and laughed. The woman never ceased to surprise her. "Well, it's not much notice. He may have plans. But I promise I'll invite him."

Several minutes later, after Cora had helped Ina to her bedroom, she eased the front door closed behind her and stepped off the porch. Though the air was cool and crisp, the afternoon sun warmed her cheeks. Every time she came to

Ina's she learned something new about Luke that only led to more questions.

What exactly *had* happened with his career? How did he feel about it? Of all places, why Laurel Cove? And what were the circumstances around neglecting his own dying mother?

Don't judge, Cora. There's always more than meets the eye. It was a mantra at the center of her method of writing mysteries. Don't assume you know the whole truth from what you can see on your own accord. Look for clues. Ask questions worth asking. Let the pieces of the puzzle click together. Her interest was definitely piqued to solve the mystery of Mr. Lucas Bassett.

One thing, however, was perfectly clear. Ina was right. He was nice to look at.

Luke wiped his forehead against his arm then pulled off his glove, reaching into his pocket for his buzzing phone.

"Hello?"

"Hey, Luke. It's Cora."

Luke smiled even as a strong wind redistributed some of the leaves he'd just raked. He propped the rake against the side of the house and joined Toby in the shade of the porch. The creaking of the rocking chair he sat on gave him pause, but when it held strong, he rested against its back and rocked gently.

"Already have some brilliant ideas to run by me? I'm impressed."

"I wish. No, but I'm curious if you have plans for dinner."

The rocker stilled. *She's asking me to dinner?* His pulse thumped hard down his neck. He sure hadn't seen this coming. "Uh, no. No plans."

"I'm just heading back from Ina's. I offered to bring her dinner and she wondered if you'd join us, too."

Ah. Thinking she'd ask him for a date was insane. Would accepting, even if she had offered, be a good idea? Luke pushed his foot against the porch floor, resuming the back and forth of the rocker. "Oh, sure. That'd be great. What's on the menu?"

"Well, I sort of offered to do this without much thinking. My pantry is limited to canned soup, eggs, and some good crusty bread. I may have to go into town for a few things. Any ideas?"

Now this was where he really shone. "Well, I was planning to roast a pork loin with veggies tonight. We could have that."

Her chuckle danced through the phone. "You were going to cook a whole pork loin for yourself?"

"Well, sure. Makes great leftovers." He surveyed the little bit of yard he had left to rake and tapped a finger on the arm of the chair. "If you want to come over here in about an hour, you could help me make it. Then we can head over to Ina's together."

Luke craned to listen through the silence from the receiver. Yesterday she wouldn't even walk through his house to the backyard. Now, he expected her to spend part of the evening with him cooking? Then again, they'd made cookies together at her place.

She cleared her throat and Luke refocused. "Yeah, that sounds fine," she said. "I'll bring the bread, too. See you around five?"

Luke smiled and reached down to rub behind Toby's ear as the dog stared up at him. "Five sounds great. Bye."

His steps were light as he descended the porch. With the rake in hand, he headed for the line dividing the exposed grass and pile of leaves. Each day since he'd arrived had held one surprise after another. And after the rocky start with both Cora and Mrs. McLean, he never would have guessed he'd be having dinner with both of them tonight. He made quick work of cleaning up the leaves then dashed inside for a quick shower.

About an hour later, just as he finished running a brush through his damp hair, a knock sounded at the door. His insides flipped as he opened it to find Cora's bright blue eyes staring at him, extra striking against the black coat and scarf she wore.

"Hi," she said, pulling a brown bag to her chest and shivering. "It's turned extra chilly tonight."

"Hey, come on in." Luke reached for her coat, swallowing hard as the aroma of warm vanilla and spice enveloped him.

She looked comfortable but stunning in jeans and a red cable-knit sweater, her hair pulled up in a casual knot. Focusing on cooking might be the hardest of the tasks ahead of him this evening.

He hung her coat by the door and turned to find her taking a neatly folded apron from her purse. She pulled it over her head and tied the strings behind her as they walked to the kitchen, apparently ready to get to business. Luke stifled a chuckle.

"I'd make a fire but it might not be worth it if we're gone in an hour or so."

"Oh, that's fine. I'm sure things will heat up nicely in here." She set down the brown paper bag and her purse on the small butcher block island and pushed up her sweater sleeves.

Luke just stared, head cocked, and waited. As observant as he'd become over the years, intuition told him she wasn't flirting. But it sure would be fun watching her get out of this one.

Her subtle smile disappeared and eyes grew as wide as the moon over the lake the first night he'd come to town. She eased herself down onto the stool by her side. "Oh my gosh. I, um...I didn't mean that the way it sounded."

Unable to help himself, Luke busted with laughter. When she reached to cover a cracked smile, he leaned onto the edge of the island dramatically, as if he needed support to avoid falling over. "I'm sorry, but that was wicked funny."

Cora finally gave into a sweet, musical laugh. Her face glowed in the flickering light coming from the candle sitting in the middle of the island. Luke couldn't believe how much brighter her whole demeanor became when she let her guard down. She took a deep breath and sighed. Reaching into her purse, she pulled out a small, beat-up black book. "That's too good. I've got to write that down."

"Your books don't really have humor like that in them." Luke pulled a few spices down from a cabinet as she scribbled in the book.

Without looking up, she shook her head softly. "No, they don't. But I'm working up an idea for a mystery romance.

This would make a sweet moment for two characters on the dawn of a budding romance."

Luke pulled open the door to the refrigerator and pretended to search for something. His flushed cheeks cooled, but it took several slow breaths before his heart rate started to come down. She'd casually thrown out the observation, clearly not in the least bit applying it to them. And why would she? He was no more than a neighbor she'd just started to befriend. And something told him another man still held her heart.

"I don't know any hobbyist home chefs with this kind of knife collection." Cora stared at a wooden box Luke had just lifted onto the counter. It was slightly larger than the one that held her mom's silverware. He lifted the lid, revealing small pointy knives, long serrated knives that squared off at the end, fat knives, skinny knives, and at least a dozen more in between.

Luke picked through a few before choosing a long one whose blade was covered in a clear plastic sleeve. He shrugged his shoulders, showing it to her. "Some guys collect signed baseballs or something. I like nice kitchen utensils and gadgets. I got this whole set in Japan. It was an investment, for sure, but I'll pass them onto my kids one day."

Cora stiffened and looked around the kitchen for something to do, maybe a change of subject. She reached for the oven door. "Well, it's sure starting to smell good."

"No, no, no." Luke set the knife down then threw an arm in front of her. "Remember, we don't want to disrupt the temperature inside. That's why we've got the digital meat thermometer in there."

That was easy. Cora held her hands up and mouthed *sorry* as she stepped back over to the wooden island. With the pork and vegetables cooking, there wasn't much left to do. She scanned the interior of the cabin.

Much like hers, it had exposed wooden-paneled walls, but this one was a more traditional roof slope compared to her A-frame. The simple furniture and décor definitely gave more of a summer-getaway vibe than a home. Cora thought back to what Ina had said about Luke retreating here. It was possible he didn't even intend to stay very long. Let whatever dust needed to settle, then get back to his life. What had life been like for him before coming here?

Ask questions worth asking. Solve the mystery.

"Can I ask you something?" Cora took a seat on a stool and watched as Luke started sharpening the long knife back and forth against a steel rod.

His eyebrows arched but his view was glued to the knife. "Sure, go ahead."

"What brought you up here—to the cabin, to Laurel Cove?"

He slowed his pull on the knife, set the rod down and carefully picked his thumb across the edge of the knife's blade. After he wiped it with the kitchen towel draped over his shoulder, he set it down and took the stool on the opposite end of the island. His eyes were thoughtful when they finally found Cora's.

"You want the long or short version?"

Cora glanced over to the boxy green numbers glowing above the stove. "Timer says we've got eighteen more minutes. Long?"

"Ok, you asked for it." He tilted his head to one side and smiled playfully. "I'm a photojournalist. Have been for a long time—almost two decades. Last year, I landed a big opportunity to follow a politician on his Democratic nominee campaign for a piece I'd been wanting to do on documenting small-town American voters. The photos published in a magazine just a few months ago and got a lot of attention, including that of a writer who read a lot into one of the photos. He wrote an op-ed piece that, in turn, earned the politician a lot of speculative press. That turned into the politician having a lot to say about me. None of it particularly kind. Dozens of requests for interviews started coming in daily, and his campaign staff was breathing down my neck. I needed a fresh start."

He pressed his lips into a thin smile and shrugged his shoulders. "So here I am."

It wasn't much more information than Ina had already told her, but it was nice to hear it from him. Cora crossed her arms on top of the island and leaned in. "What was the photo of?"

"It wasn't so much what but who." Luke drew in a deep breath and let it out slowly. "He'd just wrapped up a small rally in Iowa and was making the rounds. I got a great shot of him crouched down to shake hands with a small boy, maybe four years old, wearing an Uncle Sam outfit. Fake beard and all. But it turns out the woman standing behind the boy, with a hand on his shoulder, was an old flame of this politician. During his first year as senator, there was speculation he'd had an affair with this woman—which was just about four years before the campaign."

"Oh." Cora's eyes grew wide as she connected the dots. What a mess to be wrapped up in.

Luke nodded. "Yeah. Quite scandalous considering his platform to bring ethics back into the office." He leaned onto the island and rubbed his face into his hands. "I photographed thousands of people during that campaign. There's no way I could have known who she was. And the chances that photo was one of a dozen I chose for the feature—it's just bad luck, I guess."

His voice trailed off. He seemed to be talking to himself, really, as if trying to make sense of it. Cora watched him stare into the flickering candle between them, now a sea of melted orange wax.

After giving him the space of a few breaths, Cora continued. "Not all bad luck, right? Ina mentioned one of those photos won you a Pulitzer. That's huge, Luke."

"She told you about that, huh?" He met her eyes, a genuine smile brightening his face. "Thanks. I'm thankful to have had a short time to enjoy that before all this hit. But I think the notoriety put the feature under more scrutiny. I gave a lot of interviews following the award, but once this came out, I haven't said yes to even one."

"Why?"

"The photo itself doesn't need defending. If his actions in relation to someone in the photo do, that's his business and has absolutely nothing to do with me." Luke stood, brow furrowed and voice a low growl. "It's not what I want a year of hard work to be remembered for."

He stepped over to the oven and reached for the door.

"No, no, no..." Cora echoed his earlier warning and stepped to his side, placing a hand on his arm. "We've got the digital reader thingy in there, remember?"

Luke looked down at her, face stoic, eyes searching hers. Her chest warmed under her apron and sweater. Slowly a grin crept across his face until the small dimple appeared.

"Digital reader thingy?"

Cora stepped back, suddenly aware of how close they were. "You would have regretted it all night."

"You're right. That was close." He let out a breathy laugh as he settled against the side of the counter.

"So," Cora said, doing the same against the counter opposite him. No reason to stop the investigation now. "You needed an escape. Why Laurel Cove?"

Luke looked around the cabin, eyes settling on the sliding glass door leading to the back deck past the kitchen. Cora glanced behind her in the same direction. The early evening sky was painted with pinks and purples, the smooth mountain range across the lake already black.

He sighed. "This was my mom's cabin. Maybe you met her before she died. Ellie Bassett."

Cora studied Luke, whose gaze was still fixed on the door, the lake, or maybe a memory. In his face she found something familiar. A longing. It pricked at her own wounded heart. "Yes, I knew Ellie. She was lovely. I was sorry to hear of her passing."

"Yeah, she was lovely. I wasn't able to..." His eyes fell. Crossing his arms across his chest, he looked to Cora. "Truth is, I didn't make the time to come see her those last few years she was up here. I didn't know how to process her illness, so I stayed away too long. By the time we got her back to

Boston, I'd missed the chance at quality time with her before..."

Before. A lump swelled in Cora's throat as his voice trailed off. She rubbed a hand across her neck.

He coughed and straightened, picking up the kitchen towel from the island and absently running it across the already clean countertop. "Anyway, this cabin holds a lot of great memories from when I was a kid and we came during the summer. You know, hiking, swimming in the cold lake, and campfires."

Cora nodded when he looked at her, smiling softly. Their eyes locked for several seconds until the oven timer buzzed, startling them both. Luke pressed a button and it quieted.

With a hand on the oven door, he paused. "I don't have anyone in my life who brought me peace like she did. I guess coming here makes me feel as close as I can get to her now. Is that crazy?"

Swallowing past the lump, Cora shook her head. "Not at all."

The mystery of Luke Bassett wasn't so complicated after all. He was grieving. If there was anything Cora understood, it was how grief for a person anchored you to a place. She suddenly found herself aching to tell her own story. Maybe Luke was exactly the one she needed to tell.

CHAPTER Eight

Screams of sirens pierced the darkness with a dizzying effect. The muscles of Cora's throat pulled, aching to make her voice heard. Her knees hit the pavement as she watched through eyes blurred by cold rain and warm tears. A shroud of smoke and steam rose from the mangled heap of steel on the far side of the two-lane highway. Suddenly someone was at her side, pressing fabric to her face.

Christopher.

Cora pushed the man away, desperate to keep the car in her sight. The rain fell harder as a sharp, hot pain ripped through her abdomen, throwing her to the ground. On her hands and knees, she watched drops of blood fall onto the white line painted on the asphalt. Was it hers? As the pain subsided, she choked on her own cries.

Then an explosion.

Christopher.

Stumbling to her feet, Cora lunged forward. Her body and soul wailed, but nothing sounded. A high-pitched level tone filled *her ears, drowning out the symphony of horror. She fought against thick arms holding her back as sobs wracked her body.*

In the glow of the blazing fire, stillness slowly took over. Numbness set in. No more sound. No more feeling.

Then the sharp, hot pain tore through her again. She doubled over the arms holding her and heaved violently. With each wave of pain, darkness increased. Please, God, no. *Gasping for breath, Cora craned for one last look up at the inferno, veiled now by a thick curtain of rain. She reached for him.*

Christopher.

One last blinding stab hit, bringing blackness. And the end of her whole world.

Cora choked through deafening sobs, blinking through her tears at a bright light. Heaving for breath, she pushed away the hair stuck to her face and looked around frantically at her surroundings. No rain. No sirens. She pressed a hand to her cheek. No blood, but a smooth scar.

Christopher.

Sitting atop her bed, tangled in flannel sheets, she rested her sweaty face in her hands and wept. With every nightmare came new tears for a refreshed grief. The trauma ripped open to expose ever-raw, stinging nerves.

Gradually the sobs turned into wails, which faded to whimpers, and eventually became sniffles. When deep breaths finally quieted her cries, Cora stood and walked to her window. A light frost sparkled across the leaves and grass below. The lake was placid, reflecting the colorful mountains.

Like a needle piercing through silk, Luke's red kayak pushed soft ripples through the water as it glided toward the cove from the far side of the lake. Cora drew in a jumpy staccato breath chased by a lingering sniffle. Talking and cooking with Luke and then dinner at Ina's yesterday had been so nice. It had brought a reprieve from the suffocating grief. She'd lived.

Cora balled her fists as her eyes slammed shut, breath quickening again. *It's not fair!* Why was she sentenced to relive the most horrific day of her life? Why not relive one of the thousands of happy, fulfilling, joyous days with Christopher? She couldn't bear to continue looking backward.

She opened her stinging eyes and found the kayak entering the curve of the cove. What she'd give to feel the sense of freedom of being on the water, gliding effortlessly. Maybe she'd ask Luke to take her out again sometime, to feel the breeze on her face and crisp air in her lungs. Maybe she'd ask to go to the far side of the lake where the winding shore hid a tiny island. She'd explore something new and make new memories...and live.

When Luke stopped rowing and let the kayak glide along the pristine surface, the motion felt like floating on glass. He hadn't seen the water this calm since he arrived in Laurel Cove. Just in the last few days, the temperature had dropped several degrees, and less green peeked through the autumn confetti sprinkled along the mountain ridge. Bright yellows and oranges now covered the trees and the ground equally.

Luke inhaled deeply, the cold air rushing all the way to the bottom of his lungs as he sliced the paddle through the dark water. The delicate splash of the ripples he made was the only sound on the lake that morning, except for an occasional squawk of a goose or song of a bird call. With the exertion of his morning trip behind him, he coasted into the cove with an even breath.

Cora's cabin caught his eye and he smiled. He was learning to not set expectations around here. A simple detour to Ina's to deliver mail had turned into reason for concern and a chat with Cora while making cookies. Just as unexpected had been cooking dinner with Cora for a fun evening with the two women who were strangers just days ago.

Luke's eyes moved across the frosty downstairs windows of her home to the one window at the top of the A-frame roof. Was she downstairs getting tea and making breakfast, or still upstairs just greeting the peaceful morning? Another glance at the second-story window and his smile grew, thinking he could make out her faint silhouette. He faced forward and pushed onward toward his piece of shoreline.

For a woman so unwelcoming and gruff at their first meeting, Cora was becoming easy to talk to and even, at times, funny. The dinner last night had been easy and lighthearted. Ina told stories of how life in Laurel Cove had both changed and stayed the same in the eighty years she'd lived here. How she and her husband had built their home with items from Bowdon's Supplies. About mills that had come and gone, bringing jobs then taking them away. The people who made the place such a pillar of Southern hospitality and kindness.

Cora mostly listened, as she was good at doing. She was also good at not divulging too much about her own past here.

But man, he wanted to learn more. Become the friend he thought she needed.

Luke pushed deeper into the water for the final few strokes and leaned forward as the kayak ran ashore enough for him to hop out onto semi-dry land and pull it in the rest of the way. On his way back up to the cabin, he pulled one arm across his chest and then the other, feeling the pull of tired muscles. After one last glance back at Cora's cabin through the thinning trees, he grabbed a few logs off the woodpile then stepped inside, kicking his shoes off.

When the fire began to crackle, Luke pulled an armchair close and propped his cold feet up on the stone hearth. Toby circled the floor a few times before curling up nearby. As the flames danced, Luke's mind returned to part of his conversation with Cora as they waited for dinner to cook. He'd told her the cabin was more than fond childhood memories; it was also the last connection he had to his mom. The last place she'd really lived.

His eyes pulled away from the fire to the built-in shelves lining the wall of the living room past the fireplace. Stacks of old books stood next to chunky pieces of pottery and other knickknacks. Dusty candles in silver holders that needed polishing flanked a frame holding a photo of Luke and his sister as children standing on the shore in tank tops and swimsuit bottoms, holding fishing poles.

Luke stood, the wooden floor cool against his toasty socked feet. A small spiral notebook on a lower shelf caught his eye. Lying across the top of it was a silver pen. He picked it up and turned it until he could read the small etched letters on the side: ERB. *Elinore Rose Bassett.* An ache tugged at his chest. He returned to the chair in front of the fire with the pen and notebook.

Luke stared into the flickering flames. He'd seen his mom with notebooks like this one as long as he'd known her. Back when he was young, he'd asked her what she wrote in them. She'd placed her hand on his cheek and whispered, "Prayers and feelings and secrets."

Luke swallowed and ran a hand across the simple blue cover before opening it. The familiar elegant cursive penmanship filled the lined page. Luke's breath caught at the sight of a date written in the upper corner. His sister had come from Oxford to move their mother to Boston at the end of the same month. This was likely her last journal.

As if the fire offered some solace, Luke watched it for several moments. Was he ready to read the prayers and feelings and secrets of a dying woman? A dying woman who'd faced the final chapter of her life virtually alone? Luke closed his eyes and let his head fall against the back of the chair.

You owe this to her. Don't be a coward like you were before.

Luke let out a low grunt and shook his head, eyes finding the page. He began reading aloud.

"It's a gorgeous day, though I do long to see the daffodils push up from the cold ground. God, maybe You'll gift those to me before I have to leave? Yesterday's treatment was the hardest yet. To be so tired and yet unable to sleep soundly is a curse. While lying awake last night, Luke was on my mind again."

Luke's heart skipped a beat. He ran his finger over the letters of his name as if reaching out to touch her. He inhaled a full breath and continued reading silently.

Lord, I know when you give us children, they are not really ours. We raise them for a season, then turn them out into the world and hope for the best. What best did I hope for Luke? For him to be a good, kind man—he is. For him to find a purpose and passion in the world—he did. For him to find someone to love and cherish—I pray that you help him find her. For him to not forget me—I must trust that he will not. Be with him, Lord. You are good and faithful. Amen.

Blinking away threatening tears, Luke swallowed past the ache in his throat. Her words were at the same time a soothing balm and sharp knife, full of pride and longing. As he sniffled, Toby stood, rested his head on Luke's knee, and peered up at him with concerned eyes.

Luke closed the notebook and watched a log settle in the fireplace, sending glowing embers dancing up the chimney. He had spent so much energy over the years arguing with a father whose behavior left him craving acceptance and affection that he'd never find. All the while, he'd neglected spending time with a mother who overflowed with pure love that didn't need to be earned or deserved.

What a waste.

Luke pressed his palms to his eyes, stood, and walked to the back door, drawn again to the peaceful lake. When his father told his mother several years ago he wanted a divorce, the only thing she'd asked for was enough money to buy the cabin. Was she seeking the same peace then as Luke so desperately sought now? Had she found it within these humble walls, in the gentle rise and fall of the quiet mountains, and in the steady presence of the calm, dark water?

God, I pray she did.

The short burst of a horn startled Cora. Her eyes darted up to the green traffic light then in her rearview mirror. She gave a quick wave as she lifted her foot off the brake, easing through the intersection before pulling into a parking spot in front of the post office on Main Street. She cut off the engine and sat with her hands in her lap, the chill returning quickly with the heater no longer blowing warm air at her feet.

This morning's nightmare had really done a number on her. Cora had never been a drinker, but the pounding in her head and hard-to-focus feeling had to be similar to what a hangover felt like. But she was done letting the disorienting grief control her.

She set her keys in her small purse, placed the strap across her shoulder, and reached for the large envelope lying on the passenger seat. An email from Gail waiting for her that morning included a copy of the new contract from Random House. They'd moved fast and wanted her to do the same. She'd given it a read over, scribbled a note about a provision for working a romance thread into her next mystery novel, signed it, and gotten it ready to mail off.

When she stepped out of the car, the air on Main Street smelled faintly of cinnamon. The base of every lamppost lining the street was decorated with dried cornstalks wrapped with autumn-colored ribbons. At the top of each hung a small banner advertising the Laurel Cove Fall Festival, coming up soon.

Cora managed a smile at the real black cat posing atop a stack of pumpkins next to the door of the post office. When she pulled the door handle, a cheery bell greeted her.

"What can I do you for?" A bald, round-bellied clerk peeked over bifocals as he waddled from one end of a long counter to a swivel chair behind a computer near the center of the lobby. Cora approached as he struggled to situate himself on the tall chair before folding his hands in front of the keyboard and smiling at her.

"I just need to mail this off." She slid the envelope across to him.

He eyed it carefully through his half-moon shaped lenses before looking back up at Cora. "My, my. Going all the way to the Big Apple. You know, just the other day someone sent something all the way to Japan. Their grandson is doing some sort of internship with a fancy technological company over there. Now New York. Amazing how things travel these days, isn't it?"

Cora couldn't help but snicker at the obvious amusement on his face. "Yes, it sure is."

In a matter of moments, the clerk stuck a printed label onto the envelope and flung it into a container behind the counter. She handed over her payment as the small talk continued. They agreed the crisp weather was refreshing, discussed their favorite parts of the Fall Festival, and he suggested she head to Brewed a few doors down for their new seasonal treat—a fresh cider donut.

By the time Cora stepped back out onto Main Street, her steps were lighter and head much clearer. Just days ago, it had taken a whole day of sleep to recover from a debilitating nightmare. Today, coming out of the fog so swiftly was a welcome blessing. One thing was certain, the people of Laurel Cove were the most friendly she'd encountered anywhere.

She glanced to the left and spotted the sign for Brewed hanging from the line of storefronts several doors down. A cider donut and hot tea sounded perfect right about now. As she bundled her coat and started walking, the black cat darted in front of her and scurried across the street.

After watching to make sure the animal crossed safely, Cora looked forward again. She froze as her eyes met those of the man walking toward her on the sidewalk.

"Hello, dear."

"Hi, Harry." Cora leaned in lightly as Christopher's father placed a kiss on her cheek. She took a step back and averted her eyes to the cat across the street, now grooming itself in front of a bookstore. The Bradford genes were strong. When she looked at Harry with his light-gray eyes and youthful face that never seemed to age, all she saw was Christopher. Maybe that was why visiting her in-laws had been so difficult in the years following the accident.

"It's good to see you. Laura will be glad to hear you're well." He paused, then continued when Cora finally looked at him. "*Are* you well?"

"Yes, I'm fine. And you? Laura?" She crossed her arms, fingers gripping her elbows tightly.

He nodded, smile soft and genuine. "We are. Just got back from our annual trip to Arizona last week. And Laura's quilting group will have a booth at the festival. She's been as busy as a bee. I hope we'll see you there?"

"Um, maybe." Cora chewed on her lip, gazing past him to the café sign. "Well, it was really nice seeing you, Harry. Please tell Laura I said hello."

He adjusted the flat cap atop his head before putting his hands in his pockets. With a smile, he nodded. "I will. You take care, dear."

Cora released a deep breath as they parted ways. Several steps down the sidewalk, she turned and watched him get into his car. They'd lost their only child, and life seemed to be moving right along for them. Why was it so much harder for her? What was she doing wrong?

Maybe it was as simple as choosing to do one thing at a time. Getting out of bed even though her body still trembled from a nightmare. Leaving the house despite wanting to hide. Smiling and chatting with a friendly postal clerk.

Even though every fiber of her being begged her to run for her car, Cora placed her hand on the cold handle of Brewed's door, pulled, and stepped inside. Today, along with feeling the pain, she'd also enjoy one of her favorite fall treats.

CHAPTER *Nine*

The canopy of trees covering the lake road bounced in a gentle breeze, letting the late-afternoon light shine through in small bursts. Gravel crunched as Luke turned onto Cora's driveway and pulled to a stop next to her car. He smiled at the sight of a few pumpkins sitting to either side of the steps up to her porch.

Smiling felt good, refreshing. He'd spent a good bit of the day in a chair by the lake, watching the water and thinking of his mother, her journal, and her prayer for him. *For him to find someone to love and cherish. For him to not forget me.* Finding the journal was a comforting reminder of how tender and good his mother had been. It also fed the guilt and regret twitching inside him.

Luke grabbed his phone from the console and read back over the earlier texts with Cora before shutting the truck off.

CORA: S'MORES FOR DINNER?

LUKE: IS THAT A THING?

CORA: IT IS TONIGHT.

LUKE: SURE. WHAT CAN I BRING?
CORA: TOBY. SEE YOU AROUND 5.

"Well, come on, guest of honor." Luke clicked his tongue, and Toby turned from the passenger window, now covered in nose smears, and followed Luke out the driver's side door.

Cora stood at the open front door before they'd made it all the way up the steps. She wore a long-sleeved black shirt under casual denim overalls, and her long wavy hair was pulled to one side in a loose braid. She was the perfect mix of artsy, comfortable...and adorable. Luke watched as Toby bounded ahead of him right into her waiting arms, glad for the opportunity to watch her. Subtle lines creased at the corners of her eyes as she broke into a wide smile. She threw her head back, laughing in a feigned attempt to get away from Toby's affectionate tongue.

"Hey," Cora managed through a laugh as she stood, Toby licking at her hand.

"Regretting asking for the dog yet?" Luke followed Cora and Toby inside, where he was greeted by the faint aroma of warm spices.

"Hardly." Cora walked through to the kitchen at the back of the cabin, Toby her shadow.

The living room was dim, lit only by a candle on a small entryway table and a reading lamp by an overstuffed chair past the couch. Luke noticed an arrangement of deep-red flowers atop the coffee table as he passed through. The little bit of decorating hinted that maybe she'd had a good day.

Cora handed him a tray covered with aluminum foil, picked up a thermos and two mugs, and nodded toward the porch. "I've already got the fire started. Shall we?"

The deck was the epitome of a fall evening in the mountains. Bulbs strung across the deck from post to post gave off a golden glow and illuminated four Adirondack chairs around a crackling firepit. The two chairs facing the lake were draped with plaid blankets. As Luke set the tray down on a low table between the chairs, he looked out over the water.

"I can't get over the colors of the sky up here."

Cora sat the thermos and mugs down next to the tray, and they stood facing the lake together. "Yeah. Lately, it's like I'm seeing it for the first time."

He watched her face as her eyes trailed the sky from overhead to the ridge across the lake. His breath caught when she suddenly turned to him and smiled.

"I don't know about you, but I'm hungry." She took a blanket off one of the seats and sat down, covering her legs with it before reaching to take the foil off the tray. It was full of a few wrapped chocolate bars, graham crackers, and fat, puffy marshmallows.

Luke took the seat next to her, leaning forward. "I've never had traditional s'mores."

Cora narrowed her eyes and tilted her head. "You're kidding. All those summers up here without s'mores?"

"No, really. My mom made them with peanut butter cups."

Her eyes widened and mouth gaped open. "Okay, that is brilliant. We have to settle for standard chocolate tonight. But next time, we're doing that."

Luke chuckled and took another opportunity to watch her face as she worked a marshmallow onto the end of a long skewer. He liked the sound of *next time*. "Deal."

"How was your day? Get more done in the yard?" she asked, handing him the skewer.

"I blew off the deck—again." He waited for her to ready her skewer then started turning his over the fire. "But that's about it. I actually found my mom's old journal this morning. I only made it through one page before I had to put it down."

When Luke looked up, Cora's tender blue eyes pierced him. He twisted the skewer, watching the marshmallow slowly brown, and let his lungs fill with the crisp air.

She cleared her throat. When she finally spoke, her voice was raspy. "I'm sure that was hard."

"Yeah, it was. But I think it's important I face some things I can't control. So I'm sure I'll read more eventually." Luke pulled back his skewer and started to turn for the tray to finish building his s'more. "Hey, watch out!"

Cora jerked her skewer back with her marshmallow on fire. In a few quick puffs, she had the fire out but was left with a completely charred marshmallow. She shrugged her shoulders and offered a thin smile. "It's okay. I kind of like them this way."

For the next half hour, they laughed over stories of ruined food, Boston memories, and what they were like as children. When only crumbs remained on the tray and Luke had poured the last of the cider from the thermos, they sat back and watched the fire with a symphony of clicks and chirps sounding in the surrounding woods.

Luke turned toward Cora when she sighed. Her eyes stayed focused on the dancing fire as she said, "Today started rough, but this has been fun. Just what I needed."

"What was rough about it?"

She rubbed her hand across her mug, watching its contents. Through the dim, glowing light, her bottom lip seemed to quiver. "Sometimes I have nightmares. The one I woke from this morning was particularly bad."

Luke's heart sank. He sat up to the edge of his chair and resisted a strong urge to reach out and touch her. "I'm sorry."

Cora closed her eyes and inhaled sharply. She held the breath a long moment before slowly releasing it in a steady, controlled exhale. "They always get bad this...this time every year."

He watched her knuckles go white around the mug, eyes closing tighter. Luke's heart began to race as if the soundtrack to a thriller film had broken through the serenity of the woods' serenade. If she'd only look at him. Just as he began to reach a hand toward her knee, her brilliant blue eyes flew open and cut through to his.

"I'd like to tell you why."

Luke held her stare and nodded. "Okay."

It was such a simple answer for what Luke was somehow certain was going to be very, *very* complicated story.

Breathe.

Eyes closed, Cora inhaled a slow breath through her nose and focused on the feeling of her chest expanding. Releasing it in an easy stream through rounded lips, she opened her eyes to find Luke watching her patiently. Under the glow of the deck lights, he leaned on a hand propped up at his elbow on the arm of his chair. His fingers wrapped around his chin and mouth, his square jaw lending gravity to his expression. Yet, his eyes were full of a soft kindness.

You're safe.

"I'm not sure why I'm saying this tonight." She set her lukewarm mug on the table between them and worked her hands in her lap. If she didn't start talking soon, she'd chew a hole right through her lip.

"It's okay." Luke's voice was barely above a whisper.

Cora drew in a deep breath to feed her bravery and found Luke's eyes again. "Three years ago next month, my husband, Christopher, died in a car accident."

She swallowed hard then sighed as if a weight had just been lifted off her chest. Saying the words out loud had not, in fact, killed her.

Luke closed his eyes briefly and nodded, finding her again. "I'm so sorry, Cora."

As if some tricky lock had been figured out, Cora's determination to inch the door of her heart open grew. She turned her face to the stars flickering overhead and began.

"We'd been out in town all day. We had lunch with Christopher's parents after my doctor's appointment and ran several errands. It was a perfect November day, cold and crisp, but I was ready to get home and put my feet up in front of the fire. Then Christopher used his charm to talk me into driving out to a local farm stand to pick up something he couldn't find anywhere else. That charm had gotten me into a lot of trouble over the years."

"Oh, come on, babe. We're already out and you're dressed. We might as well make the most of this time while we've got it. I'll rub your feet an extra ten minutes. What do you say?"

Cora's mind replayed Christopher's words before she glanced sideways at Luke with a slight smile. "Anyway, the place was about half an hour over a mountain ridge to the west, almost to Tennessee. When we pulled back onto the two-lane highway to head home an hour later, the wind had picked up. Storm clouds rolled in fast out of nowhere. A lot like the other evening."

Luke nodded, lips thin. Cora realized her knee was bouncing under the blanket. Trying to still it, she crossed her legs.

"About the time we started back down the mountain to Laurel Cove, the little bit of daylight left had gone. It was pitch black. The rain fell so hard it was impossible to see more than a few feet in front of the car. To the left of us was the steep mountainside. To the right, a small stream and a narrow valley dotted with farmhouses."

Cora closed her eyes, her forehead wrinkling as the scene vividly sprang to life. She gripped the side of the deck chair the same way she'd held tightly to the car's arm rest. Her pulse quickened, seeing dark shadows of houses and trees pass by through the thick curtain of rain out her window as Christopher reassured her.

"We'll be out of this in no time, babe. You know how these storms are."

Deafening rain. Cracks of thunder. Adrenaline traveling in shockwaves all over Cora's body.

She heard her own voice crack as she continued. "Suddenly there was rock and...so much mud sliding off the mountain just ahead of us. Christopher swerved. But we went off the road and..."

"Oh, God. Cora, hold on."

Her head pounded, her thundering pulse begging her to not go any further. She choked back tears, eyes stinging, and shook her head as it fell into her hands.

A warm hand touched her knee. Startled, she gasped and looked up to find Luke sitting at the edge of his chair, leaning toward her. She searched his eyes desperately. "We hit so hard. A tree. It was so loud, and then...it was just...quiet."

Luke nodded, his jaw twitching as if he wanted to say something but didn't have the words.

Cora wiped at a tear as it rolled down the side of her nose. Her head told her not to, but her heart longed for that one sweet moment before the downward spiral to the end. She bit her bottom lip and closed her eyes, remembering.

Coming to her senses in the quiet car, Cora winced as she turned away from the passenger window being pelted with rain. Panic shook through her as the shattered windshield came into focus, steam rising in a white fog just outside. The mangled interior was filled with deflated airbags, lit only by flashing yellow and red dash lights. She blinked through the darkness. Christopher looked so peaceful, like he was sleeping against the headrest. Her hands reached out wildly to him.

"Christopher, honey, come on. We've got to get out!" Cora watched as blood dripped from the corner of his mouth. She frantically worked to unclasp her seatbelt, pain shooting through her side. Steel creaked as something shifted underneath them. Cora screamed, heart sinking, and scrambled to find the release for Christopher's seatbelt.

"I need you to open your door. I'll get you unhooked, but then you've got to get out, okay?"

Christopher let out a small, weak cough. Cora labored to her knees and held his face. His eyes opened narrowly. Relief rushed through her. "You scared me..."

"Go." *Another cough stole his shallow breath, and he shook his head softly.*

Cora trembled, horror setting in. Just outside the fractured windshield, something popped and small flames erupted from under the hood.

"We have to go now, Christopher. Please." *Christopher's hand was limp when Cora picked it up, pressing her lips to it.*

He offered a faint smile. "I love you so much. My everything. It'll be okay."

"I love you. I'll get help. Just hold on, okay?" *Cora closed her eyes against stinging tears, bringing his palm up to her cheek. When she looked back at him, his eyes had closed, smile faded. And the* after *began.*

Cora blinked through watery eyes and watched the flames lick the crisp air on her deck. She turned to Luke, who still leaned toward her in his chair. "I managed to get out just as the emergency vehicles got there. The owner of a house nearby apparently called. But it was too late. He was already gone."

Luke shook his head and rubbed his face. "That's awful, Cora. I can't imagine what that must have been like for you. Were you hurt?"

A phantom twinge pulled at Cora's stomach as fresh grief stepped to the front of her heart. She swallowed past a new lump in her throat, felt the scar lining her face, and nodded. "I spent eleven days in the hospital but made a full recovery."

He sat back against the chair. "I'm glad you're okay now."

And Luke was right. She was okay. For several moments, they both watched the fire and listened to the clicks and chirps from the dark woods. With a deep breath, life filled Cora's lungs and, gradually, the past faded back to the place it would always live within her. She'd told the story, allowed the pain and sorrow to accompany her, and survived.

It was enough for tonight. The rest would be there, waiting for its turn to be shared.

A curiosity satisfied wasn't always satisfying. Luke lay in bed staring at the ceiling and thinking over the evening with Cora. Even though he had figured whatever loss she'd endured was likely a tragic one, hearing the details had been horrifying, nauseating even. With her knack for using words to tell a story and his ability to see captured scenes, it was as though he'd been there. Or watched the accident reenacted.

He closed his eyes as his heart wrenched. If simply imagining it was hard for him, the nightmares surely tormented Cora. No wonder she'd been such a mess the day they'd met. Before he'd headed home earlier, Luke had thanked her for telling him about Christopher. It was nice to feel trusted with such intimate details. Still, he'd left feeling that she hadn't told him everything. Maybe that was for the best. His head and heart were full with enough for now.

Toby whimpered at the foot of the bed, paws twitching in a running motion. Luke welcomed the sight of happy dreams being enjoyed.

He turned to his side and watched the silvery moon out the window. Knowing what he knew now really illuminated

Cora's resiliency. Though the anniversary loomed ahead, she was getting out some and participating in life. Was this balancing act, riding the rollercoaster of her grief, how the last three years had been for her? She'd decided to write after all this time, so that had to be a sign that she was headed in the right direction. Right?

Moving to Laurel Cove had brought Luke a life so very different from what he'd expected, though he wasn't quite sure what that was. He had found calm on the lake. But the lingering ghost of loss was all around him here, too. The loss of his mother was in every inch of the cabin. The loss of Ina's husband was in the decades of two lives lived side by side, now separated. And the loss of Christopher lived in Cora's waking memories and sleeping nightmares.

The burden of all this loss weighed heavily on Luke's chest. With his gaze heavenward, he opened his heart to God for the first time in his adult life.

God, I want to believe you're listening. I need to believe it. Did you bring me here, to live among these women, to teach me something? I came here for peace, but it feels like too much hurt for one place.

Luke sighed, sadness and frustration wrestling inside him. Unsure how to continue, the words written in his mother's elegant handwriting came back to him.

Just be with me, God, and Cora and Ina. Amen.

As a cloud passed in front of the moon, a yawn crept up from his chest and sleep whispered to him. A peaceful calm covered him like a blanket, an answer to his prayer.

CHAPTER Ten

When Cora stepped out onto her front porch, the noon sun warmed her face. The misty clouds that had hung over the lake earlier that morning had burned off, revealing a clear Carolina-blue sky that really made the bright yellow and orange leaves pop. As she placed wireless earbuds in her ears and pushed play on a classic rock playlist, she trotted down the steps and then the driveway toward the road.

Just before she turned left to begin her walk, she glanced to the right toward Luke's cabin and her heart swelled. The other night had been such a blessing—reviving her childhood tradition of s'mores for dinner on a perfect fall night. But more than that, facing her fear of telling someone about the accident had also blessed her. It left her lighter than she'd felt in years. She had fallen asleep that night with a prayer of thankfulness on her heart, especially for Luke.

It had been a long time since Cora had made a new friend, and Luke was quickly becoming just that. The few friends

Cora had in Laurel Cove were Christopher's from childhood that she'd met when they moved back a few years before the accident. As with her in-laws, she'd mostly shut them out since the accident, only seeing them at church or here and there around town.

In the last several days, she'd grown to enjoy Luke's company. He made her laugh without trying, was easy to be around, and didn't push her. Even the other night, though he must have had more questions about the accident, he'd let her guide the conversation to wherever she felt comfortable. Though Ina was a great neighbor, there was something about being with Luke that made her not feel alone for the first time since...

Since the accident.

Cora's steps slowed, her fingertips tingling. She wasn't interested in filling the void that Christopher's death had left in her heart. Was she? She pulled an earbud from her ear to quiet the music and stopped in the middle of the road, hands on her hips. Her chest rose and fell as she gazed at the bright sky. For the first time, Cora let herself wonder if her future could one day include another chance at love.

Off in the distance, the small American flag hanging above Ina's mailbox blew gently in the breeze. It was probably a good idea to stop by and see what Ina needed from the store before she made her list for tomorrow's grocery run. Cora refit the earbud in her ear and resumed her pace down the road to the rhythm of *More Than a Feeling* by the band Boston.

Cora prickled as the coincidence of the song hit her. The words of the title. The fact that Boston was Christopher's favorite band and just happened to be the city she and Luke shared in common. It was almost more than coincidence. If she'd written it in a book, the song choice would foreshadow destiny. She turned down Ina's driveway and shook off the strange warming in her chest.

Cora: I need you at Ina's. Hurry.

Luke: On my way.

Leaves went flying in the wake of Luke's truck as he sped down the narrow lake road and past Cora's drive. Adrenaline pumped through him as he pulled down Ina's driveway, jumped out, and raced up to the porch. He blinked to let his eyes adjust as he stepped into the kitchen, the screen door smacking behind him. The room was empty.

"Luke? Back here!" Cora's strained voice called from somewhere farther into the small house.

He ran through the living room, where the television blared, and down the dark hallway. He pushed a door open to find an empty bathroom. "Where are you?"

"Keep coming!"

Luke's heart pounded at the crack in Cora's voice coming from an open doorway at the end of the hall bright with sunlight. In a few steps, he found Cora kneeling beside Ina, who was on the floor, propped up against a nightstand next to a bed. He joined them. Red seeped through a hand towel Cora pressed to Ina's forehead. Matching splatters stained the front of Ina's light-blue housecoat.

"Paramedics are on their way." Cora's worried gaze met his as she shifted slightly, applying pressure to the towel with her other hand.

Luke nodded, picking up Ina's frail wrist to check for a pulse. "Is she conscious?"

Ina's arm jerked. "Of course I am."

Startled, Luke teetered, bracing himself on a hand against the worn carpet. He peered at Ina, who still gave every appearance of being asleep, then shot a look at Cora. She rolled her eyes.

"She wasn't very with it when I found her. But she's turned slightly ornery."

Sirens sounded from a distance. Luke placed a hand on Cora's shoulder. "I'll go watch for them. You okay?"

She nodded, smile thin.

Less than twenty minutes later, Luke pulled onto the main road behind the ambulance. He glanced over at Cora, who wrung her hands as she looked ahead intently. "It's lucky you went by when you did."

She turned to him, reaching to collect her hair into a twist over her shoulder. Working the ends in her fingers, she said, "I was out for a walk and decided to stop by to see what she needed from the store. I usually go after church on Sundays."

"Did you get any sense of what happened?" Luke pressed on the accelerator to keep up with the ambulance, now a few hundred feet ahead of him.

"When I first found her, the walker was lying on the floor a few feet away. I'm guessing she lost her footing. But listen to this..." Cora's fingers brushed the top of Luke's arm.

The hair on his arm stood at attention beneath his jacket. His gaze flicked from his arm back to Cora. Her eyes were wide, staring back at him.

"After I called 911 and started tending to her head, she started mumbling. It took me a while to make out what she was saying, but I finally figured it out. 'It was enough, Charles.' She said it over and over."

Luke watched the blinking lights on the back of the ambulance, picturing Ina lying there. "What do you think *it* was?"

"I don't know." Cora placed her hands in front of the vents blowing heated air into the cab of the truck then rubbed them together. "But she seemed very peaceful, though adamant. It was as if she could see him and was offering reassurance."

Luke turned right into the parking lot of the hospital as the ambulance turned left toward the emergency entrance. Parking the car, he turned to his passenger. Cora's face, full of color a moment ago, was now as pale as a ghost. Her eyes were panicky, and her head shook in short bursts.

"I can't go in there, Luke."

His heart sank as he looked past her to the large red EMERGENCY sign on the side of the building. *Of course.* This must be where she'd been brought after the accident.

Her hand trembled when he took it in his. "You don't have to go in."

She looked out the window and nodded softly. "Yes, I do. She needs me. She doesn't have anyone else."

"You're not alone either, Cora. I'll stay with you the whole time if you want."

When she turned to him, her blue eyes held his gaze. "Yes, please."

In her eyes, Luke found both strength and vulnerability, something at the core of her character that impressed him the most. He expected, though, that she felt only the vulnerability and saw it as a weakness. In that moment, he'd have done just about anything to help her see that her strength had also survived all she'd endured.

Cora sat in a hard chair in the waiting room of the emergency department, both knees bouncing under her elbows as she leaned over and stared at the speckled linoleum floor. She hated this place. The smell of disinfectant, beeping of machines in the distance, and people carrying on with casual conversation as if this weren't a place where people's lives were altered forever.

She looked up and watched Luke walk toward her. Her breath caught in her throat seeing the deep furrow between his brows.

He huffed as he settled into the chair next to her, his arm naturally falling across the back of her chair. "All they'll tell me is that she's being admitted. Because we aren't family, we can't go back to see her until then."

Cora sat back into her chair and nodded. The warmth of his arm behind her was comforting as she bit at the inside of her lip. "If they're admitting her, then that means something is wrong, right?"

"Not necessarily. I would think at her age, it's more precautionary than anything. They need to do some scans and monitor her closely." He searched her face. "She'll be okay."

Luke's hand squeezed her shoulder, and she smiled up at him. His eyes were so tender and kind. Cora's cheeks flushed. She bolted to her feet. "Uh, think there's anywhere to get hot tea around here?"

Mouth agape, Luke scanned the lobby. He stood and nodded in the direction opposite the nurse's station. "Sign says the cafeteria is that way."

"Great." Cora pressed her lips together and crossed her arms as they started walking. She'd welcome just about any distraction she could get right now. Distraction from being in the hospital again, from her concern for Ina, and from the way Luke looked at her.

They walked silently down the white corridor and into an open atrium-style room filled with tables and chairs around a cafeteria counter. After ordering, they walked with their steaming mugs to a table near tall windows that overlooked the back of the hospital. Despite the less than ideal location, the view of the Blue Ridge Mountains in the distance was one of the best Cora had ever seen. Light-blue peaks tucked behind darker blue ones, which seemed to cap the nearby golden ridges on the outskirts of town. The tall spruces and oaks that landscaped the hospital grounds added to the natural beauty. The whole view was just the distraction Cora needed.

"Cora?"

Cora spun from the window at the familiar voice. Approaching the table was Jack Bowdon, an old friend of Christopher's that they'd hung out with a few times.

"Hey, Jack." Luke extended a hand and the men shook.

Cora sat back, puzzled.

"How's the yard coming along, man?" Jack asked.

Cora addressed Luke. "How do you two know each other?"

"It's coming along, slowly but surely, thanks." Luke turned back to Cora, smiling. "I ended up at Jack's store the other day, and he helped me get outfitted to work on the mess at the cabin."

Jack looked back and forth between Luke and Cora then asked, "What brings you guys up here? Everyone okay?"

Cora shifted in her chair, eyes glued to Luke. He gave her a little smile then answered, "Our neighbor, Ina McLean, fell at her house earlier today. We're waiting to hear how she's doing."

"Oh, man. Sweet folks. They attended our church until a few years ago when Mr. McLean took a turn. I sure hope she's all right. You've got my number, Luke. Let me know what you find out, will you?"

Luke nodded. "I sure will. And you? Everything okay?"

Jack waved a hand in the air. "Oh yeah. My wife volunteers up here sometimes. Her car is in the shop, so I just brought her." Jack studied Cora for a moment. "I think the two of you would really hit it off. You haven't met Livy, have you?"

Cora had heard Jack got married a couple of years ago. Ina had been all atwitter about one of Laurel Cove's most eligible bachelors coming off the market. "No, I haven't. But that would be nice."

Luke smiled from across the table. Why did he look so amused?

"Great. Unless your number has changed, I'm sure I've still got it. Maybe I'll connect you two soon. I better be off. It was great seeing you both. Give Ina my best." Jack turned to go, then looked over his shoulder. "And Luke, I haven't forgotten that I owe you a visit."

Luke waved as Jack headed down the corridor. Turning back to Cora, Luke smiled and shook his head. "He might be the nicest guy I've ever met."

Cora couldn't help but smile back. "Yeah. That's Jack. Christopher used to say—"

She stopped herself, feeling heat rise up her neck. She was usually so guarded and caught herself before casually bringing Christopher up in conversation, wanting to avoid any memory wrapped up in whatever topic sprang him to mind. The ease with which she'd brought him up just now startled her.

Go ahead. She let out a deep breath. "Uh, Christopher used to say Jack could make friends with a charging bull before he was halfway across the arena."

The same amused half-smile rose to Luke's face. "That sounds about right."

Just then a nurse walked up to their table. "Are you the folks who came in with Ina McLean?"

Cora's heart raced. "Yes. Yes, we are."

"You can come with me. She's in a room and asking for you. Demanding, really."

Luke and Cora stood and followed the nurse, who walked back down the corridor at a fast clip. Luke leaned down and whispered, "If she's demanding things, she's got to be doing okay."

Cora had to admit, it was a positive sign. A spunky Ina was hopefully a healthy Ina. The nurse stopped at Room 212. She pursed her lips and paused a moment. "You can go on in. The doctor will be in shortly to speak with you."

Something about the way the nurse said it made Cora prickle. She glanced up at Luke, who gave her a reassuring nod. They walked in to find Ina sleeping in the bed, looking small and frail. Not an ounce of spunk to go around.

With her arms crossed tightly around her and shoulders hunched, Cora looked every bit as frail as Ina. It took everything Luke had not to reach out and hold her as they listened to the doctor in the hallway outside Ina's room.

"I'm only speaking to you with Mrs. McLean's permission. Even though she suffered no fractures or internal bleeding and can be discharged after another day of monitoring, I'm afraid I cannot recommend that she continue living alone. I'm aware she has no family. Someone can come by and speak with her about helping to make assisted living arrangements."

Cora's eyes snapped from staring down the hall to the doctor's face. "Will you let us speak with her first, please?"

The doctor smiled and removed his glasses, letting them rest across his chest from a string around his neck. "I think it's always nice to hear things like this from friends. Just let one of the nurses know when she's ready, and we'll put in a request for a patient care advocate to visit soon."

As the doctor headed down the hall, Cora turned to Luke, shaking her head, her eyebrows raised into high arches. "She's going to hate that, Luke."

"Probably." Luke's curiosity piqued as he watched Cora continue to shake her head, mouth twisted to one side.

She raised a hand to her mouth and tapped her lips with a finger. What was percolating in that head of hers? She peered intently at the cracked door of Ina's dark room then turned to him, a fierce determination in her eyes.

She licked her lips then nodded. "She's coming to live with me."

Luke let out a small, breathy laugh. "Uh, that's a pretty big decision."

"You're right. But think about it, Luke." She nodded toward a bench under the window across the hall from Ina's room. As they sat, knee to knee, a spark twinkled in her eyes.

"I'm home all the time. I have a downstairs bedroom and bathroom. I'm already familiar with what medicine she takes. For goodness' sake, until you came along, I was the only one who she saw on a regular basis. Why *wouldn't* I do this for her?"

Luke applauded her empathy and kindness, but his answer to her question would hurt. He paused, gazing out the window past her at the end of the hall. A wild autumn wind whipped through the trees. He couldn't smell it, but it sure looked like rain may be on the way.

"What are you thinking?"

When he looked back at her, his heart about burst at the way she searched him. Without thinking, he reached out and took one of her hands in his. Her soft skin and slender fingers felt natural to hold. When she didn't pull back, just enough courage swelled in him to say what was on his heart.

"Cora, you're still dealing with big loss in your life. And even if Ina makes a decent recovery, at her age she probably doesn't have a long time left. I just don't want to see you get hurt over losing someone else who becomes a part of your family."

Her eyes stayed focused on their hands. Luke watched her press her lips together as she looked up at him with watery eyes. "She already is a part of my family, Luke. No matter when she dies or where she's living when it happens, losing her will hurt. It just feels like the right thing to do. If she agrees, that is."

As if on cue, Ina's crotchety voice—sounding not at all affected by the fall—bellowed from beyond her door. "Whoever is whispering outside my room ought to mind their manners and either take their business elsewhere or speak up so I can hear what's being said!"

Cora's eyes brightened and she laughed, pressing at the corner of her eye with her free hand. Luke nodded and instinctively squeezed the hand still in his before releasing it. She gave him a quick smile before standing and turning for Ina's room.

With a hand on the door, Cora paused and turned back to Luke. "Will you come in and talk to her with me? She likes you."

"Of course." Luke rubbed both hands down his jeans and stood. "I like her, too."

These two women he'd befriended were quite the complicated pair and full of surprises. Though he worried this was going to end in more heartbreak for Cora, he agreed that something about it felt right.

Again, the words from Marie at the market echoed in his mind, about how God could use each of us to bring comfort to one another. As Luke followed Cora through the door to Ina's room, it dawned on him that he had a role to play in this little trio of neighbors, too. This time, Cora wouldn't be alone.

CHAPTER Eleven

Late spring and early fall in the mountains were the most fickle times of the year. One day could be cool and sunny, the next downright cold and wet. This October day was definitely the latter. Cora peeked out from under the overhang of her porch and pulled the collar of her puffy coat up around her neck. The slate-gray clouds looming in billows above the house looked ready to drop buckets of rain at any moment.

As she watched for Luke to return from Bowdon's Supplies with items needed to outfit her home for Ina's impending arrival tomorrow, she bounced on her toes to keep warm blood flowing and chewed at her lip.

What am I thinking? Is this nuts? Here, in her little refuge of solitude. Where memories with Christopher were preserved in unmoved furniture, precious kept routines, and storage space allowed to hold only mementos of lifechanging events—those good and terrible. Was she ready to compromise her carefully preserved life?

Is it really the life I want to hold on to forever? Cora stilled her feet and tilted her head at nothing in particular.

Just as a roll of thunder echoed in the distance, Luke's black truck turned onto her driveway and pulled to a stop in front of the porch. Both doors opened and Luke, from the driver's side, looked up at the churning sky. "Wasn't sure we were going to beat the rain."

"Just did, I think. Better get everything inside quick." Jack closed the passenger door and both men scurried to the bed of the truck.

Cora was by their sides in several steps and took some bags from Luke as he handed them to her. "What are you doing here, Jack?"

Jack's friendly smile lit up his whole face as he grabbed the last of the bags. "Figured three sets of hands were better than two. Especially when two of the sets aren't particularly experienced with handyman work."

"Hey, you haven't seen the amazing transformation my yard has undergone in the last several days." Luke snickered as he picked up a few skinny boxes and closed the tailgate just as a raindrop hit Cora's forehead.

Her skin prickled from a gust of wind as the three of them darted up to the porch through light rain. She held the door open for them.

Jack stepped in behind Luke and surveyed the cabin's downstairs before smiling down at Cora. "I actually just helped my aunt make some adjustments to her home two months ago when my uncle came home from a hip replacement. We did a lot of research, so this was a no brainer when Luke mentioned what you were doing for Ina when he came into the store."

He raised his eyebrows and nodded as he set the bags down inside the door and pulled off his coat. "Which is really great of you, by the way. Not a lot of folks would step up like this."

Cora wrinkled her nose and shrugged. "It's not a big deal." But her chest tightened at his words, a reminder that this was a very big deal. She took his coat and hung it on a hook next to the now closed door.

Facing the wall, she peeled off her own coat and paused a moment, closed her eyes, and drew in a long breath. What if she'd made a big mistake? What if this turned out to be bad for both Cora and Ina? After all, what did she know about taking care of the elderly?

"You okay?" Luke whispered beside her, hanging up his coat next to Jack's.

"I'm fine." She shoved her worries down and offered him a forced cheesy smile before turning around. "Let's get started, I guess."

Cora ran a hand across her neck and chest. A subtle sense of suffocation threatened at the sight of not one but two men in her home. *I've been alone here for so long.* But this was good, and growth often hurt. So, she'd let it hurt.

After a cleansing breath, Cora watched the guys chat between themselves while they sorted the items from the store on the kitchen table. From the edge of the coffee table in the living room, Cora picked up the list of *Ways to Prepare Your Home for an Elderly Loved One* the hospital had given her. Maybe staying on task would help the anxiety coursing through her. She ran her finger down the few checked boxes of simple tasks she'd already done that morning.

A rumble of thunder boomed, rattling the windows of the cabin. What a perfect day to match her mood. Cora joined the guys in the dining room and cataloged the supplies spread across the table.

"Man, you guys really do have a great view out here. Even with the nasty weather." Jack looked through the window off the dining room.

"It's definitely *one* of the perks." Luke's voice showered down over Cora from where he stood next her. His words were upbeat but tender.

A heat rushed up Cora's cheeks. Did Luke see her as a perk of living out by the lake? It was remarkable how quickly he'd become a friend to her. Yet, the way he'd begun to study her with his serious but soft eyes... Did they hold more than friendship?

Suddenly, Cora's head swirled into dizzying confusion. She grabbed a box of no-slip strips lying next to a package of nightlights and turned away from the table. "I'm going to start in the bathroom."

In a few quick steps, Cora escaped to the solitude of the guest bathroom just down the short hallway off the living room. The porcelain of the tub was cool under her hands when she sat on its edge, working to slow her breathing.

She closed her eyes and called to mind the rise and fall of the mountains at the edge of the lake. Inhale on the climb...exhale on the descent. It was all too much. Ina moving in. People in her house. Adjustments being made. Luke speaking softly to her.

As Cora's heart slowed, no longer thumping in her ears, she lifted her chin and looked around the bathroom. Her eyes landed on a framed quote sitting on the vanity next to the basin sink. *All things are possible if you believe.* The Bible verse from the book of Mark tugged at her. She glanced up to the ceiling with an open heart.

God, help me believe that with you by my side I can keep learning to live again. I want to. I need to. I can't keep riding this roller coaster. Help me.

She wiped at a tear that rolled down her cheek and neck. How many times did she have to pray some version of this prayer? God was there like always, she knew it. But waiting for the shift to set her sailing, once and for all, away from her grief and into a calmer harbor was exhausting.

A gentle knock sounded at the door, which cracked open a smidge. "Cora, did you want us to..."

Had the door not closed behind her? She stood and quickly wiped at both eyes. "Yeah?"

Luke stepped in and looked at the box of strips, still unopened, lying on the vanity. His smiled faded when their eyes met. "Hey, what's up? Were you crying?"

"Oh, I'm fine." Cora bit her lip hard to keep it from quivering. If only she'd had a few more moments alone to compose herself.

He peered over his shoulder, took a step farther into the bathroom, and closed the door about halfway behind him. Her hand rubbed against her collar bone, and she stepped back until the edge of the tub met her calves.

The corners of Luke's mouth were drawn down, brow furrowed. "You don't seem fine. Are you having second thoughts about all of this?"

He took a step closer and reached out for Cora's arm, crossed in front of her. She jerked her shoulder back, the shower curtain rustling behind her. "I said I'm fine, Luke."

She leaned past him, grabbed the box of strips, and turned for the shower, flinging open the curtain. Her throat stung with a fresh collection of tears waiting to be released. Why couldn't he just leave her alone? The box ripped down the center when she yanked at the opening, sending textured plastic strips flying all over the bathroom.

With a cry from deep down in her gut, Cora spun around and lunged forward. With nowhere else to go, her face pressed against Luke's chest as sobs shook her. The dam had broken and was flooding fast.

Luke's arms splayed out in both directions as Cora clung to his middle. He wasn't exactly sure what was happening or what part he'd played in it. The pinch in his heart told him to hold her tightly, but his head—not to mention her tone a moment ago—told him to tread lightly.

She let out a whimper, then moaned through another round of sobs, tightening her grip on him. He couldn't take any more. Her shoulders trembled as his arms eased around them, tucking her into an embrace. They stood together in the bathroom until her body stilled and she began to breathe deeply through sniffles.

Then, as if someone flipped a switch in a pitch-dark room, Cora startled and pushed away from him. Her puffy and smudged eyes were wild, confused. "What are you doing?"

What? Luke threw his hands up, though there was nothing to defend. "I was just...I mean, you were upset."

She rubbed at her eyes with the palms of her hands and knelt to pick up the scattered strips. "You just caught me at a tough moment. I'm fine."

"Cora, come on. It's okay to not be okay." He bent and picked up a few strips from the floor in front of him. "I'm sure this is a big change for you to process. Especially considering no one's lived here with you since—"

She was on her feet in a second and pointed a finger up at his face. "Don't! You have no right to come in here thinking you understand what I'm feeling. I don't need your advice or your pity or whatever this is." She sniffled and waved a handful of strips around the bathroom.

"I don't pity you." Luke sighed.

She was acting more like the unreasonable woman he'd met that first day. It would be easy, and probably wise, to wave a white flag. However, when had he ever done the easy thing?

He leaned against the vanity and crossed his arms. "But it's easy to see that you're still dealing with some big stuff related to your husband's death. It's all right to let your friends—"

She shook her head and glared at him, lips pursed. "We have known each other just over a week, Luke. We are *not* friends."

Luke's stomach sank as if filled with rocks, his breath gone. He looked into her icy blue eyes and nodded shortly. "My mistake."

A crack of thunder boomed, and the lights in the bathroom flickered. Cora closed her eyes with a startled shudder. Luke waited for her to say something, anything that might rescind her declaration. This was her stubbornness speaking. There was no way she didn't feel at least some small sense of friendship between them. But she remained silent.

"Okay." Luke stood from against the counter, pulled the door open fully, and stepped into the dark hallway. "I'll help Jack get these few things done, and we'll be out of your hair."

As he made his way down the hall, fresh muffled sobs joined the percussive rain pounding the roof. Walking away was so unnatural, and yet his only option at the moment. He rounded the corner into the living room and found Jack plugging in a nightlight to an outlet at the base of the staircase.

Jack stood and offered Luke a thin half-smile. "Everything okay?"

"Did you hear any of that?"

"A little. She sounded pretty upset. Are you guys—" Jack raised his eyebrows.

Luke waved a hand and shook his head. "Oh, no. Nothing like that. I think I just overstepped and said something she wasn't ready to hear. At least not from me."

Jack placed a hand on Luke's shoulder. "I'm no expert, but it's been my experience that you can't help someone who's not ready to be helped."

Luke nodded, his heart burdened with that truth.

As the men went to work installing a motion-sensor light in the guest room where Ina would sleep, Luke couldn't stop thinking of Cora. Her obvious pain, the snap of anger and stubborn rejection. Then there was Jack's suggestion that there was something romantic between Luke and Cora. He found her attractive, that was impossible to deny. Not to mention that, to date, spending time with her on or around the lake was his favorite thing to do in Laurel Cove. But any kindling of an idea to pursue her had been snuffed out cold by today's clear message.

In the hour that followed, Cora and Luke managed to dodge one another and exchange minimal words. With a handrail and seat now up in the shower, non-stick liners added under rugs, and a baby monitor system set up between the two bedrooms, their work was done.

"Livy told me to mention that she'd like to bring over dinner one night soon. We'll be in touch." Jack zipped up his jacket at the door.

"Thanks, Jack. I really appreciate the help." Cora held the door open and Jack stepped onto the porch, the rain now a gentle pitter-patter outside.

She lowered her eyes to the ground as Luke followed. Despite a bit of a wounded heart, he wanted nothing more than for her to look up at him and give one of those bright smiles. The kind that lit up the whole room. Instead, her eyes darted at him just long enough to acknowledge him leaving.

He couldn't hold back a sigh. "Listen, I'm sorry about the way things went today. I hope Ina gets settled in well tomorrow. Please call or text if you need anything and I'll be here."

"Okay. Thanks." Her quick smile was no brighter than the gloomy autumn sky.

His skin prickled when a strong, cold wind rushed across the porch as she closed the door. Just like that, she seemed as far away as before he'd even met her.

In the hours that followed, Luke was consumed with wondering what the days ahead would hold for the constantly changing and unpredictable trio he'd found himself a part of. In many ways, it was more than he'd bargained for when he came to the lake in search of peace. These women were haunted by ghosts of lost loves. They had wounds that needed healing, care that he didn't know how to provide. And yet, somehow, all he ever wanted but never knew he needed seemed wrapped up in them.

CHAPTER Twelve

"No, not that one. The blue one." Ina pointed a shaky finger from atop the seat of her new walker. Cora grabbed the blue sweater hanging to the right of a red one in Ina's closet.

"Think that'll about do it for now?" Cora added the sweater to the pile lying on top of the bed. Moving Ina into her house today started with packing up some essentials. A pulse pounded between her eyes, increasing the ache in her head. "Remember I can always come back to get anything else you want."

Ina nodded and twisted a finger under the hospital bracelet still dangling around her thin wrist. "Tell me again why Luke isn't here? Will we see him later?"

Cora's insides knotted. She turned to grab a laundry basket from the floor at the end of the bed and started layering the hangered clothes in carefully. "I think he had some work to do at his place."

Ina shuffled her feet along the worn carpet until the walker inched up next to Cora at the bedside. She placed a cold hand on Cora's. When their eyes met, Ina's were narrowed behind her glasses.

"What happened?"

Cora resumed packing the clothes. Why was everyone around here so nosy lately? "I don't know what you mean."

"*I mean*, what occurred...what took place...what transpired between you and our tall, handsome neighbor?" Ina's voice oozed with sarcasm. "Did you have words? Did he kiss you?"

Cora gasped and eyed the old woman, mouth gaping. "No! He did not kiss me. Where in the world do you come up with these wild ideas, Ina?"

Ina rested her elbows on the low handlebars of the walker and intertwined her bony fingers in front of her. Her white eyebrows rose, deep wrinkles folding along her forehead. "My, my. It is a wonder how one could possibly fathom the notion of two attractive single persons like yourself and Mr. Bassett finding one another inclined to canoodle."

"I am *not* single." Blood pumped through Cora's veins like the raging spring streams filled with runoff from melting snow.

"Oh dear, but you are." The biting sarcasm in Ina's voice was replaced with a tender softness. "The vows we took say *'til death do us part*. You and I both are as single as the day is long, I'm afraid."

Cora's knees suddenly threatened to give up supporting her. She sat atop the patchwork quilt on Ina's bed, the sweater in her hands crumpling into a mound on her lap. She searched Ina's face and found a stoic resignation that came with a life well experienced in unfairness. "But I don't think of myself as single."

Ina looked to a window on the far wall past the bed. The day's brightness danced through sheer white curtains. After a moment, she sighed and returned her gaze to Cora.

"That's the thing about loss, dear. Those of us left on this side of heaven must redefine ourselves. It's the only hope we have of continuing to live in the here and now." She reached out and patted Cora's knee. "Otherwise, we end up doing something that only resembles living, in a version of the past that doesn't exist anymore."

Cora swallowed hard, her brain working Ina's words over. Was that what she had been doing? Carrying on an existence that merely *resembled* living? It resonated in a way that made Cora's stomach turn.

Angst percolated inside and she shook her head. "I have a hard time believing that after decades and decades with Charles, you care to define yourself as anything other than his wife."

Ina's eyes filled, lips pressed tightly. After a long pause, she answered. "What I care to do and what simply is are two *very* different things. The one and only thing I was, am, and will be forever is a child of God."

Cora bit at the inside of her lip and stood to return to her task. "Well, nothing about that has anything to do with Luke."

Ina clicked her tongue and shook her head.

Cora picked up another handful of clothes and turned to face her. "What?"

"My stubborn child, I believe it has everything to do with him."

Heat rose from Cora's toes, through her stomach and chest, and straight to her cheeks. She cleared her throat and blinked back tears. Ina could go on and on about how handsome and charming she found Luke Bassett. Whether or not he was handsome or charming or interesting or pleasant to be around didn't change the fact that he didn't know when to mind his own business.

A bell rang above his head as Luke stepped through the door of Brewed. Surprisingly, the place was hopping at noon on a Wednesday. He scanned the place as he unzipped his jacket, then spotted Jack waving from a table near a large window at the front.

"Hey, man." Luke removed his coat, hung it over the back of the wooden chair, and took a seat opposite Jack. "I had no idea this place served lunch."

"Oh yeah. Breakfast, lunch, and dinner actually. The name is kind of deceiving, I guess." Jack turned over his shoulder and pointed to a lunch menu written in colorful chalk that hung next to a window looking into the kitchen. "Menu's up there. Can't go wrong with the chili, but Greg's patty melt is killer, too."

"I've been in town over three weeks, and this is the first place I've tried." Luke glanced around.

Several customers sat at a counter past the register, bent over plates of food. Others were scattered among about a dozen tables, chatting and laughing. Behind the counter, shelves held rows of white coffee mugs and silver bags of coffee with labels matching the Brewed logo stenciled on the door. These had been his favorite kind of stops along the campaign trail.

"Restaurants like this are the heart of a small town."

A smiling woman with dark brown hair pulled to the side in a braid approached the table. "Now I like the sound of that."

Jack grinned and gestured across the table. "Meredith, this is Luke..."

"Basset," Luke said, reaching out for Meredith's hand. "Luke Bassett. Nice to meet you."

"Luke recently moved into a cabin up at the lake," Jack said.

Meredith tilted her head, looking to Jack. "Up near the Bradfords' place?"

Luke perked at the mention of Cora's name and watched Jack nod. "Yeah."

"It's beautiful up there. We're glad to have you. Laurel Cove's a great place. Did you move here with family or just you?"

"Just me." Luke smiled thinly, but the answer stirred something inside him. When he first arrived, the solitude was just what he wanted. But he'd become acutely aware of being alone in the several days since the incident with Cora.

Jack leaned onto his arms folded against the table. "You going to take our order or what?"

Meredith wrinkled her nose at Jack. "Hey, just because we're friends doesn't mean you get to push me around, mister. I'm just spreading some Welcome Wagon cheer."

The three of them shared a laugh before Meredith finally took their orders.

"It was nice to meet you, Luke. Hope we see you around." Meredith ripped the ticket from the pad she'd scribbled on and turned to go.

"Thanks, you will." Luke meant it, too. If the food was half as good as the atmosphere and friendliness, he'd be back often.

Once they were alone again, Jack sat back and looked at Luke. "Anything yet from Cora?"

"Nope." Luke shook his head and gazed out the window onto the street. He watched as a man hung a strand of black bats across the window of the bookstore across the street. Every day since Cora had practically shut her door in his face, there'd been no calls and no texts. Had Ina gotten moved in all right? How was Cora adjusting? He'd resisted the urge to stop by and check on them both.

"These things have a way of blowing over, even with estranged neighbors."

Luke sighed and looked back across the table. "Thing is, I thought we'd all started to become friends."

"Well, then I'm sure you'll hear from her eventually."

Meredith walked up with their bowls of chili and a basket of cornbread muffins. "Here you go, guys. And hey," she said to Luke with a hand on her hip. "Don't know if anyone's mentioned it, but the Fall Festival is Saturday and Sunday."

Luke laughed and gestured outside the window. "You mean the one advertised on every lamppost, the banner strung up over Main Street, the hand-painted billboard by the bank, and the flyer the grocery clerk handed me yesterday? I think I've heard of it."

"The new guy thinks he's funny." Meredith gave Jack, who smirked, a sideways smile with a thumb pointed at

Luke. When she turned to Luke, she offered him a sugary sweet smile and a wink. "Well, if that means you'll be there, look for our food truck. We'll have coffee, hot chocolate, cider, plus our new cider donuts. Y'all enjoy now."

Luke raised his eyebrows at Jack, who picked up a spoon and started to stir his chili. "She's a pistol, huh?"

"You bet. But you won't find a fiercer friend than her and her husband Greg."

The rest of lunch was filled with chatter about the weather and hikes Jack recommended in the area. After lunch was over, Jack headed back to work at the supply store, and Luke made his way back to his truck parked farther down Main Street.

Luke's mind strayed easily back to Cora and the notion of fierce friends. In all his years of traveling, making friends had taken a backseat to his career. The solitary lifestyle had suited him, the constant stimulation of new faces and new places distracting him from the void created by the absence of more permanent relationships.

Until he moved to the lake, that is. With Cora now absent from his days, something was definitely missing. His mind flashed with visions of their kayak-saving canoe ride, cooking together, s'mores on the deck, learning about each other's lives, and coming together to help Ina.

He grabbed his keys from his pocket as he approached the truck and shook his head. *No.* He did not buy Cora's claim that they weren't friends. If what they'd shared wasn't friendship, then he didn't know what was.

Before stepping into the cab of the truck, Luke picked a bright orange Fall Festival flyer from underneath his wiper blade. His heart stirred with an idea. Maybe she was willing to discard their new friendship, but he simply wasn't going to give up that easily.

Cora stepped onto the deck and eased the door closed behind her. One thing she hadn't considered when Ina moved in was how much she'd sleep. Cora welcomed the post-lunch alone time during Ina's nap, though to be fair, her new housemate had not been a nuisance at all.

The crunch of the gravel on the path mixed with the rustle of fallen leaves. Cora passed her usual chair near the shoreline, drawn to the sun-soaked dock. She walked to the end and sat cross-legged on the wooden slats, setting her black notebook beside her. The sun warmed her face as she surveyed the peaceful scene of gently rippling water and colorful mountains.

The notebook held scratches of a few ideas that had come to her over the last week, but nothing close to the well-developed concept she needed to have soon. She eyed the black cover and sighed. Instead of picking it up, she reached into her sweater pocket and pulled out her phone. She turned it over in her hands and looked out over the water. For the thousandth time in the last several days, Cora mulled over Ina's words.

My stubborn child, I believe it has everything to do with him.

Cora had so quickly dismissed those words. What about her life could possibly have anything to do with a neighbor that had shown up just a few weeks ago? He was virtually a stranger. They were connected by proximity only.

But with each passing day, God had begun to chip away at her hardened heart. What if Luke represented a new beginning? What if being his friend didn't have to threaten her loyalty to Christopher? He was, in fact, the first person she'd opened up to about the accident.

That's huge. You know it is.

A strong gust of wind sent her hair whipping around her face, the shaking of the remaining leaves in the trees behind her almost deafening. She twisted her hair into a bun on top of her head then punched in the passcode to her phone and started a new text to Luke. The cursor blinked. She tapped the side of the phone. *Nothing.* Her cheeks puffed with air as she lay flat against the dock, the sun turning the inside of her eyelids a bright orange.

Suddenly a shadow passed over and blocked out the sun. Her eyes flew open to find Luke bent over her, staring down. She scrambled to her feet, her phone nearly tumbling into the water before she caught it. "You scared me to death!"

"I didn't mean to sneak up on you." He was dressed in a gray long-sleeved athletic jacket, black jogging pants, and running shoes. Was he perspiring? "Can we talk?"

Cora rubbed a hand up her neck and looked behind him up toward the house. Surely Ina wasn't up already and had let him in. "How'd you know I was back here?"

He tipped his chin toward the cove. "I saw you out here from my place. It's a pretty day to be outside."

She glanced over at his cabin then back to him and narrowed her eyes. "I haven't been out here that long."

"I ran."

Cora chuckled, but his face was serious. "Why?"

"I didn't want to miss the chance to talk with you alone," he said matter-of-factly.

She flushed and turned to face the water. After a moment, she resumed her seat cross-legged on the dock and looked back at him over her shoulder. "You can sit if you want."

He wasted no time joining her but said nothing. Autumn continued to swirl around and between them, drowning out any sound other than the effect of the wind on the trees at its mercy. Content to wait for Luke to speak, Cora busied herself by letting stubbornness and vulnerability vie for attention inside her. All she knew, beyond any reason, was that she was glad he was here next to her.

He'd come in with such gusto, but sitting next to Cora on the dock, Luke found himself disarmed by her mere presence. After days apart, her effect on him had a new, stronger potency. With his arms draped around his knees, he stared out over the lake and waited for a brilliant speech to come. Finally, with only two words on repeat in his head, he sighed and turned to look at her.

Wavy strands of golden hair fell from a mound atop her head and blew around her. She reached to tuck several pieces behind her ear. When their eyes finally met, it was like two puzzle pieces snapped together in Luke's heart.

"I'm sorry." He drew in a quick breath and held it.

Her gaze fell to her lap where her hands fiddled with her phone. "You don't have to say that."

"Sure I do. If I pushed too hard or overstepped, that's on me."

Luke waited for her to look at him again and licked his dry lips. *Just say what you came to say.* He nodded to himself and continued. "Listen, I'm not insane. I realize we've known each other a very short time. And from the little bit you've shared with me, I'm sure there's a great deal I can't possibly understand about your life before I got here. But the bottom line is I think you need a friend."

The side of her lip creased under her teeth before she turned away from him toward the cove. She was so hard to read. Was she about to cry? Was she really listening to what he was saying, or was she still blinded by anger, grief, or some other emotion he didn't understand?

He fixed his gaze across the lake and sighed as another strong gust of wind rushed over them. When it finally stilled and the space around them quieted, he turned and spoke to the side of Cora's head, which still faced the cove. "So, I'd like to be your friend."

His shoulders relaxed as if he'd just turned in a big assignment. He'd said what he came to say. Plain and simple. Now it was up to Cora to decide if she wanted him as a friend. At least if she rejected the offer, he wouldn't go to sleep that night staring at the ceiling wondering where she stood, if she'd call, and whether he should reach out.

After what felt like several minutes of silence, she finally faced him. She opened her mouth just as a violent wind whirled to life. Cora covered her face with both hands and ducked her head. Luke's eyes watered as the cold stung them. He braced himself with a hand on the dock to keep from toppling into her as leaves from the shoreline blew around them in a frenzy.

Then just as suddenly as it came, the wind left. The silence and stillness that replaced the chaos was almost eerie. Cora's breathing was heavy, her hair a mess around her.

She looked at Luke and one corner of her mouth upturned. "I'd like very much to be your friend."

Luke's chest swelled as a smile broke across his face. Whether it was the wild winds of change that swept over her or a true change of heart, he didn't know. But it was a good starting point. He reached into his back pocket and pulled out the bright orange flyer he'd found earlier on his windshield.

"Apparently this festival is a big deal around here. I think I need a friend to show me the ropes." He raised his eyebrows and cocked his head to one side.

She eyed the flyer and grinned. "On one condition."

"Name it."

"You buy me a cider donut."

Luke laughed and extended a hand to her. "Deal."

It was the easiest deal he'd ever made. Luke would take one day at a time as they learned what being friends meant, living along this lake that seemed to have a mind of its own. Something told him it wasn't going to be easy, and this recent misstep wouldn't be the last with Cora. But if the rest of his life had taught him anything, it was that things that were worthwhile were rarely ever easy.

CHAPTER
Thirteen

Surely, for some people, adapting to change was less of a struggle than it was for Cora. The morning after agreeing to go to the Fall Festival with Luke, she wrestled with her bedsheets like a fly trying to escape a sticky spider's web. She finally kicked her feet wildly until the fabric was a bundle on the floor, then sat up to the edge of the bed with a huff.

She stood, glanced at the clock, and brushed her hair off her face as she stepped to the window. At just a few minutes after seven o'clock, Ina wouldn't be up for about another hour. Beyond the lake, the brightly-colored mountains and overcast sky matched her two-faced mood. One half of her glowed with relief that things with Luke were resolved, while the other half brooded with worry over what it all meant and whether she was somehow leaving her life with Christopher behind.

She left the window, pulled on her robe, and made her way downstairs. Passing through the quiet living room to the kitchen, her nose detected the nutty aroma of freshly brewed coffee. Sure enough, the small red light was illuminated on the coffee maker they'd moved over from Ina's. She peered back over the living room, but all the chairs were empty. Maybe Ina was enjoying an early cup in her room.

Though not usually a coffee drinker, Cora poured herself a cup and stepped out onto the deck. The air, cool and damp, smelled of a fireplace burning nearby. She looked to her left through the trees at the distant outline of Luke's cabin. Sure enough, a thin line of smoke puffed from the chimney.

"Morning, dear."

Cora jumped at the voice to her right, a slosh of hot coffee stinging her hand. She gasped and found Ina sitting in a deck chair, a blanket draped over her lap. The four-wheeled walker sat beside her.

"You scared me to death. What are you doing out here?" Cora took the other seat and set her mug on the small table as she wiped her hand on her robe.

Ina peered out over the yard. "Just enjoying God's great creation."

Cora picked up her mug and took a sip, the coffee bitter on a tongue that was used to mild tea. "You really shouldn't be coming out here alone. Just getting over the threshold of the door with your walker is dangerous. Not to mention you had hot coffee in your hand."

The woman's wrinkled chin tilted upward as she kept her gaze on the dark water of the lake. "Rest assured, today's not the day I'm going to die a tragic death traveling to the deck."

Prickles ran up Cora's arms. She bit her lip, but the words she tried to suppress wouldn't be denied. "How about we not make light of tragic deaths, okay?"

Ina turned to look at her, mug paused halfway to her mouth. With a trembling hand, she worked carefully to ease it down onto the table. "Are you insinuating I'm making light of your husband's accidental death?"

Cora averted her eyes and winced. She was trying to choose the brighter side of her mood, but this wasn't helping. She didn't want to argue with Ina, nor did she really want to have a conversation about Christopher. "I'm sorry. I shouldn't have—"

"I'm going to give you some unsolicited advice," Ina interrupted. When Cora looked back at her, Ina's eyes bore into hers. "I'm ninety-three years old and I've earned the right. You need to put to rest the power you are giving that one event in your life. Christopher died. Tragically, yes. But it was almost three years ago, dear. You're not the only one in the world who's lost someone they love."

Cora's stomach twisted and she gripped the hot mug in her hands despite the heat radiating through her palms.

"In fact," Ina continued, her voice sharp, "you're not the only one on this lake who's lost someone...or even this deck."

Guilt whirled around Cora's twisted stomach. Luke had lost his mother. Ina had lost a husband. And while many would say Charles' death was not tragic at his elderly age, it was likely nonetheless tragic to his wife of more than seventy years. Cora, however, had not gotten her seventy years. She'd not even gotten one full decade with Christopher.

Cora searched the contents of her mug and finally cleared her throat. "I seem to owe a lot of apologies lately. I don't mean to minimize your loss. I'm sorry."

Ina nodded softly and sipped her coffee.

A cool breeze blew between them, rustling the trees surrounding the cabin. Cora adjusted a corner of the blanket that had blown off Ina's leg. "I want to move on, but how do I do that without having to give up my past?"

"The past is not something to give up or to hold on to. It just *is* the past, child. Nothing you do from this day forward can change or replace the wonderful life you had with Christopher." Ina's cold hand rested on top of Cora's across the small table between them. "Let Christopher be a highlight on your life's timeline. Just don't let him be the only highlight."

It all sounded so easy. Cora's heart flustered for understanding like someone listening to a foreign language. Her eyes implored Ina's. "But *how*?"

Ina smiled and tilted her head to the left. "You can start by enjoying more time with people your own age and getting out of this cabin."

Cora followed Ina's gaze to Luke's cabin then looked back and pressed her lips into a thin smile. "He asked me to go to the Fall Festival with him on Saturday evening."

"Good, good." Ina nodded behind her mug.

"You don't think it's a bad idea? I mean, we're just going as friends."

Ina pushed her glasses up on her nose and raised an eyebrow. "I don't ever think spending time with a tall, handsome, polite man is a bad idea, dear."

A chuckle bubbled up in Cora's chest, her middle slowly untwisting. From the far side of the lake, a bright ray of sunshine broke through the gray clouds and set the colors of the gentle mountainside ablaze. It only took that one small break in the clouds to set forth awe-inspiring change below.

Maybe the one small break in the clouds for Cora was Luke asking her to the Fall Festival. One step at a time out of her grief and into the world of the living.

A log settled in the fireplace, and Luke looked up from over the edge of the book as a burst of embers danced above the flames and up the chimney. Engrossed in Cora's latest novel, he had spent all morning reading with Toby at his feet.

Ding. He reached for his phone on the side table, its screen illuminated. The clock read 10:45 as he swiped the notification to read the new text.

RACHEL: GIVE ME A CALL WHEN YOU'RE FREE.

Luke bristled. The last time he'd talked to his sister was when he phoned to tell her of his plans to move to the cabin. She'd told him he was running away from his problems and should face them head on. It was her less-than-comforting version of support and encouragement. Since arriving in Laurel Cove, he'd texted her a few times to check in but received nothing more than an occasional "fine" or "thanks."

He stood and set the open book facedown on the chair's seat. Toby stood too, stretched his front legs with his rear end in the air, then followed Luke to the back door and out onto the sunny deck. The fresh air cleared Luke's mind of Paige Price's entangling story, making way for a surprising yearning as he turned his phone over in his hand a few times.

He'd never considered the space left by the strained Bassett family dynamics to be a gaping hole. Luke had come to terms with how things were long ago. An *every man for himself* sort of thing. It's what led to independence and few obligations, which in turn made it easier to achieve the life he'd enjoyed for so long.

Then his mom died, he moved to Laurel Cove, and Cora and Ina came into his life. And everything had begun to change. In the relatively short time he'd been there, the unlikely trio already experienced ups and downs. No family is perfect, even the ones without blood relation to complicate things.

Family? Luke shook his head and chuckled. Anyone would call him crazy calling the women his family after such a short time. But there was no denying his neighbors-turned-friends, not to mention whatever he and Cora could become, had started to fulfill something inside Luke he hadn't known he wanted or needed.

For the first time in his adult life, it sparked to life a subtle yearning for his own family. He suddenly wasn't dreading calling Rachel. Maybe it was time to reconnect—or connect at all—with his one and only sibling. He drew in a cool breath through his nose and dialed.

She answered on the first ring. "Hello, this is Rachel Bassett."

Luke rolled his eyes. Surely she saw it was him who was calling. "Hey, Rach. How are you?"

"Hello, Luke. I'm doing well, though quite busy with term examinations. Hang on just a moment." The rustling of papers, then what sounded like a door closing. "Okay. I'm going to cut to the chase."

She always did. Rachel, much like their father, had never been the warm and fuzzy type. Luke stepped down from the deck to the yard, Toby close on his heels. "Okay."

He bent to pick up a yellow tennis ball peeking out from a pile of damp leaves. Toby pranced around him then raced after it as Luke threw it into the yard toward the shoreline.

"I'm getting married."

Luke's eyebrows arched skyward with both surprise and amusement. He only recalled one other man she'd ever dated, and that was short-lived. "Hey, that's big news. Congratulations. Who is he?"

"Thank you." She paused and let out a long sigh, inviting Luke to listen intently for what came next. "His name is Harley. He's a drummer in a band, if you can believe it. We met at a museum on a random rainy Sunday a few months ago. He's brilliant but hopelessly whimsical and silly. We're probably the worst match. But I can't help myself."

Luke laughed as Toby dropped the retrieved ball at his feet then barked impatiently. He threw it again and wiped his hand on his pants. "Well, Sis, I definitely can't picture you being a roadie to a guy named after a motorcycle, but I think it's great."

"We're ridiculous together."

"They say you can't pick who you fall in love with." Cora's face sprung to Luke's mind, clear as day. He rubbed at the back of his suddenly hot neck, eyes skyward. "How boring would that be anyway?"

"Boring isn't all bad, you know. Boring is predictable and trustworthy."

"That sounds *so* romantic." Luke smiled into the phone, imagining Rachel in her cashmere sweater and pearls, arms crossed and lips pursed. "But you're happy?"

Another sigh, this one labored as though it needed extra oomph to make it across the Atlantic Ocean. "Against all odds, I am."

"Then, it's not ridiculous at all. It sounds great. I'm happy for you. Set a date?"

"Oh, we're doing a quick civil registrar ceremony in a few weeks. Neither one of us wants a big fuss. We'll have a few friends over for cocktails but that's it. Still, I wanted you to know."

Luke's heart warmed. This was a big gesture on Rachel's part, very sisterly. "I'm glad you told me. And I can't wait to meet this drummer who stole your heart against your will."

It was Rachel's turn to laugh, and it suited her. "What about you? Tired of the small-town life yet? How's the cabin?"

Luke turned and eyed his sun-drenched home flanked by golden-leafed trees. "It's exactly as I remembered it, except for a few things Mom added over the years." He returned his view to the lake and found Toby sniffing along the shoreline. His gaze wondered over the vibrant mountains and calm, black water until he found Cora's cabin across the cove. "And no, I'm not tired of it yet. I've met some really great people. I think it's just what I needed."

"Any of those really great people a woman?" Rachel didn't smile often, but Luke detected she might be right then.

"No, only men live in Laurel Cove," Luke bit back, an eyebrow quirked upward. But the stirring in his heart acknowledged what she likely implied. "Of course I've met women."

"Well, it would be quite a different headline than the others about you if some simple country woman finally nabbed the ever-elusive, most eligible bachelor photojournalist Luke Bassett."

Now she was playing with him.

"This is an uncharacteristically jovial side of Dr. Rachel Bassett. If I didn't know better I'd say Harley might be rubbing off on you." Luke joined Toby at the water's edge. The dog whimpered, focused on the yellow ball that had floated out of reach into the cold water.

"You're incorrigible," she hissed, then paused. "But you're not wrong."

Luke's eyes grew wide and a smile broke. "I'm impressed you'd admit it."

"Well, I've got a lecture in ten minutes. Best be going. Bye now."

With that, Rachel was gone. Luke stared at the now-blank screen on his phone before sliding it into his back pocket. There was no telling when he'd hear from his sister again. He smiled and rubbed a hand across Toby's head when the dog stepped up alongside him and nudged his leg.

Maybe today's call would be the start of better relations. Even though they weren't close, Luke was glad Rachel had found love. He studied Cora's cabin, focusing on the deck where they'd enjoyed s'mores and she'd shared so much about her life. That had also been the night she'd made a deeper impression on his heart.

His chilly, closed-off sister had found unlikely love with a British drummer. Luke, too, had found an unlikely family of sorts here in Laurel Cove. But could he really be satisfied with just being Cora's friendly neighbor?

The Fall Festival was in two days. Right now, it was enough to spend time with her. It had to be.

CHAPTER Fourteen

"What do I need to know before we get there?"

Cora peeked across the cab of the truck at Luke as they made their way to town for the Fall Festival. He was casual in jeans, sneakers, and an olive-green knit sweater that Ina had said, in a whispered aside when he came to pick Cora up, really set off his caramel-colored eyes.

Ina wasn't wrong.

Cora swallowed past the thought. "Well, I already suggested you go back and get gloves. I really do think you're going to get cold once we're out there a while."

He smiled and released one hand from the steering wheel, wiggling his fingers. "I told you, I only work my camera with bare hands. Plus, I've got a coat. I'll be fine."

She nodded at the small camera bag sitting atop the console between them. "It'll be fun to see what you get. If you like small-town stuff, you'll be in heaven tonight."

"I'm looking forward to it." He watched the two-lane highway in front of them as they headed west toward town. "So, what's your favorite part of the festival?"

Cora worked her gloves in her lap and admired the early evening sky's bands of gold and orange and pink. It looked the same as the last time she'd been to a Laurel Cove Fall Festival, which was three years ago with Christopher. She chewed at her lip. *Nothing can replace what I had with him.*

"I really love the tilt-a-whirl."

Luke grinned like a kid on Christmas morning. "Wait! They have rides?"

She hid a giggle behind a hand. "Well, yeah. What kind of fall festival doesn't have rides?"

"Hey, I always thought the same thing until my hopes were crushed at a festival in Maine. Not one single ride. Not even hayrides." He shook his head, mouth pressed thin.

"Well, there should be a handful of good rides tonight. Not to mention the best hayride I've ever been on. Unless—" Cora paused and waited until Luke looked at her expectantly.

"Unless what?"

"Unless you're easily scared. It's a *haunted* hayride." She widened her eyes and danced her fingers in front of her face.

The grin on his face grew by another inch. "Oh, you don't know what I've seen around the world. Nothing scares me anymore. Well, maybe snakes. I hate snakes."

Cora laughed when he wrinkled his nose then shuddered. She was actually looking forward to this. "Okay, then. We can definitely do the hayride."

Several minutes later they pulled into town and started down Main Street. Cars lined the parking spots along the curb, and the sidewalks were full of families making their way up the hill toward the town square where the festival was staged. Cora pointed to the right when they rolled to a stop at the traffic light that blinked red. "Turn here. I know of a great place to park."

Sure enough, a spot was still open in the small lot behind Bowdon's Supplies. Luke parked the truck and they stepped out. The crisp air pricked Cora's face as she pulled on her gloves and they started the steady climb up the sidewalk to the square. A few kids ran past them to catch up to a couple walking ahead.

Cora focused her eyes on the sidewalk in front of them and shoved her hands into the pockets of her jacket. It was strange enough being here with Luke, even just as a friend. But being out in public at all left her feeling exposed.

Luke gently nudged her elbow and sniffed the air. "I think I smell fried food."

She smiled, thankful for the invitation back into the moment. *Just have fun.* She tipped her nose into the air and took a whiff. "I think you're right."

At the top of the hill, the square came alive with a bustle of activity under twinkling lights strung between lampposts. Cora's heart soared at the familiar, happy sight. Colorful rides sat atop the grass at the square's center and twisted in the brisk air. Squeals of delight mixed with upbeat bluegrass music coming from a stage off to the left.

"Wow. This is awesome." Luke snapped a few photos then smiled at her and let his camera rest from a strap around his neck. "Where to first?"

"The food and crafts are over here." Cora stepped to the right toward a row of white tents, tripping as she stepped off the curb and bumping right into Luke. Both hands grabbed on to his arm to keep from falling.

He chuckled, reached to place his other hand on one of hers, then winked. "Woah. I'm not going to have to start calling you Grace, am I?"

"Oh, hush." Heat rushed to Cora's cheeks, and she brushed a strand of hair from her face. What was she going to do if every time he looked at her she blushed? She pressed a gloved hand to her cheek as they meandered past a table filled with clear bags of cotton candy.

"Cora."

She turned at the sound of her name and the familiar voice of her father-in-law. *Former father-in-law.* The thought startled her. "Hi, Harry."

Harry stood in the middle of the crowded street holding a half-eaten bag of popcorn. He glanced from Cora to Luke then back to Cora. "We were hoping we'd see you out tonight. I'm glad you came. Who's your friend?"

Cora couldn't think for the sound of her heart thumping in her ears. Her gaze moved from Harry up to Luke staring down at her with a thin grin. *He doesn't erase Christopher.* A lungful of crisp autumn air helped to clear her head.

"Harry, this is my friend and new neighbor, Luke Bassett." She managed to smile up at Luke, whose wide grin was just about enough to make her float away into the perfect evening sky.

"Be sure to stop by the quilting booth and say hello to Laura. She'd love to see you. Luke, a pleasure." The man shook Luke's hand again before turning into the crowd.

"Well." Cora looked up at him and shrugged her shoulders softly. "That was Christopher's dad."

Luke widened his eyes. He wasn't sure what tonight would hold, but he'd definitely never expected to meet Christopher's father or for Cora to handle it so well. As they resumed their walk past the tents of food and crafts, he watched Cora. Illuminated under the glowing lights of bulbs strung overhead, her face relaxed.

When she paused to check out a display of hand-painted signs with clever fall sayings, he leaned in. "Are you okay?"

Her smile was faint, but her eyes softened tenderly, and she nodded. "Thanks. I'm glad you got to meet Harry. Christopher was a lot like him. A good man."

They moved on to the next table, full of homemade jarred products. Luke perked and started picking up jars to read the labels. Maybe this place would have what Handy's market didn't.

"Looking for anything in particular?" Cora asked.

Luke set down a jar of apple butter. "Yeah, my mom used to get this stuff when we were kids that I couldn't get enough of. It was some kind of strawberry jam that had jalapenos in it. Sounds crazy, but it was delicious. I think it was made locally, but I don't have any clue of course."

Cora tilted her head and held his gaze for a long moment. It was hard to tell under the dim lighting, but she seemed to have gone pale. "What?"

She shook her head and picked up a small jar from the table before setting it back down. "I don't think I see any of that here."

The lady wearing an apron behind the table was busy helping another customer, so they kept moving. After browsing a few more tables, they decided on getting food. With two corn dogs and a bag of popcorn, they took two empty seats at the end of a long plastic table on the edge of the grassy lawn.

Luke watched Cora nibble on her corndog as she observed the square full of people. She was perfectly dressed for the evening in jeans, boots, and a rusty-colored puffy jacket topped with a plaid scarf. Her hair swept across one shoulder in a loose braid, framing her face in a way that, if possible, drew even more of Luke's attention to her bright blue eyes.

"Aren't you going to eat yours?"

Luke blinked and looked at his uneaten corndog. He'd better snap out of it. *Just friends.* There was a lot of the evening left, and he didn't need to spend it pining over Cora. He took a bite, determined to keep himself in safe territory. He swallowed and asked, "I know you love the tilt-a-whirl, but what was Christopher's favorite part of the Fall Festival?"

Cora's chest vibrated with a silent chuckle. "Well, he actually hated most everything about fall."

"You're kidding? What's not to love? Pumpkins, more sugar than you know what to do with, a reason to dress up in costume, the cool weather."

She quirked her mouth to one side and shook her head. "Nope. His favorite season was summer. He used to say the Fourth of July was the most underrated holiday of them all. But he'd come to this festival just because he knew I loved it so much. He never complained, but I knew he thought most of it was hokey."

Luke nodded. There was no question Christopher had loved Cora well. "He might have a point about the fourth.

But I still say it's hard to beat a jack-o'-lantern and haunted hayride."

Cora looked up into the black sky then back to Luke, her eyes twinkling under the festive lights. "Speaking of the hayride, it's dark. Want to do that next? By the time we're done my stomach will be ready for the tilt-a-whirl."

Luke looked around them and narrowed his eyes. "Sounds good. But I'm not so sure how great this haunted hayride is gonna be right here in the town square."

"Oh, it just leaves from here." She pointed her corndog stick toward the black mountain Luke could just barely make out behind the town hall. "It takes you up through Hawk's Gap and past the old Laurel Cove cemetery before circling around to the boarded-up Hawthorne Mansion and back to the square. Takes about forty-five minutes."

She smiled at him as she took the last bite of her corndog.

Luke swallowed, a chill running down his back. "Let's do it."

He'd never admit to being a bit intimidated. They might be famous last words, but spooked or not, what could be bad about sitting close to Cora for a while?

"I don't think it's even this dark out at the lake," Luke leaned down and whispered as the open trailer bounced behind a tractor and the hayride entered the edge of the woods just past town.

Cora grinned to herself. This was going to be more fun than she'd counted on. It was almost pitch black. With no moonlight under the cover of the thick forest, she couldn't even make out the faces of the people sitting on the other side of the trailer just a few feet away. Hay poked up from the bales through her knit gloves as she braced herself against the jostling of the trailer.

"You still there, Cora?"

She whispered slowly, "Cora who?"

He poked her arm with his elbow and hissed, "Not funny."

Heat radiated from under the blanket they'd been given, his leg up close next to hers. They sure did pack people on these things. The tractor rounded a corner and soon came into a clearing. Cora glanced up at Luke to her right, his face a ghostly blue in the bright moonlight. He looked down at her with a stretched toothy grin and raised eyebrows.

"You're spooked already!" Cora doubled over with giggles. When she sat back up against the wooden sides of the trailer, Luke pressed his shoulder against hers firmly.

"Am not."

Just then several black shadows fluttered overhead, and a child across from them let out a shriek. Luke gasped and just about jumped off the bale of hay, holding tightly to the camera hanging at his chest.

Cora cracked with laughter. "You going to be okay?"

He looked down at her, mouth gaping, and nodded.

Through the rest of Hawk's Gap and past the cemetery, Luke startled at every little sound, and Cora laughed every time. When the tractor sputtered to a stop under a flickering lamppost in front of the Hawthorne Mansion, the driver turned around in his seat and announced that the parlor of the house was open for a haunted tour. They'd have fifteen minutes to explore.

Cora stood. But as the other riders exited the trailer, Luke held his seat and waved a hand. "Uh, I think I'm good. But you go ahead."

He really was spooked. Cora tried to hide a smile as the last person stepped past her. She sat on the hay bale across from him in the center of the trailer that was now unoccupied. It was adorable that a guy well over six feet tall who'd travelled the world and probably seen unspeakable things throughout his career was scared by a harmless hayride.

Luke busied himself by fiddling with the lens on his camera. "I'm not scared, you know."

"Sure you're not." She offered him a half smile.

"You don't believe me?" He raised the camera and snapped a photo of her.

She startled, a flush rising up her chest under her jacket. She unzipped the top half, letting the cool air hit her neck. "I wasn't smiling."

He lifted the camera from around his neck and set it beside him. His expression was thoughtful as he looked at her, rubbing at the back of his neck. "That's okay. I usually prefer it that way. I find the photos are more realistic when the person isn't expecting it."

Cora didn't usually care for the unexpected. But even though the night had been unexpected in several ways, it still was turning out to be pretty enjoyable. A child shrieked then laughed loudly somewhere nearby, prompting Cora to look past Luke's shoulder. "I'm just giving you a hard time, you know."

"Yeah, I know. But I admit it's creepy out here." He peered out into the dark woods surrounding the mansion and crossed his arms in front of him. "Something about not knowing what's out there."

Cora could relate. That's exactly what spooked her about her future—and about Luke. She didn't know what was out there waiting for her. When his eyes found hers again, she just stared, searching him for some revelation to calm her fears. In them, she found something unnamed that stirred feelings she was sure had died years ago.

The way Cora stared at him made Luke forget where he was—just yards away from a haunted house. He blew into his cold hands but didn't dare break the connection between them.

From somewhere over Cora's shoulder a howl echoed loudly through the woods, startling her out of her trance. She was on her feet in one second flat, lost her footing, and fell into Luke's arms. Their faces were so close that he could feel her warm, quickened breaths on his lips. The scent of vanilla and spice was intoxicating around him.

"You all right?" he whispered.

She nodded slowly before she righted herself and settled back on the bale next to him, their shoulders touching. They exchanged soft smiles as an older couple stepped back up onto the trailer, taking seats on a bale opposite them.

The woman, wearing an orange sweater covered in outlines of black cats, smiled at Luke. "You two had the right idea. Gotta steal moments alone when you can, don't you?"

Cora stiffened and scooted a few inches. A sharp breeze blew, icier than the sudden shift in mood. Luke took a deep breath and resisted the urge to reach for her hand. Within a few minutes, the trailer filled with riders, and the tractor bounced back toward the town square. They rode the rest of the way in silence until the bright lights of the festival welcomed them back.

Cora kept her hands tucked tightly into her pockets as they walked down the bustling street toward the rides and games in silence too. Luke wasn't willing to let this awkward cloud hang between them the rest of the night. They came upon a booth with a few basketball hoops surrounded by stuffed animals of all shapes, colors, and sizes hanging on its flimsy walls.

He nudged her shoulder and nodded toward it. "Bet I can beat you."

She looked at the hoops then back to him, an imaginary thread pulling at one corner of her mouth. "You're on."

Luke paid for a few tickets, and they stepped up to the edge of the booth, balls in hand. "Ready?"

"What's the bet?" She jutted a hip out and rested the ball against it.

Man, she looked cute. "Uh, whoever gets the most baskets buys the cider donuts."

"Deal. But..." She grabbed the ball and got into a stance, ready to shoot. "Tilt-a-whirl, then donuts."

The teenager behind the booth pressed a big green lever on the wall, and the red digital timer between them started counting down from thirty. Luke's first ball went in. So did Cora's...and the next, and the next, and the next. One after the other, Cora's balls effortlessly swished through the net. By the time the buzzer went off, the score was twelve to twenty.

Luke gawked at her as she brushed her hands off and tucked the white teddy bear the young man handed her under her arm. Did the woman have an endless supply of surprises?

"I thought you said you had no athletic ability," Luke said as they kept walking toward the rides.

She smiled without looking at him. "I don't."

"Then what do you call that?"

"I had one of those small hoops on the back of my door growing up. I can shoot all day long, but put me on a court and I'm totally uncoordinated and don't really understand the rules at all. I guess I figured the athletics came in when you played the game." She shrugged her shoulders and pulled her lips to one side when she looked up at him.

"Well, for future reference, that is definitely athletic." If nothing else, Luke sure stayed on his toes where Cora was concerned. Whether riding the roller coaster of her emotions or learning facts about her like secret athletic abilities, he was never bored. And as someone who thrived on adventure, Luke found himself intrigued to a dizzying degree.

At the wildly spinning tilt-a-whirl, Cora stepped in front of him and walked backward a few steps. With a mischievous grin on her face, she pointed at him. "Sure you aren't gonna get scared?"

His heart thumped in his chest. He managed a smile and shook his head. "Not a chance."

CHAPTER Fifteen

If laughter was the best medicine, Cora should be cured of all that ailed her. She stumbled breathlessly on wobbly legs down the rickety steel plank leading her and Luke off the third spinning ride they'd ridden in a row.

Feet firmly planted on the grass, she hunched over with a lingering giggle and held a hand up. "I'm done."

Luke danced around her with the agility of an NBA star, tossing an imaginary ball into an imaginary hoop above her head. "Oh, come on, Miss Secret Abilities. Don't tell me you've met your match."

"You wish." She straightened, inhaled a lungful of crisp air, then pointed past him. "But it's time to pay off your debt."

Luke looked over his shoulder to the food trucks parked in a line near the stage. He smiled down at her, sending her heart pounding to a completely different rhythm than the ride. "You got it."

They walked side by side through a sea of children running about, couples holding hands, and teenagers whispering and laughing. Cora's pulse returned to normal, her steps light. She had, for the moment, recovered from the trauma her heart had endured earlier on the hayride. It was a triple threat—finding herself in his arms, dangerously close to his mouth, and all alone. She closed her eyes, dizzied by the flashback.

Her eyes popped open as her hand brushed up against Luke's. Again, her heart raced from zero to sixty within a blink of an eye. She grunted and pressed her palms toward the ground.

Luke chuckled. "What was that for?"

Had she moaned out loud? Her cheeks flushed and she darted her eyes up to him. "Oh, I just didn't mean to bump into you again."

"I don't mind." For a man with such chiseled, strong features, he had the most tender eyes. Cora could get lost in them if she wasn't careful.

Just then her shoulder bumped into someone walking past from the opposite direction. "Oh, I'm sorry."

"Cora!" Christopher's mother, Laura, grinned with the same crooked smile as her son, pinching Cora's insides. A quilt was draped over both of Laura's arms. She wore her salt-and-pepper hair shorter than before, but otherwise looked exactly the same.

Cora leaned in and the women exchanged a quick hug. "I was going to stop by your booth later. How are you?"

"Oh, we're just fine." Much like her husband had, Laura eyed Luke. But her narrowed eyes and pursed lips weren't nearly as friendly. "Introduce me to your...friend."

Cora's mouth went dry, her guard on alert.

"I'm Luke Bassett. Just moved into a place on the lake a few weeks ago. Cora's showing me the ropes for my first Laurel Cove festival." He reached out a hand and shook Laura's that poked out from under one side of the quilt.

"A pleasure, I'm sure." Laura pierced Cora's eyes and held them for a long moment. "We're having a dinner in honor of your *husband* in a few weeks. Harry emailed you about it, but we haven't heard back. You *will* make it, of course?"

Tingles shot down Cora's arms to her fingertips. Harry's email sat in her inbox still unread. She worked to get her breath and managed, "Yes, of course, Laura."

"Well, I must be getting back." Laura nodded curtly and gave Luke another slow once over. She leaned into Cora for another barely-there embrace and hissed in her ear, "What would Christopher say?"

What? The hair on the back of Cora's neck stood up. Surprisingly, confidence surged through her, and she didn't even have to think twice. Cora straightened and squared her shoulders, voice at full volume. "I actually think Christopher would love Luke. It was nice seeing you, Laura."

Cora took Luke's hand and resumed their walk toward the food trucks. Thumping echoed in her ears as she let out a breathy sigh.

Luke looked down at her with eyebrows raised high, glancing over his shoulder at the woman they'd left standing with her mouth dropped open. "*What* was that?"

"I think she and I have actually handled Christopher's death in similar ways. She's very protective." Cora realized she still had Luke's hand in hers and released it, reaching up to fiddle with her braid. "I've had time to get to know you. She'll come around eventually."

Luke put his hands in his pockets and gazed out over the crowd. "You really think Christopher and I would have gotten along?"

"Yeah, I do." The question sent her heart soaring. If Luke cared what Christopher would think of him, then Luke cared about her. Cora willed her heart to hold on and let the ride take her where it would—climbs, thrilling dips, and all.

Luke set down two cups of hot cider on top of a picnic table and rubbed his hands together. His fingers still tingled from the feeling of Cora holding them. They slipped into the seats opposite each other, and Cora handed him one of the warm donuts they'd just gotten from Brewed's food truck.

He watched her take a bite and close her eyes. A smile spread across his face in unison with her satisfied grin.

"Oh yeah, that's what I'm talking about," she moaned.

As they enjoyed the fall treat in quiet, Luke replayed the latest surprising experience with Cora. He'd seen the signs the second Laura scrutinized him. But if meeting Christopher's father had been unexpected, Cora sticking up for Luke with Christopher's mother took the surprise factor to another level. She'd done it so quickly, too, without so much as a pause. The roller coaster of Cora continued to both excite him and keep him guessing.

"Well, look who it is." Luke turned to find Jack walking up to the table with an attractive brunette. The woman's hair was pulled to the side over one shoulder much like Cora's.

"Hey, good to see you, Jack." Luke shook the hand Jack offered.

Cora brushed crumbs from her lips and waved at the couple. "Hi."

Jack turned to the woman with her arm tucked under his. "This is my wife Livy. Livy, this is Cora and Luke. They're the ones I was telling you about who each have cabins up at the lake."

Luke perked and chuckled at being the topic of anyone's conversation, then motioned to the other empty seats at the table. "You're welcome to join us."

Jack shook his head and beamed, tilting his head toward his wife. "Thanks, but we're actually headed out. This one gets tired easily these days."

Livy placed a hand on her stomach, barely round under her coat. "We're expecting."

"Hey, that's great. Congratulations," Luke said. He glanced over at Cora and smiled, but her lips were pressed in a thin line, longing in her eyes as she looked up at Livy.

Livy turned to Cora. "Hey, Jack told me Mrs. McLean just moved in with you. I think that's just about the nicest thing I've heard of in a long time. I'd love to bring you guys some dinner. What about tomorrow? Maybe a lasagna?"

Cora's face blossomed, sending relief rushing over Luke. She nodded and said, "Sure, that's really kind of you. Thanks."

"Great. I'll bring it by around four, then you can just pop it in the oven whenever you're ready to eat."

Luke's chest swelled as he winked at Cora. This was another big step for her, letting a new friend stop by.

"Well, we'd better be going. You guys enjoy the rest of your evening." Jack and Livy started to turn, then Jack looked back to Luke. "Hey, didn't you say you're a photographer?"

"Yeah, I am," Luke said as he and Cora stood from the table and collected the trash from their snack.

"He's the best, actually." Cora nudged him with her elbow, a twinkle in her eye.

"Well, I was at the town meeting the other day," Jack said. "They mentioned doing a photo calendar of the local landscape to raise funds to fix up the bell tower." He motioned to the top of the town hall in the direction of the hayrides. "Not sure if that's the sort of thing you do, but figured it was worth mentioning."

Luke raised his eyebrows. It might be nice to do what he did best for a good cause. "Text me the name of the person I should get in touch with. I'll reach out and see if I can help."

"Will do." Jack gave a final wave before he and Livy turned to go.

Luke looked down at Cora and found her twinkling eyes still staring into his. "Thanks for the vote of confidence."

Her soft grin just about undid him.

"Well," she said as she shrugged her shoulders and turned her gaze out over the crowd. "I think it's always a good idea for new residents to get involved in town projects. You know, civic duty and all."

"I certainly want to pull my weight." Luke chuckled. But joking aside, he was beginning to feel a sense of duty to this place as a tug in his heart whispered faintly of *home*.

"Anything else you want to do?" Luke pressed a hand to the small of Cora's back as they turned into the crowd along the street of white tents and glowing lights.

Tingles traveled from the spot his hand rested against all the way up to her neck. There was something so natural and yet exhilarating about every time they came in contact. How could her firm declaration to be friends so quickly morph into these electric feelings?

The bright blinking lights outlining the spokes of the Ferris wheel at the center of the square caught her eye. She pointed and said, "How about one more ride then we head back?"

In a matter of minutes, they stepped up into one of the bucket seats, and the bar clicked in place across their laps. Cora set the white teddy bear between them as the wheel started and sent their seat swaying slowly. She tucked her hands under crossed arms as the crisp breeze blew across her face.

"You said Christopher didn't love the festival. Would he ride rides with you?" Luke looked over at her as the wheel came to a gentle stop a moment later to board more riders.

Cora nodded as a comfortable calm settled over her. "Yes and no. He would never ride ones like the tilt-a-whirl. He got dreadfully motion sick. But he could do this."

The wheel began moving again, and they rose into the cool night sky over the town. Luke took in the impressive sight. "Wow, what a view."

The lights below twinkled like fireflies on a warm summer night. From somewhere nearby, the smell of caramel drifted past. Cora studied her hands in her lap and swallowed. "Luke?"

"Yeah?" His soft voice floated away on the chilly breeze.

"I want to thank you." She looked over at him and waited for his rich brown eyes to find hers.

"For what?"

"For asking about Christopher. It's like you want to get to know who he was. I can't tell you how much that means to me."

He searched her eyes then gave a slight shrug. "You're welcome. But I guess learning about him feels like part of getting to know you. And maybe it helps you, too?"

She gazed out over the town and watched another hayride depart up the hill. He was right. For so long she'd avoided talking about Christopher for fear of what it would dredge up. That it would encourage the nightmares. Deepen the wounds. No one was more surprised than she was that, in fact, the opposite was true. "Yeah, it does."

"I've got to thank you, too," Luke said. The ride stopped as their swaying seat came to a gentle stop at the very top of the wheel. "You didn't have to give me another chance at being your friend. I'm grateful you did."

Cora's heart skipped. What would Luke say if she told him it was the best decision she'd made in a long time? And how, in a matter of days, he'd started to fill most of her waking thoughts. And how, in the biggest surprise of all, his friendship was starting to look like the most magical kind—one that turned into a sweet relationship full of hope and promise.

Their eyes locked and the happy clatter below them faded. She bit her bottom lip then swallowed. "You're welcome."

A strong breeze rocked their seat, but Luke kept his eyes on her. Cora braced herself with a hand pressed against the cold painted metal seat between them. He reached up and tucked a stray wisp of hair behind her ear. Her breath caught as his warm fingers traced slowly down her jaw.

With a jolt, the wheel thrust back into motion, pushing them both back hard against the seat. Luke hit his head on the steel cage with a grimace. "Ouch." Like a balloon popping, the moment was gone.

Cora winced. "Are you okay?"

He rubbed the side of his head and nodded, but his eyes reflected the same disappointment she felt. "Never better."

With the moment broken, they finished the quick ride in silence. Within a few minutes, the bright lights and sounds of autumn festivities began to fade as they made their way downhill toward Luke's truck.

He held the passenger door open for her and she climbed in. She watched him cross in front of the truck and smile up at the sky. The corners of her mouth pulled up, too. Nothing, and yet everything, had happened between them on that Ferris wheel. For Cora, it was the moment she realized God had answered her prayer to find hope in really living life again.

How was Luke supposed to focus on driving with Cora sitting next to him? He wasn't a big fan of romantic movies, but that moment on the Ferris wheel, complete with an almost comical interruption of epic proportions, would have made for some serious award-winning material. He glanced quickly at Cora, the headlights of an oncoming car casting shadows over her soft features. And those full lips…

"Do you really think you might do that calendar thing Jack mentioned?"

Luke whipped his attention back to the road. "I'll at least see what they have in mind. It might be a fun project."

"Well..." Cora's voice was soft through the dark cab. "You'll have to let me know. Maybe I can be your assistant or something. Did you even have an assistant before?"

He laughed and rested his arm on the edge of the window as he kept the wheel steady. His was a pretty solo set-up, but he wasn't about to turn down a chance to spend more time with her. "No. I usually handled all of my own gear. But if it turns into anything, I'd love if you tagged along."

"It'd be fun to see you doing your thing." Another car passed and he saw her mouth curl.

"Speaking of doing your thing..." He needed a new topic to keep him distracted from thoughts of kissing her. "How's the book outline coming along?"

"Since you asked..." She twisted in her seat to face him more directly. "I'm actually more than halfway done. Inspiration really struck this morning, and I worked through a lot of the idea. I think it's going to turn into something really special."

Hopefully like what's going on here.

"That's great." Luke blinked hard and stared out his window. *Pull it together man.*

No matter how hard he tried, his mind was laser focused on her. The way she'd looked at him as they swayed over the town as if they were the only ones on top of the world. How her lips pouted, and her golden hair framed her face. The line of her neck. The curves of her...

"Is it hot in here?" Luke pressed a button on his window and let a few inches of cold air hit his face.

Cora laughed and pulled her jacket up around her neck. "No! Are you nuts?"

He forced a laugh and unzipped his jacket as the window rolled back up. In another minute, he steered the truck down the lake road and turned into Cora's driveway. The porch light cast a golden hue over the front yard as the truck rolled to a stop.

Cora picked up her gloves from beside her and reached for the door handle. "I had a really great time. Thanks."

Luke rubbed both hands along his thighs and swallowed hard. "Cora, wait."

She looked at him expectantly. "Yeah?"

"I'd like to take you to dinner sometime." He pushed out what breath remained after the last word.

A warm, tender smile was his reward for being brave. She pulled at the door handle and stepped down from the truck, taking Luke's breath with her. Just before she closed the door she looked back, eyes sparkling in the glow of the porch. "I'd like that. Very much."

His chest swelled and he nodded. "Good. Great. I'll call you about a night."

"I'm free Monday." She raised an eyebrow.

"Uh, yeah. Monday's great."

She nodded and closed the door. Luke watched her head up the porch with the teddy bear that she'd won herself tucked under her arm. Before she stepped into the house and closed the door, she looked over her shoulder at him and smiled.

Luke let out a celebratory laugh as he pulled back down the driveway toward his own cabin. A few days ago, he'd been certain he'd seen the last of Cora Bradford. No one could have convinced him he would have spent the evening at the Fall Festival with her, let alone almost shared a kiss then made plans for their first date. The surprises kept coming. And if they continued on this track, he'd welcome every one.

CHAPTER Sixteen

"See what happens when you listen to your dear old Ina?" Cora smirked and rolled her eyes. She handed Ina her morning pills and a glass of water after clearing their breakfast plates. "Yes, you're so wise."

Ina swallowed the pills then carefully stood from the kitchen table and leaned on her walker. As she scooted along toward the living room, she clicked her tongue. "Though I have to say, you covered a lot of ground in one night."

Cora wiped her hands on a kitchen towel and frowned. She watched the back of Ina's head, white curls set just right. "Do you think it was too much too fast?"

Ina's head moved from side to side before she pushed down on the handles of the walker to lock the wheels then lowered herself onto an armchair. "Oh, don't get me wrong.

A handsome fella like Luke? It'd be hard to keep my hands off him, too."

"Ina, honestly!" Cora laughed and watched Ina's chest shake with a giggle.

Ina reached for the remote control on the side table and pointed it at the television hanging on the wall above the fireplace. "We're all hot-blooded women, dear. Charles kissed me three days after we met. We were engaged a month later and married two months after that. No judgement here."

Cora stood next to the couch and watched a prize wheel spin in front of three contestants on the screen. "You don't think it's a bad idea to go to dinner with him tomorrow?"

"Bad idea? Heavens, no. As long as you come home and tell me every tiny detail, that is. It's the most excitement this old lady has had in a long time." She looked at Cora, pushed her glasses up on her nose, and winked.

There was a lot to get used to, having Ina in her home. The loud television, which Cora rarely had on at all. Fixing meals for two people. Remembering medications and mobility exercises. But she already cherished the extra laughs and companionship.

Cora looked out the back door to the glimmering water. "Well, since it's so nice outside, I'm going to head out to the deck and get some work done on this outline."

"Fine, dear. I'm sure I'll be asleep before the next commercial."

Cora chuckled on her way to the desk and picked up her black notebook. "If I'm gone when you wake up, remember I've headed into town for groceries."

Ina nodded with a wave of her hand, eyes glued to the gameshow.

Outside, the sun showered Cora with warmth. The water looked so inviting that she kept walking down to her chair near the shore, where she sat, pen in hand, as ideas flowed effortlessly onto the pages of her notebook. Last night with Luke was proving excellent inspiration for the romance theme woven into this new mystery.

More than an hour had passed when she finally took a break to glance at her phone. The outline was now done, and all that was left was drafting a proposal for the publishers. She was ahead of schedule and light as a feather.

She punched in her password to the phone and dialed Luke. Her heart leaped when he answered.

"Well, hey you."

Cora looked out over the cove and smiled as if she could see him from where she sat. "Hi. How are you?"

"Better now. You?"

"I'm good. Guess what?"

"Hmm...you realized the grave mistake you made and are calling to break my heart and cancel our date." He grunted and she imagined him shoving an imaginary dagger into his chest.

Her grin widened and she brushed her fingers across her lips. "Nope, you're stuck with me."

A soft moan sounded through the phone, which sent a wave of heat rushing up her chest and neck. "I guess I can live with that. So, what is it?"

"I finished my outline." Cora squeezed her eyes shut and pulled her shoulders up to her ears. "I can't believe it."

"That's great. And just in time. I finished the book you lent me this morning."

She chewed on the bottom of her lip. Playing it cool would be waiting to see Luke until their date tomorrow. But there were no rules to this thing, were there? "I'm getting ready to head to the grocery store. But when I get back, think I could talk you into a canoe ride?"

"Uh..." Luke paused.

Cora's breath caught and she braced herself for disappointment.

When he continued, his voice was low and soft. "I think we can arrange that."

Another wave radiated through her. Despite the cool breeze, Cora fanned herself. "Um, need anything from town while I'm going?"

"Keep your eye out for that strawberry jam, will you? I thought about it again this morning when I ate my English muffin with plain old sad grape jelly." He laughed with a huff.

Cora shrank back into the chair and pulled her mouth to one side.

"Other than that, no," he said brightly. "But thanks for asking. Just head on over when you're back, okay?"

"Okay. See you in a bit." Cora disconnected the call and laid her phone in her lap. One day she really should tell Luke that she was pretty sure his mystery jelly was also Christopher's favorite. And the item he'd just had to have the night he died.

Luke's weekend just kept getting better. As he sat to pull on his sneakers, he smiled and cataloged the last few days. The almost-kiss with Cora on the Ferris wheel. Her agreeing to their impending first date. Then, he finished the book, his favorite of hers so far, and would see her soon.

On the back deck, he reached for the rake just as his phone buzzed. "Hello?"

"Luke, it's Ina. Cora's not here and—"

Luke's heart stopped. "What's wrong?"

A soft chuckle carried through the phone. "Gracious, nothing. You sure know how to make an old woman feel cared about, though. Do you have just a moment to come talk to me? We probably have an hour before Cora gets back."

His interest was piqued. What on earth would she want to talk to him about that they had to keep from Cora? "Sure. I'll be right over."

Within a few minutes, Luke knocked on the door and stepped in. "Hello? Ina?"

"Come on in, dear. Thanks for coming so quickly." She sat in an armchair that faced the front door and motioned to the couch as he stepped inside.

Once Luke settled onto the center cushion, Ina wasted no time. "Cora told me about your evening."

"Yeah, we had a nice time." Luke shifted. The way she eyed him through the bottom of her glasses with her nose up in the air pulled his eyebrows together.

Ina pointed a bony finger at him. "She's tender, Luke."

What was she getting at? He nodded. "Yes, ma'am."

She watched him for a long moment. Finally, she reached for the walker next to the chair and began to stand. He stood and placed a hand under her elbow.

"Where would you like to go?"

She pointed to the couch. He followed her as she shuffled to the end of the couch and eased herself down on the cushion next to where he'd been sitting. He smiled, quite uncertain what to expect, and resumed his seat.

Side by side now, Ina rested a shaky hand on his leg. "I wanted to look you square in the eyes. I need to see for myself."

Luke searched the woman's milky eyes behind her glasses. "See what?"

"If you love her."

His chest tightened and a fire ran up his neck. "Ina—"

"Shh-shh-shh." The woman waved a hand then slowly reached up to hold Luke's chin with her cold, weak hand. She studied him, searching his eyes.

Luke's heart raced. Was he scared of what she would see or what she'd find lacking? What did he know of love anyway? He was familiar with attraction and passion. But love?

Finally, she nodded. A faint smile pulled at the deep wrinkles around her eyes, and she released his face. "I've seen all I need to see. You can go now."

Luke laughed. "I can go? Just like that?"

"What do you want from me? I'm an old lady and I'm tired." Ina looked away and out the front window of the cabin. She was toying with him.

"Oh no, you aren't." Luke sat back and rested one ankle on the opposite knee. His arm sprawled out behind her petite frame along the back of the couch. "Spill it."

She turned to him and smiled thinly. "You love her all right."

Luke ignored the truth knocking in his heart and laughed. "We've known each other all of a few weeks, Ina.

Plus, you can't tell something like that by looking deep into my eyes like some mountain love guru."

"Oh, I sure can. And I've never been wrong." She rested against his arm. "Congratulations, you're in love."

Luke stood abruptly and looked down at her. She was so tiny, like a white-haired Yoda, sitting there with her arms crossed. "I am not. Now, if you don't mind, I've got some yard work to do."

She gazed up at him with a gummy grin. "Are too."

He sighed loudly and headed for the door.

With his hand on the knob, she called after him, "She deserves something magical. Just be good to her. Please."

"Bye, Ina."

The door clicked shut behind him, and he pulled in a long breath of crisp fall air. With the gravel crunching under his feet, he started for home at a quick clip. The old woman just flew right past quirky to completely nuts. Luke appreciated her concern for Cora. It was endearing, even. But trying to tell him he was in love with Cora? They hadn't even had their first real date yet.

Once in his backyard, he put in his wireless earbuds and started a playlist on his phone. With the rake in hand he went to work on the carpet of brown leaves and tried to think of anything but what Ina had just revealed of the inner corners of his heart.

With the groceries put away and Ina napping in her room, Cora's feet bounced down the road to Luke's. A few hours on the water with him sounded just about perfect. When he didn't answer the door, she walked around back.

"Luke?" she called out, then froze at the sight of him as she rounded the deck. Toby approached her, tail wagging, holding a tennis ball in his mouth.

Luke stood in the middle of the yard raking leaves...shirtless. His back was to her, strong muscles flexing with each pull of the rake. She really should call out to him again, but her mouth just gaped open, a small smile pulling at the corners. Then he bounced his head in a rhythm. *Oh. He's listening to something.*

Though tempted to sit back and just watch, Cora smiled and picked up the tennis ball Toby had dropped at her feet. She lobbed it in Luke's direction, missing him by several feet. When it rolled into his view he startled and spun around to face her.

He yanked out an earbud and started for her wearing a big grin. "Hey!"

Cora couldn't help but notice the sweat beading up on his chest when he approached the deck and reached for his shirt draped over the railing. As he pulled it over his head she focused on Toby retrieving the ball and tugged at the neck of her sweater to create a cooling breeze.

"Sorry. Amazing how warm it gets when you're working up a sweat." He took a swig from a water bottle sitting on the railing.

"Uh, yeah. I bet." She pressed her lips together.

"Would you rather I go shower real quick before we head out?" he asked, thumbing over his shoulder toward the house.

The last thing she needed was to be stuck in close proximity with him smelling fresh and clean. She shook her head. "Nah, that's okay. We'll just be out on the lake. It's not like this is a date."

He stepped up to the deck to let Toby inside before rejoining her in the yard. He raised his eyebrows at her and took another sip from his bottle. "Lucky for you."

"What does that mean?" She wrinkled her nose and tilted her head as they started for the water's edge.

"Oh, just that you don't know what you're in for. I'm really good at dating." He nudged her arm, his smile alarmingly charming.

Cora watched him pull the canoe off the stand. Truth was, her stomach twisted at the realization that she'd not been on a first date in nearly a decade. What if she wasn't good at it at all? She smiled as he handed her a life vest.

Minutes later they were gliding through the calm water. Cora welcomed the cool breeze on her cheeks and neck. As they cleared the cove, she glanced over her shoulder at him. He winked, and the flush that rushed to her cheeks once again overpowered the crisp autumn air. With his charisma and her newfound awareness of his bare chest, Luke definitely had the upper hand.

The water on the lake was calm and smooth as the canoe drifted effortlessly under the midday sun—a stark difference from the choppy clatter drumming inside Luke. How had he let himself get so lost in thought that she'd snuck up on him?

It was all thanks to one four-letter word pounding an imprint on his heart over and over. *Thanks a lot, Ina.*

Not to mention being caught shirtless was not his idea of gentlemanlike behavior. He'd tried to play it cool, but what an embarrassment.

Luke rolled his eyes, grateful to be out of sight behind Cora in the boat. He couldn't help but smile as she lifted her face to the sun in between a stroke of the paddle. She was so beautiful.

There went his heart again, right into the deep end.

"Hey." She glanced over her shoulder. "What do you think about heading over to the other side of the lake? I'd love to explore that little island."

Luke swallowed and gazed past her to an island that sat in front of a small inlet across the other side of the lake where the shore curved out of sight. "I haven't stopped there yet either. Sure."

"I can't promise there aren't any spooky abandoned shacks." Her eyes widened briefly and twinkled when she twisted to face him. "Think you can handle it?"

"Very funny." Truth was, it wasn't the fear of haunted buildings that kept gnawing at his insides. Thankful she turned back around quickly, Luke welcomed in a full chest of the fresh air. *There's time to figure all this out.* He nodded to himself and focused on paddling. There was no use wasting a perfectly good day with Cora by worrying about what the gnawing feeling meant.

Soon, they approached the small island and navigated its shore until they found a good, smooth spot to ground the canoe safely. Luke hopped out, foot splashing in the shallow water as he stepped to the shore and reached for Cora's hand.

He apparently pulled harder than she expected, because she tumbled forward, pressing against his chest.

"Sorry," she said softly, her sky-blue eyes inviting him to get lost in them.

He cleared his throat and let go of her hand. The pounding in his chest was nearly deafening as he pulled the canoe safely up onto the dry shore.

Hands on her hips, she looked around. "It's crazy how the shore is covered in these tiny pebbles when ours is so sandy."

Ours. It wasn't Luke's style to be sentimental, but that sounded nice. He nodded toward the woods at the interior of the island. "Shall we?"

At an opening in the tree line, a red tie was knotted around a thin pine trunk. "I bet this is a blaze marking the trail. Nice to know we aren't the first here."

"But it would've been nice to think of ourselves as the trail blazers, huh? Plus, discoverers get to name their new worlds." Cora's eyes almost glowed as they stepped out of the sun and into what shade the trees still offered now that autumn had stolen many of the leaves.

Luke worked to keep a distance between them as their arms swung. The last thing his poor pounding heart needed was the feel of her soft hand on his. "What would you want to name it? Bradford Island?"

She wrinkled her nose and chuckled. "That's a bit prosaic, don't you think? We can be more creative than that."

As they traversed uphill over gnarly roots and passed several other red ties on trees, Cora and Luke traded ideas for naming the island, from the silly to the outlandish. They hadn't agreed on even one by the time they came to a clearing about ten minutes later.

"What do you suppose this is?" Cora walked up to a stack of smooth rocks standing at the center of the small clearing. She ran her hand over the rock on top, wiping away some loose dirt.

Luke had seen plenty of these in his travels. He joined Cora next to the stack, which was about chest height to her. "They're called cairns. Usually people use them as markers on the trail, much like those red blazes. But when one's off the obvious trail, like this one, I'd guess it's just for fun or something."

"Hey, there's something scratched into it." Cora blew at the smooth surface and leaned in to inspect it.

"Here," Luke said, and poured a little water from his bottle over the stone. They both watched as letters appeared. He read it aloud, slowly. "CM + IR '46. What do you suppose that means?"

Cora looked at him as though he'd said the moon was made of cheese. "They're initials."

Luke eyed the letters again, head cocking to one side. "Like of people's names?"

"Yes, people." She laughed and rolled her eyes. "Probably of a couple who came here in 1946. You know, like how a guy would notch out his and his love's initials on a tree trunk? Honestly, Luke. If you're so good at dates, where's the romance?"

Luke furrowed his brow and crossed his arms, walking to the other side of the stones to get a different look. He may or may not know yet if he could love Cora, but no one was going to question his romantic abilities. "Like I said, you just wait."

Suddenly, Cora gasped. Luke looked up to find her eyes wide and her hand covering her mouth.

"What?"

"CM...what if that's Charles McLean, and—"

Luke darted his eyes back to the rock, tingles racing down his arm. "IR is for Ina."

They exchanged huge grins. Cora's laugh was breathy as she pulled her phone from a zippered pocket in her jacket and hovered it over the stone to click a photo. "I can't believe this. That would make Ina...yeah, nineteen. Man, can you believe this? I can't wait to show her."

The twisting inside Luke tightened. He would never have a love story for the ages that spanned so many years. But as Cora lit up at the sentiment behind the stones, the twisting deep inside him began to resemble longing. What if his love story for the ages was just beginning? What if right here in front of him, on a deserted island near the place he'd visited as a young boy, was the woman he'd one day carve his name with for all eternity?

Knees weak and breath shallow, Luke leaned against the stack of stones and slowly sipped his water. What if Ina was right?

Few things had excited Cora in recent years as much as asking Ina about the stone she and Luke had found. She just knew those initials had to belong to Ina and Charles, and the story behind it promised to be worth hearing. With the canoe tied up to her dock, Cora and Luke left the island behind them, their footsteps crunching the gravel on the way up the hill.

The warmth of the cabin soothed her chilled muscles as they stepped in through the back door. Ina's walker sat next to the armchair, its back facing the deck door. "Hi, Ina."

A waving hand poked out from the side of the chair. "Well, hello, dear. How was the ride with our handsome neighbor?"

Luke winked at Cora and pressed a finger to his lips. He waited until he was next to the chair, leaned down, and gave Ina's cheek a quick peck. "It was very nice, beautiful."

"Oh, my." Ina giggled and pressed a trembling hand to the spot he'd kissed. Cora raised her eyebrows at the blushing woman and took the seat on the couch closest to Ina's chair. Ina patted her cheek and pointed to Cora. "You may get the first date, but I got the first kiss."

Laughter sprinkled between them as Luke took the seat next to Cora on the couch. Cora's heart raced when she took out her phone and navigated to the photo of the stone. Luke smiled and nodded.

"Ina, Luke and I wanted to show you something we found today. We stopped at that small island across the lake. Do you recognize this?" She reached the phone out to Ina, who took it.

Ina studied the photo through the bottom of her bifocals. Cora watched for the moment Ina's memories connected to the photograph.

A trembling hand slowly reached to cover her mouth. "My gracious. You found it."

Cora looked to Luke, whose smile was so big she thought it'd surely break into a laugh any second. When she turned back, Ina's eyes were still glued to the phone. "They're your and Charles's initials?"

Ina nodded and handed the phone back. She rested against the back of the chair and stared out the window at the front of the cabin. The late-afternoon light flooded in like honey on the wooden floors. "Yes, they're all ours. All those stones."

"How often did you add one? Special anniversaries or something?" Luke asked.

Cora's heart pulled as Ina's face puckered, her eyes quickly filling with tears. Luke took a tissue from the box on the coffee table and stood to offer it to Ina. She dabbed at her eyes as Luke sat back down next to Cora then looked to them both. "We started the stack the day of our first date after we enjoyed a picnic. We added the second rock to signify our wedding. Then…" Her voice caught and she cleared it before continuing. "Then we added a rock for every unborn child we lost."

The air left Cora's lungs as if someone had punched her. In its wake was a familiar, aching emptiness. It had never occurred to her this discovery represented anything but happy memories for her neighbors. There had to have been at least six or seven stones representing lost babies. The magnitude of that loss was suffocating.

Cora focused on the rhythm of her own breath before she eased to the edge of the couch and reached out to hold Ina's hand. "I'm so sorry."

"Thank you, dear." Ina patted her hand and offered a thin smile.

Luke scooted up to the edge of the couch too, his knee pressing against Cora's. "When did you add the top rock with your initials?"

Though not meant for her, the tenderness in his eyes and softness in his voice soothed Cora.

Ina sighed deeply. "About twenty-five years ago, if memory serves. For years and years, I harbored a lot of guilt over the loss of those babies. Charles was unwavering in his gentle support through my tumultuous grief over our family that wasn't meant to be." She paused and pressed the tissue to the corner of one eye.

Cora swallowed past her own threatening tears as Ina continued. "On our fiftieth anniversary, he took me out to the island and placed that rock you saw on top with our initials and the year we were married. He told me that day that despite the heartache, our life together had been enough. Despite all the years praying for what wasn't to be. All the grief. All the disappointment. Even so, he wanted me to know it was enough."

It was enough.

A tear rolled down Cora's cheek. She turned when Luke touched her knee, and took the tissue he offered. The sadness she found in his eyes, too, shook something loose in her, and she had to bite hard on the inside of her lip to keep a sob at bay.

For a long moment, the only sound in the room came from an applauding audience on the television. Luke finally broke the silence between them. "That's a very special gift he gave you, to be told you're enough."

His words were a salve on the open wound of Cora's heart. She looked up and found Ina nodding. "Yes, but he said *it* was enough. Not just me. He meant our life together. Full of ups and downs. Imperfections, including all of my own as well as his. Together, willing to keep going and trust God...that was enough."

Keep going and trust God. Cora invited the message into her soul. She and Luke exchanged a tender glance. She'd try every day forward to keep going, keep living.

Cora startled as the clock on the fireplace mantel chimed four times. "Wow. I didn't realize how late it had gotten. Livy will be here soon with dinner."

With the tissues wadded up in her hand, Ina sighed, but a contentment showed on her upturned mouth. "Why don't you join us for dinner, Luke?"

Luke stood and stretched from side to side. "That's kind of you, but I'd better get back before it gets dark. Toby will be wanting dinner, too."

Disappointment stirred inside Cora as she also stood. "Well, let me walk you out."

Ina placed a hand on Luke's arm. "Keep taking her to that island. It's a special place."

He just nodded and patted her hand. Between the simple excitement of being with Luke, their discovery of the stack of rocks, then hearing the sweet yet heart-wrenching story of it, Cora's heart may not be able to take any more emotional swells.

She led Luke through the dining room and to the back door then held the door to the deck open. He stepped out then turned. "Pick you up around six-thirty tomorrow?"

With the fluttering in her chest, all Cora could manage was a nod and smile.

His eyes locked on hers. Did he want to say something else? After a moment, he nodded too and said, "I can't wait. Have a good night."

"You, too."

The door clicked shut behind her, and Cora made her way back into the living room. She couldn't help but think of the loss shared between the three of them. Surveying the living room, now empty, she found Ina's bedroom door closed.

How very wrong she'd been to think no one else could understand the grief she both clung to and was haunted by. Cora was drawn again to the back door. Luke was now a shadow as he reached the dock. She, too, had the choice to decide that life, with its ups and downs, would be enough.

CHAPTER
Seventeen

Smoke rose in wispy ribbons above the firepit and disappeared into the shadows of the trees silhouetted against the cotton candy autumn sky. His hand was warm, thumb gently brushing against the back of Cora's hand.

"This one always makes me sad." She closed her eyes as music drifted from the cracked window of the cabin.

"The minor keys always do."

Cora could hear the tender smile in the timbre of his low voice. Like waves on the ocean, she rose on the uplifting melody of violins and fell gently on the cradle of the cello. In her mind's eye, the graceful dance was mirrored in the mountains across the lake. This was peace.

"Cora."

"Yes?"

"I need to tell you something."

A smile pulled softly at her lips. Behind her closed eyes, she saw his face watching her. "Okay."

"I want you to have a good time tomorrow."

Cora squeezed his hand, the brooding notes of the cello matching the sudden ache in her throat. She sat up and searched his eyes. "I knew you would. But it feels like just yesterday we sat here listening to Beethoven after dinner."

He shook his head slowly, lifted her hand, and pressed his lips against her fingers. "It's been three years, Cora. A memory is worth remembering, not reliving."

"You sound like Ina." She sighed and lifted her eyes to the sky overhead, now a deep purple.

When she looked back over at him, he winked above a playful smile. "You gain a certain wisdom on this side of things."

The ache in Cora's throat threatened to break. "I miss you."

"I know."

The breeze blew, carrying more smoke and music up toward heaven.

"I like him, you know." The tone in his voice was light and matter-of-fact.

"I do, too." Cora focused on their intertwined fingers.

"And one more thing."

"Yeah?"

Cora found his kind gray eyes again and studied every detail of his youthful face.

"Wear that black dress. You know the one."

"Honestly, Christopher. You're incorrigible." Cora looked into the fire, but it wasn't the flames calling a blush to her cheeks.

His thumb swayed against the back of her hand in unison with the quartet playing the soundtrack of their brief time together. She leaned back against the cool chair and closed her eyes again. The music was sad, but it also roused a subtle hope inside her. One that invited her to climb without fear of falling.

When Cora blinked, it was against a soft light and warmth on her face. As sleep fell from her eyes, she sat up and found herself in her bedroom.

Alone.

Outside, the bright sun crested over the mountains and set the lake ablaze. With a smile that dawned from deep within, she greeted the new day. She'd waited so long for a happy dream. One that didn't send her begging God for mercy. No, today's prayer was simple.

Thank you, God.

She stepped into waiting slippers and made her way across the room. With a quick shuffle through her closet, she reached in and pulled out the only black dress she owned. The one she'd worn on the last anniversary she'd not celebrated alone. With it hanging on the back of her door, she smiled and started for the stairs with light steps.

Thank you, Christopher.

By the time Luke stepped from his truck in front of Cora's cabin, the sun was tucked away behind the westward mountains for the evening, the sky brilliant with millions of twinkling stars. A gentle but crisp breeze teased the air. If he'd ordered perfect weather for their date, this would be it.

Luke tugged at the cuff of his white dress shirt under his sweater and smoothed the front as he bounded up the porch stairs and rapped on the door. *This is it.*

The excitement that had compounded with every passing hour swelled to the brink as the lock unlatched. Behind the open door, Luke found a grinning Ina in a light-pink bathrobe.

"Well, aren't you a sight for old, sore eyes." She let out a whistle. He followed as Ina hobbled back to her armchair in the living room. "Cora will be down in a moment. I told her a lady should never seem overly anxious by being ready the moment a date arrives."

"Wise advice, I'm sure." He laughed with a quick glance up the darkened staircase. Was she looking forward to this as much as he was? Did she feel ready? Though the rush of his heartbeat preferred he keep upright, Luke took a seat on the couch. The stiff brown paper wrapped around the flowers he'd brought crinkled as he set them down on the coffee table.

He leaned against his knees to keep them from bouncing. "What do you have planned for this evening?"

"You're looking at it. Game shows and leftover lasagna." Ina wiped at a lens on her wire-framed glasses before setting them gently atop her nose. She squinted through them at Luke and pursed her lips.

Luke's mouth pulled to one side. She was so easy to read. "What is it?"

"Oh, nothing, dear." She picked up a nail file from the side table next to her and ran it across a nail. "But if I had any advice for you tonight—"

"All right, let's have it then." Luke rested against the back of the couch and crossed his arms. He knew it. She was incapable of *not* having something to say.

Ina cut her eyes to Luke and pointed the end of the silver nail file at him. "Just because you love her doesn't mean you have to kiss her tonight. As a matter of a fact, *since* you love her, I would recommend against it."

Luke choked out a laugh. Not only could Ina *not* not say something, she had the innate skill to shock him with her lack of boundaries. "Well, we haven't even successfully enjoyed dinner. I'd say that's the first step."

"Right you are. Good man." Ina's head bobbed up and down as she returned her attention to her nails.

Luke rubbed his hands down his thighs. He'd labored all day at tempering his expectations for tonight. This was more than a simple first date for Cora; it was the first date since her husband died. One didn't have to be an expert on emotions to know this scenario required careful handling. *No need to rush anything.*

At the sound of footsteps descending the stairs, he stood and spun on his heels. With his heart galloping ahead, his legs lost the ability to carry him as Cora slowly stepped into view. She stole his breath in stylish brown ankle boots and a black dress that fell just below her knees. It hugged curves Luke had up until this very moment only imagined.

"You look so s—*great*. You look just great." He ran his hand across the back of his neck and searched for his breath as her bright blue eyes found his and smiled.

Ina cleared her throat and darted her eyes to the coffee table.

"Oh, right." Luke picked up the flowers and willed his legs to carry him over to where Cora stood at the narrow table in the entryway that held her purse. She fiddled with the purse's clasp, for a moment resting her eyes shut. Her chest rose with a deep breath. How could he put her at ease?

He pressed his lips together then whispered, "These are for you."

"That's so sweet. They're beautiful." She took them and nestled the petals under her nose. "Thank you."

Luke helped her slip into a fitted jean jacket, and an intoxicating fragrance enveloped him as she fluffed her hair around her collar. "We shouldn't be too late, Ina. Anything you need before we go?"

"Nothing at all, dear. Don't worry about me." Ina flitted her hand in the air and grinned widely. "You two have a good time."

Luke welcomed the chilly air on his hot face as they stepped out into the night. Before he knew it, they were sitting in the dark truck on their way into town.

"You look very nice." Her voice was soft.

"Thanks." On the dark stretch of the two-lane highway, he couldn't make out much of her except the graceful silhouette of her profile as she studied the road ahead of them. He clenched his hands around the steering wheel and cleared his throat. "Let's clear something up, okay?"

She turned toward him, but it was difficult to read her expression. "Okay."

"There's no pressure tonight. We're simply out for dinner to have fun and maybe learn a little more about each other. I just want you to enjoy yourself."

A long silence lingered. She finally said, "That sounds perfect. Thanks, Luke."

When she said his name, life pulsated with a hint more vibrance. Whatever the night held in store, he was right where he wanted to be.

In a matter of minutes, Luke turned at a lit sign for "Jillian's at the Summit" and the truck climbed upward on the winding road. He eased into one of the few empty spots out front of a quaint white cottage. Its sign matched the one at the road just next to a wraparound porch lined with pumpkins of various autumn colors. Old lanterns flickering with a gentle glow hung on either side of a red door.

Luke twisted the key in the ignition, quieting the engine. "Wow, Jack was right. This place does scream date night. Ready?"

"Um, maybe we can wait just a minute?"

Bathed in the parking lot's dim glow, Cora's eyes were wide and fixed past the windshield. Harry and Laura Bradford made their way across the porch and down the steps arm in arm. Cora chewed at her bottom lip and turned hard for her window as they walked in front of the truck on Luke's side.

Luke's brow furrowed. She'd defiantly stood up to Laura at the festival, defending being seen with him. For all they knew, the night at the festival was a date. Why was tonight any different? He placed a hand on her shoulder. "You all right?"

She sighed heavily. The smile that followed was thin, but the softness to her eyes melted Luke. "Yeah, sorry. Let's head inside before I freeze."

Luke's capacity for patience and understanding had wide margins where Cora was concerned. He stepped from the truck and made his way to open her door. Only time would tell how much healing would come to her, when the fragments of her life before Luke would float to the surface.

For now, he'd trust in the hope of the future—one moment at a time.

The last thing Cora had expected while on her date with Luke was to see Harry and Laura. It was a small town, but what were the chances? As she and Luke climbed the restaurant's porch, it was hard to tell if the racing of her heart had more to do with imagining what Laura might have said had she seen them, or the touch of Luke's hand pressing against the small of her back. For now, the crisis was averted. She willed herself to be thankful for the serendipitous timing and return her focus to the evening ahead.

Jillian's indeed checked all the boxes for a romantic date night. Cora ticked them off as she settled in her chair and beheld their surroundings. Intimate table for two next to a window overlooking the lights of town below. Fireplace crackling nearby. Warm glow of candlelight, white linen tablecloth, and fine china. She traced a finger along the handle of a silver fork.

Then there was Luke sitting across the table, studying her from behind his menu in that way that sent warmth rushing up her chest.

"What?" she whispered, tucking her hair behind her ear.

In his face she found a mix of tenderness and affection. He shook his head slightly and kept his eyes locked on hers. "You're beautiful."

The warmth in her chest flamed to her cheeks. She smiled, focusing on the entrée options typed on the menu. "Thank you."

How could he do that? Make her feel both treasured and desired all at once? The only other man to ever make her feel that way had been Christopher. She'd missed it.

A waiter stepped up to the table and took their drink orders. While he told them about the night's specials, Cora took her chance to study Luke. His crisp white collared shirt and slim-fitting black sweater accentuated his chiseled features, making him look a little bit like a GQ model. His hair, slightly graying at the temples, was perfectly combed, but she was glad he'd not shaven the scruff off. What she'd give to rub a hand across his rugged cheek.

"Ma'am?"

Cora pulled her gaze up to the waiter staring down at her. "Oh, I'm sorry. What was that?"

"Would you like to start with butternut squash soup or an autumn fruit and nut salad?"

She darted her eyes over to Luke, who returned an amused smile and arched eyebrows. "Uh, the soup. Thank you."

The man stepped away, leaving no buffer between Cora and her distraction. She bit her lip and dared to cast him another glance. Luke rested against the back of his seat and tucked his arms across his chest, that dimple taunting her.

"Oh, don't look so smug. You were just staring at me, too."

"Oh, I'm not complaining."

The twinkle that danced in his eyes yet again fanned the flame blushing her cheeks. Cora resisted the urge to use her menu to cool herself. He was right—he was really good at this. She, on the other hand, was back on the dating bike, wobbling like an uncoordinated amateur. At this pace, she just hoped not to make a complete fool of herself by the end of the evening.

A few minutes later, Luke hovered his spoon over the steaming bowl of soup in front of him. "How about a rapid-fire round of first date get-to-know-you questions?"

"Sure." Cora chuckled. Her shoulders relaxed. Quick, easy questions she could handle. "Do you answer, too?"

He nodded through a bite, then started. "Okay, favorite meal?"

"Easy," she said. "Cheap Mexican with endless chips and salsa. You?"

"Steak and potatoes. Best vacation you've ever been on?"

She hesitated, twisting her mouth to one side. Would it ruin the mood to mention Christopher? But Luke was clued in to the situation. Nothing about her past seemed off limits now. "Switzerland. We went for our honeymoon, and I still dream of going back one day. You must have some exotic, off-the-map place in mind."

Luke set aside the small empty soup bowl, and leaned both his arms against the table. "Well, I know you may not believe me, but it's right here. Some days I still wake up and think it's too good to be true. No matter where I've been around the world, it's always been this place I've dreamed about."

Cora watched his gaze drift off to the lights of town outside the window. "I bet your mom would love knowing you're back here."

The flame from the candle near the window danced in his deep caramel-colored eyes when he faced Cora again. "I think so, too. I just hate that I was too late."

Even though they'd quickly skirted past the lighthearted Q&A, Cora didn't mind. She reached across the table and rested her hand on top of his. "Can I admit something to you that might sound a bit backward?"

"Sure." His pinkie finger wound around hers.

Prickles ran up her arm as she watched their hands. "It's oddly comforting to hear you talk about your mother. Your regret and how you wish you'd had more time."

Their eyes met and Luke's head cocked to one side. Cora's head swam as she searched for the right words. "What I mean is, for so long I convinced myself I was the only one who could possibly know the pain I've endured. Our experiences are very different, but I guess there's something universal about grief, isn't there? I'm glad we've been able to share our stories. It's meant a lot to me. Thank you."

Luke gently moved his hand on top of hers and squeezed. When he spoke, his voice was low and tender. "It is crazy how loss has the ability to both isolate and attract people, isn't it?"

"Yes." Cora once again watched their intertwined fingers. For a time, isolating had equated survival. She realized now that the isolation she'd inflicted upon herself these three long years had only fed her grief, nourishing it to grow stronger. She'd missed out on so much by grieving alone. It hadn't honored Christopher's zeal for life as much as living her days to the fullest would have.

She pressed her lips together and searched Luke's eyes. She released her lips along with a long exhale. "I'm done isolating."

A gentle desire flickered in Cora's blue eyes like the delicate candlelight. That, along with her petal soft skin against his, was enough to undo Luke.

Being with Cora was like riding a teeter-totter. One minute her playfulness sent him soaring into the sky, euphoric with excitement and hope. The next moment, their talk of loss and disappointment and trauma brought them back to the ground, often with a thud. But with her hand in his and those electric eyes of hers, both the ups and the downs thrilled him. Through the bobbing, an intimacy wove around them like a caterpillar crafting its cocoon. What metamorphosis lay ahead for them?

Dinner came and went amongst more of that up and down conversation. Soon, creamy wax dripped into puddles on the base of the brass candlestick at the edge of the table. Luke signed the receipt the waiter had just delivered and closed the small black leather folder. "Ready to head out?"

"Yes and no." Cora folded her napkin and placed it on the table, raising her chin just enough to reveal an upturn of her full lips.

Luke stood and helped her into her jacket then followed her through the small dining room to the front door.

A young woman in all black smiled as they passed the hostess stand. "You folks have a nice night, now. And if the wind isn't too cold, be sure to take the porch around back and check out the view. It's even more spectacular out there."

"Great, thanks." Luke held the door open for Cora, inviting in a chilly breeze. The wooden boards of the porch creaked underfoot as they stepped out into the night. He extended a flat palm toward her. "Want to check out that view?"

She stared at his hand long enough that he retracted it, shoving it into his pocket. *Okay, too much.*

The white puff of her breath disappeared above her head and she nodded. "Yeah, I'd love to see it." She grinned sheepishly and extended her hand to him.

Well, look at that. Luke's face split with a wide grin. He slid his hand into hers, which was already chilly. In a few steps, they rounded the porch's corner to find that it wrapped around to encase half of the back of the small restaurant, too. Unlike the front, there were no flickering lamps across the back.

They stepped up to the railing and looked out. Below, the lights of town were pinpricks of white and yellow and orange. Above, the full moon cast a silvery-blue hue over Cora's milky skin.

"Wow." Cora's voice trailed out into the night sky, as wispy as her breath. "I've never seen Laurel Cove like this."

Luke's heart pounded inside his chest. Being alone, in the dark, and in such a romantic setting sent his instincts and his common sense into a frenzied fight for control. The crisp air stung the back of his throat.

Cora softly pulled her hand from his and tugged her jacket tighter around her middle, hands tucking under her arms. "Whew, it sure is colder back here. Guess it's the wind coming up from the valley or something."

Luke gave in to the instinct to protect and reached an arm around her shoulder. She stiffened briefly, then relaxed into the crook of his arm. Had fireworks begun thundering over Laurel Cove, Luke would still have only been aware of the rhythm of Cora's breath and the sweet aroma of her hair.

A sharp wind blew in a burst up from the steep drop-off past the railing. Cora turned into Luke, shielding her face against his chest and wrapping an arm around his waist. Her breath was hot through his sweater.

After the wind subsided, Cora peered up at him. Luke searched her. If they were going to break the embrace, she was going to have to do it. He brushed a hand against her cold velvety cheek.

Her breath stuttered as her eyes closed, and she leaned into his hand. Luke swallowed and studied her full lips.

Because you love her, you should not kiss her.

Luke lowered his hand to hold Cora's, now flat against his chest. Ina was right. Rushing through any part of courting Cora—wasn't that what they called dating in the South?—only invited the risk of things getting messy.

"We should get going. Can't bring you home chilled to the bone," he whispered down at her.

She leaned against him and nodded ever so slightly. "There's no chance of that."

Good grief, this woman was testing every limit. Luke managed a chuckle and reached to tuck a stray wave of golden hair behind her ear. Reluctantly, he took her hand and they made their way back around to the front of the house. At the truck, he opened her door and let her climb in. Her smile was thin as he closed the door.

The truck purred through the darkness as they made their way back to the lake. Unsure what to say, Luke let a comfortable silence linger between them. Well, he hoped it was comfortable for her. It allowed him to volley between pride in his self-discipline and frustration in missing out on what, for all practical purposes, had been the perfect scenario for a movie-worthy first kiss. Surely even Ina would have agreed.

Gravel pinged against the truck's undercarriage as they slowed to a stop in front of Cora's house. He'd barely set the gear shift to P before she pushed the passenger door open. Chilly air mixed with the warmth from the heater as she stepped to the ground.

"Thanks for a nice dinner, Luke. I had a great time. Have a nice night."

"Well, wait, I..." Luke scrambled to release his seat belt as she closed the door. Between quick glances down to the stubborn buckle, he watched helplessly as she raced up the steps to her porch. Finally, with a click, he was free. He threw the belt off his shoulder, pushed his door open, and stepped into the night.

"Cora!" His door closed with a crack just as her front door thudded shut. A moment later the porch light went off, leaving him standing in her driveway watching dust dance in the beams of his headlights.

Luke deflated. He climbed back into the truck and sighed heavily as he shifted into reverse. With a look over his shoulder, he spoke into the silence. "You should have kissed her."

Hopefully, this wasn't his first and last date with the woman he was more certain than ever might just be his one and only.

CHAPTER Eighteen

Bacon hissed from a skillet on the stove as Cora pulled the steaming kettle off the back burner. She poured the water over a tea bag waiting in her favorite mug then filled the other mug with black coffee from Ina's pot.

"Are you waiting for Christmas? I need details." Ina accepted the mug of coffee from Cora and gingerly set it down in front of her at the kitchen table.

Cora turned the bacon with a fork then joined Ina at the table. "It was very nice. The restaurant was lovely, very romantic with candlelight and soft music. Food was great. We had good conversation."

Ina waved a hand in small circles in front of her and nodded her head quickly. "Yes, yes. But how *was* it? Was there chemistry? You know, that little something that sparks inside you when he looks deep into your eyes?"

Cora inhaled, holding the breath before blowing it out in a quick puff. She leaned against the table and cradled her cheek in her hand. "Well, I thought there was."

"What does that mean?"

The tingles that had rushed over her as her hand touched Luke's across the dinner table last night sprang back to life. The electricity that had pulsed through her when she'd taken his hand on the porch. And her quickened breath, expectant, as Luke's strong arms held her tightly in the moonlight. She shook away the vivid memories, stood, and returned to nursing their sizzling breakfast.

"I don't know. At the end of the evening, I was certain he was going to kiss me. The moment was perfect. More than perfect, really." With a piece of bacon dangling from the fork in her hand, Cora recalled the intensity in his eyes. The way he'd focused on her lips.

Grease popped, stinging her thumb and yanking her back to reality. Cora rubbed her hand against her thick flannel pajama pants and opened the fridge to grab the eggs.

"And?" Ina encouraged.

"And nothing. He just said it was cold and we should head home." Cora closed the refrigerator door and looked back to the old, curious woman, eggs in hand. "I just don't get it. I hope I didn't do anything wrong or discourage him somehow."

Ina's nose pointed toward the ceiling. "He was being a gentleman. Good for him."

"How would kissing me, in such a sweet moment, be ungentlemanly?" Cora knew she hadn't misread the chemistry between them. And while Luke was respectful and kind, he didn't strike her as the type to shy away from an undeniably charged moment.

Ina clicked her tongue. "It really is a pity the low standards you young people have these days. Frankly, I'm impressed he listened to me."

Cora froze. "Wait, what do you mean? What did you say to him?"

Ina ran a finger across the lip of her mug. "I advised him against moving too fast where the two of you are concerned. Especially considering—"

"Ina, that's not really any of your business." More grease popped from the skillet, and Cora reached to move it to a cold burner. "Besides, it would have just been a kiss. If you're worried about virtue or something here, there's no need."

Cora took a bowl from the cabinet and began cracking eggs into it, tossing the shells into the sink one by one. Had Luke really refrained from kissing her because of advice from an old woman? As she whipped the whisk through the bowl and sloshed the eggs into a clean pan, she smiled to herself. It was actually kind of endearing.

Ina cleared her throat. "I've watched you flounder these past years, treading water to stay afloat through your grief. I just didn't think it prudent to rush headlong into any new romance. I had your best interests at heart, my dear."

Cora sighed and worked the eggs with a spatula. "I believe you did. And thanks for that. But weren't you also the one who told me I had to find a way to live again?" She turned the burner off and walked over to the table, taking one of Ina's hands in her own. "That's what I'm doing, Ina. I'm trying to live again. Luke is very much a part of that."

Ina's eyes glistened before she looked to their hands and patted Cora's. "I did say that, didn't I? Well, I never meant to ruin a moment between you two. But rest assured, my sweet dear, I'm not the only one who has your best interests at heart."

Cora followed Ina's gaze in the direction of Luke's cabin. She knew it. He *had* wanted to kiss her. Her heart soared with a renewed hope and echoed with the thundering passion still fresh from last night. She longed to be in his arms again.

A smile rose up from her toes, stirred her stomach, and tingled through her cheeks. She stood, her breath quickening as she flitted around the kitchen on light feet. "Here," she said, placing a plate in front of Ina a moment later. "You go ahead and get started. I, uh...I'll be back in a few minutes."

"Wherever in the world are you going right now?"

Cora grabbed the red scarf she'd worn last night from the hook near the front door and wrapped it around her neck. Her keys jingled from her hands as she yanked the door open. She glanced back through the living room to Ina at the kitchen table, staring with her mouth hanging open. "I've got to go see about a gentleman."

Ina's eyes doubled in size. "You're in your pajamas!"

Cora gave a quick wave before pulling the door shut behind her. The air stung her face as her slippers crunched along the driveway, but it was no match for the embers of excitement smoldering inside her. She steered the car onto the lake road and sped toward Luke wearing her frumpy pajamas, slippers, and a wide grin.

So, this is living.

Toby's bark startled Luke almost as much as the unexpected knock at his door. The clock on the mantel read half past eight as he passed it, tossing the newspaper onto the couch seat he'd just risen from. Toby sniffed the edge of the door then whimpered and danced around excitedly. *What in the world?*

Another knock sounded. "Coming."

Running his fingers through his uncombed hair, Luke grabbed Toby by the collar then inched the door open. Cora stood before him, chest heaving as though she'd just run there. She was in an oversized set of flannel pajamas and slippers, cheeks flushed and nose pink.

"Well, good morning." Luke widened the door to let her step inside. She nuzzled the top of Toby's head but kept her bright eyes locked on Luke's as he closed the door. "To what do I owe this—"

The whole world stopped as Cora was suddenly on her tiptoes, her full, soft lips pressed hard against his. His wide eyes slowly melted shut, and his arms enveloped her, pulling her in tightly. For a long moment, all that existed was the two of them. His hand caressed her soft hair as her hands rubbed up his back. Finally, she pulled back and brushed one more peck across his lips before returning to flat feet.

"Whoa." Luke released her and sat against the arm of a chair, working to process what had just happened.

She gently ran a few fingers across her lips then giggled quietly. "I'd apologize for showing up so early unannounced, except I'm not sorry."

Luke's head swam as he trailed a hand up her arm. From where he sat, perched along the chair's arm, they were now eye level. "Uh, no. Do *not* be sorry. But I am curious."

"I spoke to Ina this morning."

"Oh yeah?" Luke followed the rise and fall of her collarbone as it disappeared behind the fabric of her pajama top. He gripped the chair underneath him. *Get it together, man.*

"Yeah. She gave you some advice, I take it?"

Luke's pounding heart came to a sudden halt. Surely Ina hadn't revealed what he'd only recently come to admit to himself could be true. He looked down at his socked feet. "Well, yeah."

"It made me realize you did want to kiss me last night." She took a step closer to him, her plump mouth upturned slightly. "You just thought it wasn't the gentlemanly thing to do."

Her close proximity was intoxicating and stole his ability to form words. Luke reached up, and their fingers wound together. "Mm-hmm."

"I figured this way you maintain your status as gentleman, and I get my kiss."

In a million years, Luke would never have dreamed this turn of events would come so soon after last night's disappointing end. Before heading to bed, he'd vowed patience and to let her lead the way. And boy, had she done that.

She leaned her forehead against his. He sighed, contentment filling him up more than he knew was possible. "You smell like bacon."

The laugh she let out was infectious, and soon they were both roaring. The raucousness excited Toby into a fit of barks, separating them. Cora's laugh trailed off as she reached for the doorknob.

Luke's brow furrowed and he grabbed her other hand. "You're going already?"

Her smile was tender. "I left Ina eating breakfast alone. But can we see each other later today?"

"Yes, please." He stood, eyes resting on his equipment stacked on the other side of the room. He could actually use her help. "I'm heading into town in a bit to take some photos for that calendar fundraiser. Come with me."

"Oh, I'm so glad you're doing it," she said. "I'll get Ina settled with lunch, and then we can grab something to eat in town?"

"That sounds amazing. Pick you up around noon." He gave her hand a little squeeze as she nodded, opened the front door, and let the chilled air rush in.

Just like that, she was gone as quickly as she'd arrived. Luke was left alone in the cabin with Toby. He stared at the dog's blank expression. "Can you believe that?"

Luke was in the business of believing in things he could see, things he could capture through his lens for future observation. But there was no film or digital technology to properly capture the way his heart soared at this moment. The way hope rushed through him like a raging river, the lightness to his soul like autumn leaves picked up by the wind. Believe it or not, it was official. He loved Cora Bradford.

The back of Cora's thighs screamed. She paused a moment on the leaf-littered dirt trail to readjust the strap of a camera bag hurled over her shoulder. Chills rippled through her body as the wind whipped. Despite the bright sun shining high above them, it couldn't cut through the cold of the high altitude. "I guess I underestimated the distance."

Cora didn't remember it taking this long to get to the spot she knew would provide an ideal shot for the photo Luke needed to finish the calendar project. The last few days, she'd followed him to the most picturesque spots around Laurel Cove. The beautiful red barn tucked into the valley of New Hope Farm. A faded mural on the side of the pharmacy. The Laurel Cove Inn, perfectly charming with its wraparound porch and white picket fence. Luke even had shots of old guys in overalls sitting at the counter at Brewed and families walking down Main Street.

Luke had become acquainted with the town's charming personality, and Cora had reacquainted herself with the home she dearly loved.

"You sure you're not trying to get lost in the woods with me?" Luke winked at her, a collapsed tripod tucked casually under his arm. Sure, he was cute, but how was he not winded after their fifteen-minute uphill climb?

"All right, Olympic medalist hiker. Let's go. It can't be much longer." With a few deep breaths that stung her lungs, Cora shifted the bag behind her hip and continued up the trail.

Sure enough, in minutes they came upon the large boulder she'd always said resembled a bear up on its hind legs.

Luke on her heels, she turned her chin to her shoulder. "It's just up here."

With every step, a familiar rushing sound filled Cora's ears. Just beyond several trees bursting with deep red leaves, the trail opened up to a rocky ledge on one side. Cora gently lowered the camera bag to the ground at the foot of a rustic log railing. With one hand on her aching neck, she swung her other arm in front of her in a grand gesture. "There it is."

"Wow." Luke leaned the tripod against the railing and stared out over the steep rocky embankment.

Across a narrow gorge raged a majestic waterfall framed on both sides with all the brilliant colors the North Carolina mountains were known for in autumn. Water thundered in a veil of misty white that eventually faded calmly into the deep, dark pool below.

"It's spectacular." Luke reached out for Cora's hand and pulled her to his side.

She smiled, her mind's eye remembering the last time she'd been to the falls. "Christopher and I came here often. But my favorite time to visit is in the fall. The colors and the crispness. It just doesn't get any prettier."

Luke's eyes blazed with intensity. "Yeah, it does." He pressed his lips to her cheek, invoking a wild rush as mighty as the waterfall through her veins.

Cora brushed a hand over her face as he released her and began to set up his equipment. He operated with a swiftness that proved his expertise. Within minutes, he stood hunched behind the camera perched atop the tripod, twisting the lens and inspecting shots as he snapped them.

"You know, I can't for the life of me remember what this waterfall is named. I know I used to know." She lifted her phone out of her jacket pocket, pulled her glove off using her teeth, and pressed the screen.

"I've noticed things around here have some pretty interesting names." Luke straightened from behind the camera and peered out over the sun-drenched waterfall. "I drove by a road sign for Lazy Farmer's Gap the other day."

Cora's laugh trailed on the bone-chilling wind. He was right. There was something both charming and silly about many of the monikers in these parts. Cora twisted her mouth when nothing loaded in the internet window of her phone. She noticed the single tiny shaded bar out of five in the top corner of the screen. "I forgot how bad service is out here. I'll have to look up the name of these falls later."

"You know, so far you've just watched me. Want to take a few shots yourself?" Luke tilted his head toward the camera.

"Sure," Cora said and stepped over as he moved to the side. The camera she owned took nice shots but was way less intimidating than Luke's set-up. She rose to her tiptoes, unable to see through the viewfinder. "Um..."

Luke laughed heartily and rested a hand on her shoulder.

"Here, let me lower the tripod, shorty." He knelt down and twisted at the legs one by one until it was eye-level for her.

She swatted his arm. "Hey, not all of us were given the gift of height."

He stood, placed a hand on his waist, and pouted his bottom lip dramatically. "Aw. Are you cranky because you're..." He darted his eyes side to side before delivering two final words in an exaggerated whisper. "...vertically challenged?"

Cora gasped and placed a hand over her heart. Oh, he was cute when he teased. *Two can play at this game.* "Are you cranky because you're...you're..."

Apparently two could not play at the game of cute teases.

Luke raised his eyebrows and poked her side, chuckling. "Oh, you really told me."

Cora rolled her eyes and swatted him again. He dodged on nimble feet to avoid her reach. A satisfied sigh escaped, a good accompaniment to the loud rush of the falls. It felt good to be playful.

"Are you going to spend all day picking on the short girl, or are you going to actually show me how to use this fancy thing?" Cora mimicked his raised eyebrows and gestured back to the camera.

Luke held up both hands in defense. "Okay, okay. The lens should be all set. Just find the viewfinder and pan the camera up, down, or side to side to find the composition you want. Falls in center, half falls and half trees. Focus on the rocks at the top of the falls. Whatever you want. Then push here." He leaned in and pointed at a small black button on top of the camera's body. A warm, intoxicating scent enveloped her.

Mercy. Focus took extra determination this close to him, but Cora pressed one eye to the small rectangular viewfinder. She scrunched her nose and backed away. "Uh, it's all blurry."

"No way." Luke looked for himself. "Huh. Must have shifted a bit when I lowered the legs. This lens can be really sensitive. Let me show you how to adjust it."

Cora watched him point out a few adjustable parts along the cylindrical lens. As he rambled on using some photography terminology foreign to her, she noticed a few stray gray hairs mixed into the dark scruff along his chin and cheeks. The muscle along his strong jawline flexed as he talked. His neck had pinked slightly from the midday sun. Flecks of gold danced in his brown eyes.

His eyes. He was looking right at her. Cora drew in a quick breath of cold air and snapped back to the present. "Sorry, what were you saying?"

"You weren't listening." One eyebrow and corner of his mouth both pulled upward as if attached to the same thread.

Cora shook her head slowly, lost in his eyes again. Her heart pounded in her ears, drowning out the deafening rushing water.

He closed the short distance between them and cupped her cheek, his jaw tightening as his eyes dropped to her lips.

Cora pushed up on her toes as the bright world around her went dark under the shadow of Luke's towering frame. His warm lips took over hers, hand firm on her waist. Though they'd shared a few kisses, the effect of this one was no less potent than their first. As his hand worked up from her waist to behind her neck, the thundering of Cora's heart eclipsed the rushing of the mighty falls. Like when she watched a good kissing scene in a movie, Cora's breath caught in her chest as she willed time to stop and suspend the perfect moment.

Raucous laughter suddenly crashed through, the sweetness and sensuality tumbling around them like falling boulders. A threesome of hikers approached from down the trail. Her heels met the earth, slamming a heavy door shut on their moment. She pressed her fingers to her lips.

As the hikers passed by, the young man in the center of the threesome put a hand on each of his buddies' shoulders and pushed them forward. "Let's give the love birds some privacy, fellas." Cora stepped backward, Luke's hand dropping from her waist. The men exploded with laughter again and trotted farther down the trail, around the bend and out of sight.

Cora's cheeks burned. The warm current that had flowed through her while in Luke's embrace was replaced with a prickling electric heat up her neck. They saw her and Luke as a couple. Most of their time together was spent on the uninhabited lake, quite alone and out of the public eye. Did a date and a few kisses make them a couple?

Love birds.

Her mouth was suddenly so dry. She swallowed and rubbed a hand up her tightening throat. What did she know of love anymore?

Alone again, the roar of the waterfall the only sound now surrounding them, Cora risked a glance up. Like every word of an old song coming back to her, she recognized a profound truth in Luke's gold-flecked brown eyes. After all this time and all her pain, she at least still recognized love.

Cora's face drained of color. Was her shift in mood simple embarrassment at being caught in a public display of affection, or was there more? Luke reached for her hand, and she flinched briefly before holding his tightly. "Don't pay them any attention."

With a quick shake of her head, her mouth quirked upward. She waved a hand in the direction the hikers had travelled and said, "Of course not. Guys will be guys."

"Well, sure." Curiosity mixed with concern pricked at him. "That seemed to rattle you a bit. Why?"

A brisk wind shifted, showering them with a cold mist. Luke pulled a thin plastic sheet from the camera bag, settled it over the tripod, then ushered Cora over to a large flat boulder at one end of the ledge. It provided some shelter next to the trunk of a large oak. Side by side they sat, and Luke rubbed Cora's cold hand between his.

"Thanks, that feels good." Her blue eyes almost glowed up at him. "I'm not sure why I reacted the way I did. I guess parts of this still take some getting used to."

"It's new for me, too. We're figuring each other out." He picked a small yellow leaf from her hair.

Truth was, Luke had never been interested enough in a woman to figure anything out before. Boy had that changed in these weeks with this beautiful, complicated woman. The new territory worked heart muscles he'd never used and awakened fresh emotions. Add to that knowing what she'd endured and still carried with her and it was dizzying to navigate at moments like this. All he knew to do was trust his instincts.

Cora cleared her throat and studied their hands. "I know I come with a lot of baggage."

Luke sighed with a chuckle, though the truth of her statement stung a bit. It was as though she'd read his mind.

"Not so much baggage as experience, maybe. But don't we all bring our experiences into new relationships?"

Her eyes darted up to his, stealing a pause before Luke squeezed her hand and continued.

"Relationships with new colleagues, new postmen with awful delivery skills." He winked, hoping the power of humor could lighten the mood enough for her to wander back to a place of comfort. "Or even an annoying neighbor, turned friend, turned shockingly handsome suitor."

One corner of Cora's mouth crept up as she scooted a few inches closer to him. "Suitor? You sound like Ina."

That's more like it.

"I'm okay with that." He shrugged. A tug at his heart urged him. "Just promise me something."

"What's that?"

"First, that you'll talk to me. I know earning each other's trust takes time. But if I don't know what you're thinking or feeling, I can't know what you need to try and help."

She chewed on her lip and gazed out into the dense forest across the trail for a long moment. Luke watched as her head began to bob up and down softly. "That's fair. I promise."

"Good. Now, if the coast is clear," Luke said, shifting his eyes side to side, "I'd like to sneak one more kiss in before we finish up. I'm freezing!"

She shuddered, either from amusement or the cold, as their lips met again. Luke wrapped his arms around her and then nuzzled into her neck, causing her to squeal and jump up off the boulder.

"Goosebumps!" She danced around and pulled up on the collar of her puffy vest.

With the mood light again, Luke made quick work of snapping a few photos of the waterfall before dismantling the camera and tripod. Soon they were on their way back down the rocky mountain trail.

With the equipment safely in the back seat and the heater roaring at their feet, Luke pulled out his phone before heading out of the small parking area.

His heart sank. "Hey, I've got a missed call from Ina."

Cora frowned, looking up from her phone. "Me, too. Thirty-two minutes ago."

Luke yanked at the gear shift and pressed a foot on the accelerator as Cora lifted her phone to her ear. His pulse rose along with the speedometer as he maneuvered the steep winding roads down the mountain.

"No answer."

Cora's shaky voice fueled the thumping in Luke's veins. "It'll be okay."

He glanced at the time glowing on the dash. At best, the lake was fifteen minutes away.

God, let her be okay.

CHAPTER Nineteen

A surge of adrenaline swirled wildly with the sourness of worry in the pit of Cora's stomach—an all too familiar sensation that made her nauseous. She gripped the armrest on the door of the truck as Luke steered sharply onto her driveway. Before it came to a full stop, her feet found the gravel and she sprinted for the door.

Please be okay.

"Ina?" Cora blinked rapidly as she pushed through the door. The television blared at its usual offensive volume, but the living room was empty. She covered the distance of the living room in a few steps, heading for Ina's room.

"Ina!" Luke called as he followed through the open front door, ushering in a chill that matched the one running up Cora's spine.

The white coverlet on Ina's bed had been smoothed neatly and tucked under the thin pillows. Nothing was out of place.

Cora spun on her heels and reentered the living room as she watched Luke step out onto the back deck.

"Cora, out here!"

Luke sprinted off the deck and ran at full speed through the yard toward the shore. With her heart suspended in her chest, Cora followed. Her feet crunched onto the path as she spotted a tuft of Ina's white hair from above a wooden chair near the water's edge.

Oh Lord, please.

Ahead of her by several paces, Luke reached the chair and dropped to his knees, saying something Cora couldn't make out. His shoulders slumped and he caught himself with a hand on the ground.

"Ina?" The desperation in her own voice brought instant tears to the surface.

She fell to her knees at Luke's side, breathless, and rested a hand on Ina's leg, covered in her long baby-blue housecoat.

"Heavens, you two sure are in a snit."

Cora's chest heaved as she found Ina's wide eyes shifting between her and Luke. "Thank God."

The pine-covered ground was cold through her jeans as Cora settled against it. A tear spilled down her cheek. She noticed Ina's pale, bare toes poking out from underneath the thick terrycloth fabric. Next to the chair, lying under a few fallen leaves, the shiny black of Ina's clunky phone reflected the midday sun.

Luke rested a hand on his hip. In between catching his breath, he asked tenderly, "Ina, what in the world are you doing out here?"

Cora's eyes scanned the small clearing around them. "And where is your walker? Why don't you have any shoes on?"

Ina glanced down and wiggled her toes. Her clouded eyes were forlorn, mouth twisted into a pucker. "I can't quite say, dear." She raised her head, gaze absent and fixed across the lake.

Cora knew that look. It was one rooted in loss, anchored deep by grief. Drawn by what whispered a kinship to maternal instinct, Cora scooted closer and slipped her hand under Ina's.

"I saw Charles, just there." Ina's voice broke. She lifted her free hand, trembling, and pointed to the end of the dock littered with yellow leaves. "Next thing I knew, I was here. But he was gone."

The woman's thin lips were as pale as her feet, wrinkles of her face deeper set than when Cora had left just a few hours before. She needed to get inside.

Luke's brow furrowed over concerned eyes, tugging at Cora. He looked away from Ina to her. "I'm going to head inside and start a fire, then I'll be right back down with her walker."

"Thank you." Cora found a natural empathy in him that was more than endearing. It was comforting. Strong. Sustaining.

As Luke climbed the path back up to the house, Cora rubbed over Ina's icy hand. "You didn't hurt anything, did you? Didn't fall? We saw that you called us both, but our phones didn't have service up on the trail. I'm so sorry."

Ina pulled away from the lake and found Cora's face. "No, dear, nothing's hurt. I just seemed to have forgotten where I was once Charles disappeared on me. I sat here until my mind returned. When it did, the little sense I do have left told me there was no way I was going to make it back up that hill. So I waited."

"I'm glad you did." Several times Cora herself had lost her footing on the loose gravel going up the hill.

"What I'd give for just one more moment with him."

Cora followed Ina's gaze as it fixed back across the lake. She wiped at the tear that had fallen moments ago, its trail dried in the cold breeze, and swallowed past the lump in her throat.

Subtle ripples glimmered on the surface of the water. Bathed in a wide swath of sunlight, the colorful treetops crowning the small island on the other side glowed bright. The beauty of God's creation in a moment of pain punctuated the journey of grief that had become so ingrained in Cora's daily life up until recently. The return of its rhythm in this moment, after the reprieve of the several past weeks with Luke, called her back like a siren from the dark depths.

It would be so easy to welcome back the debris bobbing to the surface from the wreckage. The jagged-edged memories that haunted. Cries and moans that had become her nightly companions for so long.

"Dear?"

"Yes?" Cora locked eyes with Ina.

Cold pricked Cora's cheeks as Ina held her face. "We've used up our moments with them, Charles and Christopher. And my goodness were they wonderful moments. Weren't they? Now enjoy your lifetime of moments with that one."

The familiar crack of the backdoor closing echoed through the woods, and Luke started for them, walker in hand. Just as tempting as the call of her grief was the call of hope in a happy future with Luke. A fresh, sharp pang poked at her heart.

Luke joined them. He caught Cora's attention and mouthed, "You okay?" as he set the walker in front of Ina.

Cora pushed to her feet and brushed pine needles from her knees. With a quick wipe at the corner of her eye, Cora nodded curtly.

"What do you say we get you inside and warmed up?" Luke offered Ina a hand and helped her to stand.

The three of them plodded their way back up to the cabin. Cora's prayers for Ina's health and safety had been answered, but today's episode shed light on a new level of care Cora would need to consider.

Her head was a dizzying cacophony of thoughts. Two particular ones inched their way forward, fighting for her attention. How would she care for Ina's failing body and hurting heart? And what if she grew to love Luke and, like Christopher, he too was taken from her?

At the deck, Cora held the walker as Luke tucked a hand under Ina's arm, and together, they gingerly climbed the steps. She'd gone from losing everything to a second chance at family with these two.

She bit down hard on the inside of her lip and followed them inside with her heart opened heavenward. *Lord, help me set aside my fear and trust in your gift of new beginnings.*

Relief covered Luke like a warm blanket where he sat on Cora's couch. She pulled the door to Ina's bedroom, and it clicked softly before she joined him.

"She'll be asleep soon, I'm sure." Cora's head sank into the soft cushion, her eyes closing as a deep sigh escaped her.

"I'm so glad she's all right." Luke's words were just as much to reassure himself as Cora. The incident with Ina was worrisome. Different scenarios played out in Luke's mind like pages in a flipbook. She could have fallen on the path. She could have wandered off in her confusion. Or worse, she could have made it to the dock and succumbed to the frigid lake water. A shiver wracked his body.

He would have felt so guilty had something happened in their absence. It was hard not to draw comparisons to the regret of not being there for his mom when she needed him most. But while he couldn't change that part of his past, he could be grateful for today's positive outcome.

Cora's lips pressed together, a deep crease between her closed eyes. Her pants were still cold when Luke placed a hand on her knee. "Ina's okay."

In an instant, Cora was in his arms. Muffled, breathy sobs warmed his neck. He stroked the back of her head and held her tightly, letting the flood release. When it slowed to a trickle, she squeezed him tightly before sitting back against the couch.

"Sorry," she sniffled, wiping at both cheeks. "I needed to get that out."

"I'm glad you did. Feel better?"

"Yes, some." She pulled a tissue from the box on the coffee table and dabbed at the corners of her eyes.

Despite the crying, Luke marveled at the clarity of her crystal blue eyes when she looked up at him. Would he ever tire of staring into them?

She licked her bottom lip then swallowed. "Luke, I'm scared."

"Of what?"

"Losing Ina."

The break in her voice about did Luke in. His heart in the pit of his stomach, he scooted a few inches closer to Cora and held her hands. "I'd give anything to assure you you won't lose her. And I wish loss like that, and the pain it brings, wasn't part of life."

Her head bobbed. A fresh tear escaped down the side of her nose, over the edge of her mouth, and landed on her bottom lip. Luke caught it, tingles traveling up his arm from his finger as it brushed against her chin. Was this loving someone? Willingly sharing in their heartache and discomfort? If so, he loved Cora Bradford with every inch of his existence.

"I know she's going to die," she whispered as if it were a secret. "She's in her mid-nineties. But it just dawned on me today that she will likely die here. I will find her. Not today and maybe not tomorrow, but one day."

"Oh, sweetheart." The pit in Luke's stomach was bottomless. He squeezed her hand tightly.

Her eyes were wild, mouth quivering as new tears welled. "I don't know if I can do it, Luke. Not alone."

He'd worried about this from the first moment Cora told him of the idea outside Ina's hospital room. But Luke wasn't going to let the demons of her grief steal the strength he knew she had to do this generous act. It was just as important to her healing as it was for Ina.

He tipped her chin gently and looked deep into her eyes. "You can do this, and you are *not* alone."

"But you have your own life, Luke. You didn't sign up for this."

You're my life. Luke swallowed the words that should seem an exaggeration after mere weeks together. Now wasn't the time to make some grand declaration. "I'm not exactly running off to assignments across the world, either. We both have the luxury of time. Between the two of us, we can figure out a schedule of making sure one of us is with her at all times."

She worked her hands in her lap. "I don't know. It feels like a lot to ask of you. Plus, what if you get tired of seeing *me* all the time?"

"Not possible." He chuckled and knocked his knee against hers. When she didn't return a smile, he inhaled and tried a different tactic. "How about this? Let me come and sit with Ina when you run into town on Sundays. I'd also like to come and cook dinner on Tuesdays, Thursdays, and Saturdays for the three of us—that is, if you don't mind me using your kitchen."

A moment passed before her shoulders relaxed. She gave a sideways glance, the corners of her mouth upturned just enough to spark a fresh smile across Luke's face. "That would be great."

"Good!" He patted her knee a few times then pointed a finger at her, eyes narrowed. "But you have to promise that you'll tell me if I can do more or if you need extra help. It's a deal breaker."

The corners of her mouth pulled tighter. "Deal. I promise."

Luke wrapped an arm around her shoulders and pulled backward until they fell against the fluffy cushions. Her breathy laugh danced on the air like the wisps of smoke above the crackling fire.

Here at the lake, with her in his arms and the ups and downs of life floating around them, was the only place Luke wanted to be. It was messy, complicated, and wonderful.

Muted shades of yellows and browns replaced the vibrant hues blanketing the mountains as October came to an end. Loading the last of the groceries into her trunk, the hair on the back of Cora's neck stood up as a stiff wind howled through the parking lot.

She closed the trunk and turned to steer the empty cart back to the nearby corral. "Oh!" Her heart jumped at the sight of a young girl in a pink princess costume standing next to her car, staring at her.

"What are you going as for Halloween?" Green outlined the girl's lips, matching the sucker in her hand.

"Honey, don't bother that nice lady." A harried young woman set a baby on her hip and shut the back door of the minivan parked next to Cora's SUV.

"Oh, she's not bothering me." Cora twisted her mouth and tapped a finger against her chin. "How is the Beast today, Belle?"

The girl's face lit up. She looked down her yellow dress and curtsied clumsily. "Oh, he's grumpy so I left him at the castle."

Cora stifled a snicker, smiling at the young woman who stood next to her now. "Wise decision. No one likes a grump at the grocery store."

"See, I told you," the mom said to the girl, then shifted the fussy baby onto her other hip. She offered Cora a grateful smile before taking the little girl's hand. "You're great with kids. Thank you."

A wicked pang struck Cora's gut, but she grinned through it as she'd grown accustomed to doing these past three years. "You guys have a nice day. And you have fun tonight, Belle."

With that, Cora pushed the cart into the corral another space past the minivan before returning to her car. Just as she pulled the door open, the little girl hollered down the parking lot.

"Happy Halloween!"

Cora waved, her smile big, and climbed into the car. On the way back to the cabin, she thought about how this night could be so different. Last-minute adjustments to costumes. Photos on the porch with plastic pumpkins in hand. Sorting candy before bed and taking what Cora's dad used to call "the Parental Tax" after bedtime.

In another life. A sigh filled the silent car, though the empty spot in Cora's heart ached less than expected. She rolled to a stop in the driveway, the thick blanket of brown leaves crunching louder than the gravel.

The front door opened, and Luke stepped out, making his way toward her. She pulled her keys out of the ignition and sat for a moment watching him, a warmth creeping into the edges of that empty spot.

These first days of their new routine with Ina had gone better than she'd expected. His homemade dinners were a welcome treat, as was the extra time with him. Ina's moods were hit or miss, though most of the time she seemed like her old spunky self. Luke and Cora had even started taking short early-evening walks down to Ina's place after dinner just to keep an eye on it. She found herself looking forward to it more and more with each passing day.

Cora popped the trunk open and met Luke at the back of the SUV. "Who won?"

"Who always wins?" He let out an exaggerated huff as he wove his hands through the straps of several canvas bags. "The woman is a rummy professional."

"Well, you did just learn."

Before picking up the weight of the bags in his hands, Luke paused. "Hey, listen. Just thought you should know Ina gave me a hard time about taking her medicine."

That couldn't be right. "I gave those to her just before I left for town."

Luke pressed his lips together and raised his eyebrows. "No. I found them sitting in a napkin next to her chair when she got up to take a nap just a bit ago. I asked her about it, and she got pretty sour. She finally took them, but it's probably something to keep an eye on."

"Thanks. I will."

On the way up the steps to the porch, bags in hand, Cora felt the weight of not only the five-pound bag of flour but also the responsibility of caretaking. She'd have to add watching Ina take her medicine to the list of tasks. What else was she missing? Thank goodness Luke was willing to stand in the gaps so attentively.

A few minutes later, while her hands dipped in and out of the grocery bags sitting on the kitchen table, Luke placed a hand on Cora's hip and a kiss on her cheek. "I'm going to head out. Are we walking later?"

Her pulse jumped. *Yes, please.* "Well, it is Halloween. Don't want you getting spooked after dark."

"Very funny." He pulled a grape off the bunch Cora placed in the basket at the center of the table and popped it in his mouth. "But let's go on the earlier side, now that you mention it."

Cora threw a hand over her mouth to muffle a hearty laugh and darted her wide eyes to Ina's closed bedroom door. It felt good to laugh.

"Shh!" Luke teased. He grabbed another grape before turning for the door. "See you later. I'll be the one with the extra-bright flashlight."

As the front door clicked shut behind him, so began the countdown to Luke's return. Missing him was a welcome change to missing Christopher. That was like comparing a sweet apple to a prickly cactus. One was full of expectancy and hope. The other was miserably void of either. On a day ripe with what was never meant to be, she was grateful for something—or someone—to look forward to.

Luke blinked at a bright golden light streaming through the front windows of the cabin and rubbed his eyes. He shifted in the chair, sending the book he'd been reading falling from his chest to the floor. When was the last time he'd napped in the middle of the day? Hanging out with Ina was rubbing off on him.

With a start, he looked at his watch: 4:30. If he didn't get to Cora's, the little bit of daylight left would be gone. He bolted up and, in a few steps, reached for Toby's leash hanging by the front door. The dog sprang from his spot in front of the dark fireplace, circling Luke with excitement. Luke grabbed for his coat as they bolted out the door, the air pricking his cheeks.

As they turned onto the road, Luke's phone buzzed in his pocket. It wasn't surprising Cora was wondering why he was late for their walk. But when he looked at the screen, the number of his favorite magazine editor surprised him. When had it become so foreign to think about work?

"Sadie, how are you?"

"Hey, stranger. I'd be better if you were still in the game."

Luke let Toby sniff at a pile of leaves and curled his lip. She never did mince words. "Yeah, well. You of all people know the break I needed was warranted."

"Listen, that issue sold us more copies than the previous three months combined. No hard feelings. But seriously, how are things in the woods?"

Heading down the road with Toby in the lead, Luke watched the thin line of white smoke rising from the tip of Cora's chimney just over the trees. "Good, Sadie. Things are really good. How are you?"

"Oh, you know New York. Fast-paced and frantic. I love it."

For a long time, Luke had thrived on that never-stop rhythm. It had taken him all over the world snapping one project after another, chasing an invisible finish line. To begin with, even the firestorm that followed the Dennison campaign oddly thrilled him. Until the thrill more resembled an insatiable monster, taking everything he had to give.

But Luke had found the peace he never knew he wanted and needed right here in Laurel Cove. It clicked with something inside him that he hadn't realized was out of alignment.

He drew in a full breath of the chilly air. "What can I do for you, ma'am?"

"Did you really just call me ma'am? What have they done to you?" Her laugh was as hearty as her personality. "Anyway, listen, I've got a job for you if you want it. It's big."

Luke used to live for those words.

Now? Now he couldn't imagine anything more alluring than walking hand in hand with the woman he loved. The usual rush of adrenaline that followed an assignment offer was replaced by only a slight curiosity. "I'm not really looking for work right now, Sadie. But thanks."

A scoff hissed through the phone. "Wow, I never thought I'd see the day Luke Bassett nonchalantly turned down a story. At least tell me you're shooting. Something? Anything?"

"Well, it's not the magazine's kind of stuff, but you know how much I love small-town America. This place is a gold mine for that." Laurel Cove had more than made an impression—it'd really grown on him. In fact, it'd started to feel like home. "I'm just wrapping up edits on photos for a calendar fundraiser in town. I know it's small potatoes, but I've really enjoyed it. And the photos are great."

"Hmm. I've actually got a colleague putting together a digital feature on the best underrated small towns or something like that." She paused then continued, "Why don't you send me a few of the best you've got, and I'll pass them on to her?"

"Yeah, sure. Laurel Cove *is* pretty great." The pavement of the road gave way to the loose gravel of Cora's driveway.

Luke hadn't considered doing anything else with the calendar photographs, but one of the photos from the waterfall had turned out to be his favorite from the whole project. It would be fun to get the town a little shout-out and surprise Cora with seeing the photo published.

As he and Sadie hung up, he reached to unhook the leash from Toby's collar. The dog bolted for the porch, where Cora sat with a steaming mug.

"Well, I thought you'd forgotten about me," she said as Luke climbed the steps.

In between Toby's energetic jumps on her lap, Luke leaned down and pecked her lips. She was every bit his home as Laurel Cove had become.

"Not a chance."

CHAPTER Twenty

If October was the lake's most colorful month, November was its coziest. One week into the month, Cora was bringing firewood in from the deck more often, and just yesterday, she'd pulled out her double-lined puffy coat. She yanked at its zipper on her way down to the dock.

The lake called to Cora on mornings like this, when a misty fog swirled just above the surface of the glassine water as if it were boiling. Like snuggling down under the bed covers, it was as though the lake reached around her in an embrace. She welcomed it, needy for the comfort after the second night of dreaming.

Her light steps padded against the boards. At the end of the dock, she released her arms from across her chest and inhaled deeply. The air was crisp and sweet and still. No wind rustled the trees, no burrowing animals shuffled the leaves, and no critters chirped.

Peaceful.

She'd not dreamed nightmares of the accident. Nor had Christopher visited with encouragement. These were the dreams full of the most acute longing for things that were not meant to be—faceless shadows and echoes of laughter. These were the dreams Cora had yet to find the courage to speak out loud to anyone.

She sighed and watched a line of low-flying geese cut through the mist on their way into the cove. She found the faint glow from a window of Luke's cabin, and her heart fluttered. This morning's dream had woken her in the earliest moments of dusk and included him. In fact, he was the only part of her dream not smudged out or faded or vague. Every detail, from his tender smile to the gray hair feathered at his temples, was sharp.

He was the part of her life in focus.

Cora chuckled, then brought her hands together in front of her mouth and let her hot breath warm them. How appropriate to use a camera metaphor where Luke was concerned.

She reached into her pocket to snap a photo of the serene lake to show him later. Just after she snapped the picture, a box popped up with the preview of a new text message. Prickles raced up her arm at the sight of Laura's name. She'd bet anything she knew what Laura was writing about.

A few taps on her screen led her to the message.

LAURA: HELLO, CORA. CHRISTOPHER'S DINNER WILL BE ON THE 14TH AT 6:30. CRAB LEGS LIKE USUAL. WILL YOU BRING THE CHEESECAKE? YOUR FRIEND LUKE IS WELCOME, TOO, IF YOU'D LIKE TO BRING HIM. SEE YOU THEN.

Cora pressed the button on the side of her phone and slid it into her coat pocket. She turned away from the water and blew into her hands again as she marched the length of the dock. Just when peace had begun to settle over her like the comforting fog hugging the lake, reality blew in like a stormy gust and grunted, "Not today, Cora."

It wasn't that she didn't want to honor Christopher. She just didn't want to glorify the day of his death any longer. It did her no good. Why not celebrate his *life* on his birthday or something? She stole a deep breath as a cold breeze whipped around her, then climbed the yard. The Bradfords were entitled to remember their son any way they wanted. Their grief was theirs to navigate and survive. Just like her grief was hers.

As she climbed the deck steps, she saw Ina's white hair peeking out over the top of the armchair in the living room. Instead of going in, she crossed her arms and sank into one of the chairs facing the water.

But invited to bring Luke? That was sure something. Cora's shoulders relaxed, though inwardly she weighed the unexpected change in Laura's attitude toward Luke. Had she really accepted that Cora had someone new in her life? It sure would be a welcome blessing.

Her lip pinched between her teeth. There was no denying that having Luke by her side made anything easier. But what if he didn't want to go? It was asking a lot.

The sun shone brightly over the lake, the breeze having carried off any lingering mist. Cora took the clearing as a sign to stay positive. She stood and nodded shortly toward the shiny water now rippling in the cold wind.

At dinner that evening, she would ask him. *I'll ask Luke to go to the dinner honoring my dead husband's tragic accident at his parent's house.* She raised her eyebrows, the crack of her laugh trailing on the breeze at how insane it sounded. What could go wrong?

"Well, this dinner just got interesting." Ina's fork clanked against the side of her dinner plate. She rested her elbows on the table, and her chin nestled on top of her folded hands.

Luke chewed a bite of baked chicken slowly, processing Cora's news that he'd been invited to the dinner on the anniversary of Christopher's death. Knowing the difficult date was approaching was one thing. Being invited into the intimate family experience of it was another thing entirely.

"I was surprised, too, when Laura offered." Cora's mouth twisted across the table. "And I completely understand if you'd rather not go."

Hesitation pulled him away from his instinct to support and protect Cora at all costs. Luke sipped his iced tea, carefully setting the glass down on the quilted placemat. "And you're sure everyone is okay with this?"

"I can't imagine she would have offered if she wasn't." Cora shrugged lightly, biting at her lip. It wasn't exactly the confidence he was looking for.

Ina cleared her throat. "No one asked my opinion, but I'm going to give it anyway."

Luke and Cora exchanged smirks.

"If you ask me"—Ina pushed up on the bridge of her glasses and continued—"God's working on something big here. This could be the closing of one chapter and beginning of a new one for you both. A bridge, if you will."

Luke understood the analogy to Cora's life. But how would a likely awkward dinner with Cora's former in-laws matter to the trajectory of his story?

Cora's striking eyes peered at him over the rim of her glass, but it was the narrative behind them that really struck a chord. In these past several weeks, he'd witnessed the ups and downs of her grief. The details of Christopher's life and death were woven into Luke and Cora's time together. While getting to know her, he'd come to know Christopher, too.

Maybe Ina was right and attending this dinner was crucial to Luke's own life story. Could holding Cora's hand through her hardest evening of the year bridge the wide gap between his long chapters of loneliness and still unwritten chapters of happily ever after? What if he couldn't have one without the other?

Luke set aside the hesitation and followed his instinct, trusting God was at work. He reached across the table for Cora's hand. "Of course I'll go."

Cora placed the last dry plate in the cabinet and hung the damp kitchen towel on a hook by the stove. A rush of frigid air sent a shiver through her as Luke walked in from the deck with an armload of wood.

"That cold front they talked about on the news has definitely arrived. It's freezing out there."

She followed him into the living room, where Ina sat in her armchair, an afghan over her lap, reading something on her tablet. The woman was an anomaly, equally holding tight to old fashioned ways and embracing the modern world. Cora tucked her legs under her on the couch and watched Luke work to get a fire started.

Cora's life wasn't much different. She clung to this house and its reflection of her past. She glanced over her shoulder, the box from the accident pulsing from within the coat closet like a treasure chest at the bottom of the sea. On the mantel above Luke's head sat a photograph of her and Christopher on the porch the day they moved into the cabin.

Ina clicked her tongue and whispered, "Well, that's ridiculous," under her breath. She set the tablet down on the side table and picked up the remote control. The screen glowed to life, and she found a crime drama.

Dawning awareness pulled at the corner of Cora's mouth. She thought back to Ina's metaphor of a bridge between the past and future. Ina herself served as a bridge, in a way. Cora found comfort in Ina having known Christopher and being able, in the present, to carry her memory of him alongside Cora's own healing. And yet, Ina was also a guide of sorts for Cora and Luke both. Not exactly a matchmaker, still she continually served as an active participant in their budding relationship.

"Well, clearly the husband did it. They're all blind." Ina waved a hand at the television then pointed the remote at the screen and clicked through channels.

A chuckle bubbled up in Cora. *Thank you, God, for that woman.*

Then there was Luke, embodying her present and at least the hope of her future. Crouched in front of the fireplace, he wiped his brow and stoked the logs under growing flames. Cora's smile dimmed.

She desperately wanted him at her side at Christopher's dinner, but butterflies swarmed in her stomach at the idea of inserting Luke so deliberately into the intimate, carefully curated environment of shared family history and loss.

Luke pushed to his feet and set the iron stoker in the stand of fireplace tools then crossed the room. An earthy smokiness accompanied him as he sat down next to her and rested an arm across her leg, squeezing her knee.

"Want to play cards?"

His question, so matter-of-fact, stirred something different than the jittery butterflies. Cora scanned the cabin. The kitchen dark after being cleaned up from a homemade dinner. Ina watching television in her housecoat and slippers. The crackling fire. Luke cozied up next to her on the couch.

This was family.

She swallowed past the swelling emotion and nodded at Luke. He grabbed a deck from the basket under the coffee table and began shuffling.

"I'm going to sit this game out," Ina said, eyes glued to a black-and-white movie Cora couldn't place. "At least give you a shot at winning, dear." She bounced with silent laughter, cutting her eyes to Luke.

Luke laughed as he dealt two hands. "You're so kind." He handed one stack to Cora, paused before letting go of them, and winked. "Go easy on me."

"Hey, I haven't beaten her at rummy yet either, so I'd say we're well matched."

"I'd say so." He leaned in and pressed his lips softly against hers, stealing her breath.

Cora rubbed the back of her fingers against his scruffy cheek and searched his eyes. The fireplace wasn't the only area he had a knack for stoking fires. She repaid with another peck before sitting back and fanning herself with the cards in her hand. "You're just trying to distract me."

Ina cleared her throat. "There's nothing good on tonight. I'm going to turn in early. Plus, you two don't need me here."

Luke set his cards aside and helped Ina to her feet. Once firmly set in front of her walker, which already faced her bedroom door, she swatted at him. "Fine, fine. Thank you. I'll manage from here. You go tend to your game and your flirting."

Luke held up both hands and stepped out of Ina's way. "Now, there's no need for jealousy, Ina. You know I've only got eyes for you."

Cora rested against the back of the couch and covered her amusement with her cards. She loved the rapport between those two. And Ina wasn't wrong. Christopher had always been sweet and loving, but Luke had an undeniable mastery for flirting that obviously made knees weak across generations of women.

Ina's grin was a mile wide as she shuffled toward her room. "Don't patronize me, young man. Good night."

"Night. Sleep well," Cora said.

Luke returned to the couch and picked up his cards, bringing a fresh whiff of the fire's aroma.

"I just had a thought, Cora." Ina paused in the doorway of her room. "What if I came to the dinner with you also? Maybe my being there could help in some way."

Cora sat up at the inspired idea. Having another outsider at the dinner could definitely help diffuse her anxiety. And as she'd just realized, Ina had known Christopher and was every bit as much family to Cora. "I'd like that very much, Ina. Thank you for offering."

Ina nodded sharply. "All right then. Good night."

"Good night."

As the bedroom door clicked shut behind her, Cora glanced at Luke, who was rearranging his cards. "What do you think about that?"

He looked up and pressed his lips into a thin smile. "I think we're going to need everyone on our side we can get."

Cora stiffened. "You're worried?"

His mouth twisted and he looked over into the fire. "Worried is a strong word."

"Then what?"

He shifted to face her squarely. "I just think it's possible that Christopher's parents could have a harder time seeing you with someone else than even they think. Harry seems in a better place than Laura. Sure, she's had time to process meeting me at the festival. But that wasn't the most enjoyable interaction."

Prickles ran up Cora's arms. Being optimistic was the only way she was going to get through this. "I really don't think she would have invited you if she wasn't okay with the idea. I'm not worried."

"I'm not either. Really." Luke placed a hand on Cora's knee. "But I do think it'll be nice to have Ina along. Plus, then we won't have to find someone to come stay with her for those few hours."

"True." Cora looked at her cards again. Why hadn't she even thought of that part of going to the dinner? Of course they didn't want to leave Ina alone. Could that have been one of the reasons Ina invited herself along?

"Are we going to play or not?" Luke gave Cora's knee a slap. "I'm ready to crush you."

"Oh, it's on."

Cora willed her mood to stay up, like creating momentum by pushing hard against the ground to send a teeter-totter skyward. She'd even said to herself before that Harry and Laura had clearly moved past their grief better than she had. They'd travelled, resumed old hobbies, stayed involved in town activities. Perhaps they were ready to see Cora move on, too.

Four games and a bowl of popcorn later, Luke threw his last card on the coffee table. "Rummy! Best of five, I win."

He stood and pranced in a victory dance, pointing down at a wrinkle-nosed Cora. She sank into the couch with her arms crossed. "Good game."

"Aw, don't feel bad. You put up a real good effort."

She cracked a half grin. "Yeah, sure."

A slow ballad crooned from the television. A dewy-eyed couple in the old movie Ina had left on floated across a grand ballroom. Luke extended a hand down to Cora. "Dance with me."

Her sarcasm faded into tenderness. She slid her hand into his and stood to face him. In a few steps they moved to the other side of the coffee table in front of the fire. But the heat that rose from his toes to his neck had nothing to do with the flames.

Luke pulled Cora's hand to his chest. His other hand pressed into the curve between her shoulder blades as she leaned her head against his chest. They swayed slowly, her breath hot against his hand that held hers. His eyes fell shut. He could do this forever. How did she fit so well into the place he hadn't even known was empty, waiting for its perfect match?

"I haven't danced since..." Her voice trailed off. She rubbed her hand up and down his back then rested it on his shoulder and sighed.

His heart pinched, recognizing the pain she'd live with forever, even if time continued to dull it. He reached under her chin and tilted it gently until their eyes met.

"I know you probably haven't made your mind up about us yet." Her cheek was soft under Luke's thumb, and the flames danced in her eyes. "But I will never expect you to stop loving him."

Cora's lips parted, her chest falling as she released a breathy sigh.

He tightened his grip around her waist and their steps stilled. "Maybe make room for me, too?"

"There's room." Her words came out in a whisper. She focused on his lips and squeezed his hand.

His chest thundered at the tender but intense passion he saw in her smoldering gaze. He slid his hand under her thick hair until he held her neck. She rose on her toes and her mouth met his, a sensuality blossoming in her. The intensity ignited Luke's imagination. When she buried her face in his neck, he wrapped both arms around her waist and lifted her, finding her mouth again for a deeper kiss.

After a long moment, she gently pushed against his chest, her breaths shallow. She lowered back down to the floor and brushed her fingers across her plump lips.

Luke's ears rang, his head dizzy. "Sorry."

"That is nothing to be sorry for." She closed the short distance between them and rested a hand on his chest, her smile playful. "You're really good at that."

Luke wouldn't have thought it possible, but his heart raced even faster at her teasing. He pushed her hair back and ran a thumb down her neck. Loving her was getting easier and easier. "I just want you to feel wanted, Cora. Treasured and desired. Because I do...want you. In all the ways."

"I know you do." Her eyes were soft and tender. But did sadness or maybe uncertainty linger along with her attraction?

He held his breath and searched her gaze, waiting. But for what? He ached to profess his love, but what if it wasn't the same for her? The chemistry between them could start a raging fire, but Cora's emotions were surely more complicated to figure out beyond the spark from a kiss.

She reached for his hand and pressed her lips against the back of it. "Thank you."

Luke let out his breath. Her words weren't a warning to back off, but he retreated nonetheless. If he was in this for the long haul—and he was—there was no deadline to meet. She had moved through to the other side of her grief enough to welcome him into her life. Luke had to have faith that she could welcome in new love, too.

On the television, a man in glasses announced the next classic movie about to begin.

"I'm not really ready to go home." Luke squeezed her hand and winked. "But I love *Singin' in the Rain*. Want to watch?"

Cora smiled and nodded. They returned to the couch, her head nestling into the crook of Luke's shoulder. The overture of the movie began to float into the darkened room. He'd heard before that God's timing was perfect. Maybe getting the anniversary of Christopher's death behind them would help to create a more perfect time for Luke to love her openly and freely.

CHAPTER Twenty-One

Cora blinked slowly, then let sleep settle again. She nuzzled into the warmth and comfort beneath her. Another sleepy blink brought into focus sunshine pouring in from the deck onto the kitchen table.

I'm downstairs?

She sat up to the edge of the couch and tugged at a sleeve of her blue sweater, pushed up on her arm, then rubbed her watering eyes. White-socked feet not belonging to her rested against the floor, attached to two long legs in jeans. She whipped her head, wincing at a stiff pain that shot up her neck, and found Luke asleep.

How did I let this happen?

With one hand on her sore neck, she darted her eyes to Ina's bedroom door. She sighed, grateful it was still shut.

"Luke!" she hissed, shaking his knee with her free hand.

He stirred, his hand gently rubbing hers still on his leg. She tried to ignore the tingling his touch set off up her arm. She shook him again. "Luke, wake up."

"Hmm?" A smile crept across his face as his sleepy eyes found her. "Well, hey."

Good gracious, his gravelly voice made her stomach somersault. She reached for his shoes under the coffee table, setting them in front of him, and stood. "Luke! It's morning. You've got to get up!"

He rubbed his cheek then grabbed her hand, pulling her back to him. The cushion was still warm where she had lain, his arm hot around her. She giggled but pushed against his chest when he nuzzled into her neck. "Luke, honestly! What would Ina say if she came out and found us here?"

"We're probably going to be in a lot of trouble."

Cora melted as his low, gruff voice whispered in her ear. Knowing his flirting was even more intense in the morning undid her resolve in a single heartbeat.

Is this what it would be like when we...

Her eyes popped open and she shook away the rest of the thought, tearing away from him. She pushed to her feet for the second time and pressed a palm outward toward him. "That's enough, Casanova."

He raised both hands in surrender then stretched through a yawn before standing. Cora grabbed the bowl filled with a few uneaten pieces of popcorn and started for the kitchen.

Luke followed her, rubbing at his face again. "Looks like it's going to be a nice day."

Cora set the bowl on the counter and picked up the tea kettle, starting to fill it at the sink. A glance out the back window revealed glints of sunlight dancing across the lake. Cora tried to let the serene landscape calm her nerves.

Luke leaned against the counter next to her and blocked her view. "You're even more beautiful in the morning."

"Luke, for goodness' sake. Snap out of it." She rolled her eyes, becoming more rigid with each passing moment. Getting used to the idea of having a boyfriend was one thing, but last night had been the first night she'd kissed a man other than Christopher in this house. Waking up with Luke here, in any capacity, was borderline alarming. She willed her breath to even out.

Don't overreact.

"Fine." When she looked up at him, his mouth was pressed into a thin line. "I'll go."

"I just think it's best you're not here when Ina gets up."

"Too late."

Cora's heart sank, and she turned sharply at the sound of Ina's voice.

Her white hair wrapped around small pink foam rollers, Ina looked from Cora to Luke and back again, lips pursed. "What's going on?"

The thundering of Cora's heart drowned out any thoughts that had been trying to form. She looked to Luke, pleading.

His brow furrowed before he turned back to Ina. "We fell asleep on the couch watching a movie last night."

"Luke!" Cora snapped. The last thing she wanted was for Ina to think anything dishonorable was happening between them. She scowled at him before stepping to Ina's side and pulling out a kitchen chair for her. "Ina, it was just an accident. It got really late and—"

"You don't owe me an explanation, dear." Ina lowered slowly into the chair. "You are grown, responsible adults, and this is your home. I'm not worried."

"Well, I'm going to take off." Luke brushed past Cora, pausing to press a soft kiss against Ina's forehead. "You have a good day, Ina. I'll see you for dinner tomorrow evening."

Cora stood back and hugged her arms across her middle. He moved to the living room and sat on the couch, swiftly sliding on his shoes before standing again. Cora chewed on her lip as she followed him to the front door.

He reached for the knob but stopped short of opening it. When he looked down at her, his expression was stoic, jaw tight. "Listen, I get that we didn't plan to fall asleep, but I don't understand why you're so embarrassed."

Cora shifted her feet and bit down harder on her lip, willing the threatening tears to stay at bay. Again, words wouldn't come.

He rubbed the back of his neck then sighed heavily. "Maybe it's not my job to understand. It won't happen again."

Cold air rushed in, pricking Cora's face as Luke pulled the door open and stepped onto the porch. "Luke, I..."

"It's really okay, Cora." He leaned in and pressed a short kiss against her cheek then offered her a half smile. "Burgers and homemade fries tomorrow?"

"Sounds great." Her fingers dug into her arms. She watched him walk away carrying a piece of her heart with him. As the door closed, Cora's eyes landed on a photograph of her and Christopher down by the lake. She sat on his lap, both of them mid-laugh.

In her quest to find a balance between remembering Christopher and learning to love Luke, the scales kept tipping back to the past whenever her future gained a little momentum. Two steps forward and one step back, as the saying went. She either felt guilty for being disloyal to her dead husband or guilty for pushing Luke away. Was the balance she sought even possible? Did a guilt-free scenario exist?

Her eyes travelled to another photo hanging on the wall nearby, of her and Christopher at a church picnic. Then to the wooden-framed photo of them at Christmas on the mantel. She stepped to her desk and traced a finger along the top of a small frame showing Christopher standing next to the waterfall she and Luke had hiked to.

Christopher was everywhere she looked. How was she supposed to move forward with Luke when she was constantly reminded of her first love? Cora walked to the back door and squinted at the sun glaring off the glassy water.

"You okay, dear?" Ina asked from where she sat quietly at the kitchen table.

"Yeah." Cora nodded, but she felt anything but okay.

Her conflicted heart pulled her eyes shut. All this time, Luke willingly pursued her even with these photos surrounding them. Not once had he seemed dissuaded, and he somehow managed to stay respectful to both her grief and Christopher's memory.

Maybe it was time to pack away the past and, just like Luke had asked, make room for him in her heart once and for all. She was tired of asking God for help, and yet she knew it was her best hope despite herself. With her chin tilted up, she pleaded heavenward.

God, you've helped me begin to heal. Now, help me love again.

The afternoon sun shone brightly over the square as Luke pulled into a parking spot in front of the town hall. It was a stark difference from his brooding mood. He cut off the engine and watched a couple stroll along the sidewalk hand in hand.

Why did things have to be so complicated with Cora? He didn't want to change who she was or easily dismiss her life experiences. And up until yesterday morning, he'd been confident in his ability to patiently wait as their relationship matured.

But now? The way she embarrassed so quickly and left him to defend something that didn't need defending left him needing space. Space to think and clear his mind.

He stepped out of the truck and slung his bag over his shoulder. A crisp breeze rustled the trees in the center of the square as he climbed the town hall steps two at a time. Inside, he headed in the direction of a hanging sign that read "Mayor's Office."

A half hour later, Luke descended the same steps after turning in the photos for the calendar. His bag also held a signed photography release that would allow him to submit some of them for the feature Sadie had mentioned.

"Luke?"

Harry Bradford was crossing the street and headed right for him. Luke's jaw flexed. The day just kept getting better and better. He extended a hand when Harry stepped up onto the sidewalk. "Hi, Mr. Bradford. How are you?"

"Well, thank you. How are things up at the lake?"

Could be better. "Couldn't be better, thanks."

"I'm working down a honey-do list from the Mrs. Enjoy your day." He nodded toward the line of store fronts past the town hall.

Luke gave a short wave and stepped off the curb at his truck, relieved by the brevity of the encounter. "Thanks. See you next weekend."

"How's that?" Harry stopped and turned to face Luke.

"At the dinner for Christopher. It's next Saturday, right?"

Harry's bright smile fell into a prominent frown. Under other circumstances, the severe shift would have been almost comical. But given the actual details Luke knew surrounded the event and people involved, only dread stirred inside him.

"You're coming to dinner with Cora?" Harry closed the distance between them.

Luke swallowed hard. "Yes, sir. Laura extended the invitation just the other day, I believe."

"Ah. I wasn't aware of that." He gazed out across the square before looking to Luke again. "Do you mind if I offer you some unsolicited advice?"

"Sure." Luke's jaw clenched again. Experience told him unsolicited advice often struck under the belt.

"Speaking for myself, you are certainly welcome. I'm prayerful Laura's invitation is sincere, but she tends to be quite raw on the anniversary. I'd come guarded if I were you."

"Thank you. If you don't mind my asking, what would I be guarding against?"

"The storm of a mother's deep anguish, I suppose." Harry smiled at a mother and small child who trotted down the sidewalk, then continued. "Laura is particularly sensitive to others' sense of loyalty to Christopher. I believe she's terrified he'll be forgotten."

How interesting that the two women tied most deeply to the same man shared a similar fear. "I can't speak for Cora, but I feel it safe to say she will never forget your son. From what she's told me, he was a remarkable man."

"That he was." The brightness returned to Harry's face, his mouth slowly transforming again. "You're an answer to my prayer, Luke."

The words stirred Luke. "How so, sir?"

Harry gripped Luke's shoulder tightly. "Ever since Christopher died, I've prayed God would bless Cora with another someone special. Not a man to replace my son, but to continue fulfilling the things Cora needs and deserves in his own unique way. Are you that person?"

A sudden tightness in Luke's throat threatened to betray him. He cleared it and looked Harry square in his gray eyes. "I hope I am."

Harry's smile grew another inch. "Then, son, you are."

Luke's chin tipped softly, afraid more words would break whatever resolve he had left in his voice. Harry's confidence was a welcome salve to Luke's fragile certainty. Still, the dinner sounded more ominous than ever.

Harry let go of Luke's shoulder and stepped back a few steps. "I'd best get on with my chores. See you Saturday."

Luke rubbed the back of his neck and twisted his mouth. "Would you mind if I mention our chat to Cora? It may help to prepare her for the dynamic as well. And please know if I don't come, it's only because we've decided together it may not be best."

Harry's nod was swift. "Always wise to keep the lines of communication open." His hand was firm in Luke's when they shook again. "But I do hope you'll come."

"Thanks, Harry."

Luke climbed in the truck and watched Harry step through the door of the dry cleaners. The truck came to life, and he set his hands in front of the vents blowing warm air. He couldn't have more respect for Harry. After losing a son, the amount of grace he'd extended to Luke was priceless.

Surely Luke could extend some of that grace back to Cora herself. The encounter with Harry gave Luke the courage to let her know his concern about the dinner. And now he knew he wasn't the only one.

The warm scent of cinnamon and apple from the candle burning on the console table surrounded Cora as she closed the door to the coat closet. She'd wasted no time acting on the realization that had hit her that morning. The box from the accident now also held an envelope holding most of the photos of Christopher from around the cabin. The empty frames stacked on the coffee table now waited for snapshots of memories to come.

Her eyes trailed up the staircase to her bedroom door. She had left one photo, though. A reminder of the heights Christopher had taken her to during their life together, literally and figuratively. A picture of them atop the Swiss Alps from their honeymoon remained on her dresser. It faced the view of the lake he'd loved so much.

Cora's phone vibrated in her pocket as she moved through the quiet cabin. She pulled it out and slid her finger across the screen to accept the call from her agent. "Hi, Gail. How are you?"

"Good, good. Do you have a few minutes to chat?" Always to the point.

Cora's eyes fell on Ina's closed door then the clock on the mantel. Naptime would probably last at least another half hour. "Sure. What's up?"

She grabbed her black notebook and a pen and stepped out onto the deck. The reliably cold November breeze rustled the nearly bare trees around her and made her thankful for her double layers. A chair in front of the empty firepit creaked as she lowered herself.

"I just got off with Random House," Gail said. "They're so thrilled with the proposal you sent over that they want to see if you could have a draft to them by the end of the year. Apparently, it fits well into a list they're pushing, but it would need to be done fast."

Cora's mouth went dry. All she could manage was, "You're kidding."

"I know it's been a long time, Cora. But you used to hammer manuscripts out in weeks. It'd be like getting back on a bike once you got going."

The world spun. Cora leaned back into the chair, her hand resting over her eyes. "How fast is fast?"

"Ideally, first draft by Christmas. Hang on." Gail's muffled voice chatted with another voice in the background.

Not too unlike the intoxication Luke caused her last night, this familiar rush of excitement over a new project energized Cora. Her pulse rushed, flushing her chest. She looked through the window to the kitchen.

What about Ina? Cora had admittedly written her other books within two months or less. But in those days she'd had the luxury of holing herself up from distractions. Christopher had made sure of it. How in the world would she get an entire book drafted in about six weeks while caring for another person?

"Sorry about that. It's a zoo around here," Gail huffed. "So, what do you think?"

"Well, I don't—"

"There's two other things you need to be aware of before saying no. First, they're offering a 15% increase over the original advance if you can make this new deadline."

Cora stiffened. "I don't care about the extra money, Gail. You know that. What's the second thing?"

"The studio that bought the movie rights is moving forward. In some miraculous chain of events, they've already signed on producers and have started talks of casting some huge names. It *never* happens that fast."

"Wow." Cora felt as though she was on an out-of-control merry-go-round. She sat up and leaned against her knees. "How does that make a difference as to when I write the book?"

"Well, Random House would like as much distance between the new book and the movie as possible. Moving the book up gives a better chance of that. Either way, you're looking at some busy seasons ahead. What do you say?"

Breathe. Cora focused on a deep inhale and exhale, willing her scrambled head to still. "I need to give it some thought. How long can you give me?"

"They need to know by ten tomorrow morning."

Cora pushed to her feet and paced the length of the deck. "Gail, that's insane!"

"You know how the business works, Cora. But yeah, it's fast. Take the evening and call me first thing tomorrow."

Cora nodded to no one. "Okay."

"This is good, Cora. Really good." Suddenly without its professional edge, Gail's voice was almost motherly. "The proposal is truly inspired, Cora. I know you've got it in you."

"Thanks, Gail. We'll talk in the morning."

Cora's feet thumped down the deck steps as she ended the call. The white noise of the shifting gravel helped to drown out the roaring sea of new information in her head. She planted her feet at the water's edge and stared at the rise and fall of the mountains across the lake.

Every year, these ancient hills ushered in seasons of change. Without fail, the drying up of leaves and dormancy of winter was only an interlude to the new life and growth that came with spring. The land didn't have to worry about what change would bring. It knew. It trusted.

Why was change so painful for her? Why had growth taken so long to come after the loss she'd experienced? And when new love finally began to show signs of life with Luke, why was it so very hard? Would saying yes to the challenge of writing so fast eventually allow her to reap the harvest of a new season?

Cora folded her arms and closed her eyes, letting the cold wind refresh her face. If there was any chance of pulling off this deadline, she needed help. She needed Luke.

Long shadows fell across Cora's backyard. The deck was empty when Luke started down the path, avoiding going through the house as she'd asked. When she'd called and asked him to stop by to talk, it'd saved him from having to do the same. Maybe they could get on the same page about this dinner.

"Hey." Luke bent to kiss her cheek before taking the empty chair. His hands warmed quickly in front of the small fire crackling in the stone-lined fire pit between them.

"Hi, thanks for coming." She closed the black journal on her lap.

"Doing more work on your outline? I thought you'd turned that in."

"Actually, that's one of the reasons I wanted to talk." She scooted to the edge of her chair and reached for his knee. Her eyes reflected what was left of the brilliant afternoon sky. "But first I want to apologize. I'm sorry for how I reacted this morning. I was caught off guard."

The words pulled a sigh from deep within Luke. He covered her hand with his and squeezed. "Thank you. I can understand how waking up with me there was jarring. I just don't think we have anything to be embarrassed about."

"I know you're right." She studied their hands then pulled away, sitting back into her chair again. Her eyes lifted to the lake. "I am trying."

Her tone was soft, but Luke didn't know what to make of her body language. He leaned on his knees, the fire warming his face. "I know you are. There's no instruction manual for any of this."

Silence sat between them. Luke squirmed under a subtle awkwardness. It either lingered from his chat with Harry earlier or Cora's hesitancy. He missed the casual, easy way they teased when all was right.

When she didn't say anything, he rubbed his cheek and settled back into the chair. "You mentioned another reason for asking me here?"

She drew in a long breath. "Oh, right. My agent called today."

"Yeah?" Luke perked. He listened intently as she recounted the conversation about writing her next book. "That is fast, but sounds like they've got a lot of faith in you. How are you feeling about it?"

She shifted in her seat, eyes holding a hint of sparkle. Her whole demeanor changed when she spoke about writing. "Somewhere between excited and terrified?"

He wasn't going to let her talk herself out of this. It was too important. "Sometimes we've got to do things we're scared of."

It was advice to live by. Luke wasn't very familiar with fear. In his line of work, he'd learned to shove the emotion down in order to get the story, regardless of any dangers or possible pitfalls. He liked to think it was how he'd gotten so far.

That being the case, why the hesitancy about attending the dinner at the Bradford's? If Luke and Cora had to deal with an awkward conversation, at least they'd do it together.

"I think you're right." Cora interrupted Luke's thoughts. "But I'll need your help."

"Name it."

"If I want any chance at finishing the book in time, I'll need more help with Ina. Would you be willing to come over more often? I know you've probably got other stuff to do, but I'll need to focus several hours a day."

An energy bubbled up inside Luke. She didn't realize how little twisting she'd have to do to convince him. One thing they shared in common was an innate love of work and purpose. He'd felt it himself when the simple calendar project for the town fed him a rush. "Of course. But where will you write if we're here?"

She tilted her head up the hill toward the cabin. "If you'll help me move my small desk up to my bedroom, it'll be perfect. It's not like you guys will be throwing parties downstairs."

"Only when you type The End." Luke danced his fingers across her hand resting on the arm of the chair.

Her icy cold fingers wrapped around his. And just like that, they eased back into their sweet spot. Luke's shoulders relaxed as leaves scattered around their feet.

"Okay then," she said. "I'll tell Gail we've got a deal. Thank you, Luke."

"It's my pleasure." That was one challenge solved. Luke filled his lungs with the brisk, cleansing air. Even though he was resolved to not let his fear keep him from the dinner, Cora still deserved to know about his chat with Harry. "Hey, I ran into Christopher's dad in town earlier today."

Her eyes darted to his. "Oh?"

"He didn't know Laura had invited me to dinner."

Faint lines formed between Cora's eyebrows. "That seems strange."

Luke's head bobbed up and down. Thank goodness she agreed. "Harry and I thought so too. He thinks it's wise to just be on guard if I go."

Cora's face fell. "If?"

"I'll still go if you want me to. But I also understand if you think it may cause trouble. The day isn't about me."

Her golden hair danced gently around her face as the wind picked up. She tucked it behind her and wrapped her arms around her middle. "I really think it's going to be fine. You don't know Laura. I promise she wouldn't invite you if she wasn't totally okay with it. You'll see."

Luke's stomach knotted, warning him. If anyone knew what grief could do to someone, it should be Cora. "Maybe that's true of the Laura you knew before the accident, but there's a chance she's more fragile than she used to be. It's understandable that she'd have trouble seeing you with someone else. And at an event to honor the son you used to be married—"

"Luke." Cora's eyes pleaded with him. "Please just believe me. It'll be fine. I need you there."

The tightly-wound knot unraveled in an instant. That was all he needed to hear. "Okay, then I'm there."

Her heavy sigh floated away on the breeze along with the wispy smoke from the dwindling fire. If it meant supporting the woman he loved, he'd do it scared.

CHAPTER Twenty-Two

"I've never seen dahlias this shade of orange. Thank you for getting them, dear." Ina fingered the bouquet wrapped in brown paper and a crimson ribbon sitting on the coffee table.

"Sure. I think the Bradfords will appreciate the gesture." Cora adjusted a bobby pin holding a curl at the back of her head, knee bouncing over the edge of the couch cushion.

Every other day of the year, she mourned Christopher privately and on her own terms. But today, at the Bradfords' annual dinner honoring his memory, it became a painfully public—and usually awkward—collective effort. The Bradfords had grown to respect Cora's need to grieve alone. In turn, she gave them this one chance to turn the day Christopher died into a party.

To be fair, the event had grown more cheerful each year. This year, however, included Luke. Sure, he made *her* more cheerful, but the warning Luke relayed did give Cora pause.

One thing was for certain, though. They'd not start on a good foot with Laura if they were late. She hated tardy guests. Cora stood from the couch and walked to the window to stare at her car parked alone in the driveway.

"It's not yet six. He's not even late yet."

"I know. I'm just antsy, I guess." A large black crow landed on the porch railing. Its beady eyes stared Cora down through the window. She inched away from the glass with a chill running down her spine. "Well, that's just great."

"What is, dear?"

The bird cawed once before taking flight westward into the golden sky. Cora sighed and resumed her seat on the couch. "A big crow just landed on the porch right in front of me. They're a sign of death and bad luck."

"Come, now. Don't be so morbid." Ina picked at a piece of fuzz on her sweater. "Charles actually used to say crows represented destiny. When he saw one, he'd say 'Ah, good. This must be the way I should go.' Maybe that crow visited you as an affirmation that this evening is indeed a part of your destiny. Embrace it with gusto."

Cora couldn't deny a chuckle as Ina's fist shook at the air. The woman had such a way with words. "Well, I do like your version better."

"While we wait," Ina said, "I meant to ask you. Don't you think it's exciting about Luke's photos?"

"The calendar? Yeah, he said they turned out great." The few photos Cora had seen before he turned them in were impressive. She couldn't wait to see the finished product.

"I mean the other project. The one the magazine editor from New York called about."

Cora perked, her mind speeding from zero to sixty faster than a race car. "No, I don't know."

"Earlier, while you were writing, Luke said he'd just received word that the job was all going to work out. In just a few weeks, I believe."

"I...I hadn't heard." All breath left Cora as though she'd been punched in the gut.

Luke had taken a new assignment? She hadn't even known he'd been looking. How could he keep something like this from her? But he'd told Ina? A wave of heat rose up all the way from her feet and flushed her cheeks. But it was the lump in her throat that pained her the most.

She'd let herself believe Luke was around for good and that being alone forever might not be her only fate. However, he'd never actually made the promise of being in Laurel Cove permanently. Still, he'd been so convincing in his devotion to her, and to Ina and this place they shared at the lake.

Cora pressed chilled fingers to her temple to calm the pounding in her head. Her eyes pinched closed. *How could you have been so naïve? He's a world traveler. A Pulitzer Prize winner, for goodness' sake.*

Cora jerked at the sound of a car door closing outside. She stood, head dizzy.

Breathe.

The doorknob clicked, and her heart stopped as Luke stepped through the door. Should she ask him not to come? *No.* Right before the hardest night of her year began was too late to create a scene. There wasn't time to tell Luke how he'd let her down in the worst way possible. He was leaving.

"You both look so nice." Luke especially had eyes for Cora in the black dress she'd worn on their first date. As much as he dreaded this evening, being by her side made everything more palatable. He stepped toward her, but she shuffled right past him and headed for the kitchen. It seemed he'd been right to anticipate the evening would stir up some tension in her.

"Grab those flowers, will you?" Ina motioned to the coffee table as she gripped the handles of her walker and labored to stand.

Luke picked up a bouquet of flowers and called into the kitchen, "Anything else I can get?"

Cora emerged with a covered tray in her hands. "No, I've got the cheesecake. That's all. Let's go."

A few minutes later the three of them rode quietly down the two-lane highway under a dark sky. Luke glanced over at Cora. The gentle slope of her nose and curve of her lips were outlined against the soft moonlight. "You look beautiful tonight. I like your hair pulled up like that."

She turned away toward the window. "Thank you."

Luke reached over and wrapped his hand around Cora's, which lay across the top of the plastic tray in her lap. With eyes glued to the night beyond the windshield, she pulled her hand away, gripping the underside of the container instead.

A frown pulled at his mouth. "You all right?"

"Fine."

Concern nagged Luke like a incessantly itchy bug bite. Cora's mood was more like a cold shoulder than general anxiety. The only other words Cora spoke to him on the drive were instructions on where to turn. By the time he parked the truck in front of a large ranch-style home, worry bubbled up full-force inside him. Something was going on with her, something other than this stressful dinner. But now wasn't the time to get into it.

Luke stepped out and helped Ina from the back seat, unfolding her walker and placing it in front of her. He glanced up the short driveway, thankful it was paved and flat. With the flowers laid atop the seat of the walker, she started to shuffle forward.

Following close behind Ina, Cora and Luke walked side by side. He nudged her arm with his elbow. "It's going to be fine. I'll be close by the whole night."

She narrowed her eyes and pursed her lips. Her head tilted sharply as if challenging him.

Luke prickled. "What's going on with you?"

Of all the people not on his side tonight, he'd least expected Cora to be among them. Yet, as she glared forward, she hardly felt like an ally. At the front door, Ina pushed a button and a chime sounded from within.

"Hi there!" Harry's smile was warm, his hand firm in Luke's as he answered the door. He leaned in and whispered, "Good man. Glad you're here."

Harry then placed a hand on Ina's hunched shoulder. "You must be Mrs. McLean. We're so glad you're joining us."

"I very much liked your son." Ina patted Harry's cheek then pointed a shaky hand at the flowers. "Those are for you and your wife. Thank you for having me."

Luke's tense shoulders released a bit at the warm and welcoming start they were off to. Maybe his prayers from earlier would be answered and all would be fine. His smile seemed to go unnoticed by Cora, who stared straight ahead as they stepped into the house.

As unassuming as it was on the outside, the inside of the Bradfords' home was tastefully decorated with tailored curtains and furniture that looked uncomfortable to sit in. They rounded the corner into a large room occupied by a handful of folks standing around holding drinks. As if a spotlight had flipped on, the chatter quieted, and all eyes landed on them.

Luke swallowed hard and stood close to Cora, who stopped a few feet into the room. No matter her mood, he wasn't leaving her side. Harry introduced Ina and Luke to the others, and the chatter resumed. Ina settled into a chair near the roaring stone fireplace.

Laura crossed the room and leaned into Cora's cheek. "Hello, Cora." Her steely eyes, however, stayed glued to Luke. She straightened and shifted her eyes between them. With a tight grin, Laura ran a finger along the edge of her wine glass. "Well, you two do make a nice-looking couple, don't you?"

Luke's stomach dropped at her frosty tone. Guess Harry's warning was warranted after all.

The man himself walked up just then, the flowers from Ina in hand. Luke widened his eyes and subtly tilted toward the women, hoping Harry caught on to the tension brewing. Harry's brow furrowed. Thank goodness for the man's astuteness.

"Laura, look what Mrs. McLean brought us. Wasn't that thoughtful? Why don't you take that delicious cheesecake from Cora and come show me which vase you want the flowers in."

Harry ushered Laura, with dessert in tow, toward the kitchen on the far side of the living room. Luke's neck ached as he rolled it back and released the breath he'd been holding. "Well, that was a bit icy."

Cora squared her shoulders. Her arms crossed tightly. "Was it?"

"Uh, yeah. It was." The snap of her words drained any remaining patience. Luke held the back of her arm and guided her to the entryway they'd just come through. "Okay, what's going on?"

She cut her dagger eyes to a large framed painting and sighed dramatically. "It's just a tough night."

"Cora, please look at me."

She jerked her head up. "What?"

Luke prickled at the fire that blazed in her stare. It was a heat not born of the grief he had seen before in her, but an intense anger. He'd come guarded against Laura but wasn't prepared for Cora's hostile advances. He wouldn't fight her. Not here. Not now. But if she would just tell him what fueled this mood, he wouldn't have to wonder all night.

"There is something going on other than the stress of tonight. You're obviously angry, Cora. It's been building since I picked you and Ina up. What happened?"

Her lower lip began to tremble and her eyes filled with tears, disarming him. She suddenly looked so small and fragile. Luke closed the short distance between them. Desperate to touch her, he picked up her hand by her side.

This time, her sigh was softer. "Ina told me about—"

"Dinner's ready everyone. Come take your seats," Laura called from the other room.

Cora shuddered, eyes closing. "I can't do this right now, Luke."

"Cora, please."

Her fingers trailed out of Luke's hand as she walked away. What had Ina told her that was so upsetting? How could it have anything to do with him? His hand rubbed hard against his freshly shaven face as he followed, alone, in Cora's wake.

Maybe he wasn't cut out to ride her roller coaster of emotions. When things were good, they were so very good. But as he walked into the dining room, the belly of the beast where there was no telling who was his biggest threat, he already felt utterly defeated.

The legs of Luke's chair were the last to scratch against the floor as he took the empty one next to Cora. Thanks to the way he'd looked at her, she'd been so close to falling apart in the foyer. Laura announcing the start of dinner had saved her, but she'd also give anything to get everything out in the open.

Cora looked past Luke and Ina to the head of the long dinner table. Laura stood next to Harry and clinked her glass, her lips puckered into a tight smile. The woman's cold demeanor was undeniable.

When everyone quieted, Laura smiled curtly and began. "Well, it's hard to believe another year has gone by without our boy. You all were the nearest and dearest to him." Laura's eyes cut to Luke. "Well, most of you."

From the other side of Luke, Ina turned from their hostess and eyed Cora. The wrinkles between her cloudy eyes were deeper than usual. Cora couldn't ignore the heavy thumping drumming faster and faster in her chest.

Should Cora interject? Her leg bounced under the linen-covered table. Laura wasn't wrong, exactly. Luke wasn't near or dear to Christopher. Or anyone else here, for that matter, except Cora and Ina.

Harry cleared his throat. "Well, as usual, as we start eating we'll go around the table and tell a favorite memory or story about Christopher. Cora, would you like to start?"

Hot pinpricks ran up Cora's arms as people started passing plates of crab legs and side dishes. Why'd she have to start? Her mouth went dry as she scanned the many sets of eyes on her. She tensed as Luke rested his hand on her leg.

"Well. It's hard to pick just one." She drew in a slow breath. A conversation with Luke sprang to mind. "So, Christopher never liked the Fall Festival, but—"

Laura scoffed and took a swig of her wine. Harry leaned in and whispered something to her, which the woman waved away abruptly.

"Well…" A dizzying haze joined Cora's racing pulse. Luke patted Cora's thigh, his eyes encouraging. "He was great about taking me every year even though he thought most of it was cheesy and—"

"Why didn't you take any crab?" Laura's biting voice cut Cora off. All eyes rested on Luke, who'd just passed the platter to Ina.

"Oh, I'm actually allergic." Luke picked up a bowl filled with roasted potatoes and began scooping some onto his plate. "But there's plenty of other delicious food here. Thank you."

A short, incredulous laugh erupted from Laura. Harry reached for her hand as she pushed up from her chair and flung a hand in Luke's direction. "He's disrespecting us and Christopher's memory by not—"

"Laura, for goodness' sake, the man's allergic." Harry pulled at her. "Sit down and let's be nice."

Cora couldn't do anything but stare, mouth gaped open, when Luke turned to her, eyes pleading. The same high-pitched tone that often accompanied her worst nightmares filled the silence that hung over the dining room like a thick fog.

She should say something, stick up for Luke like Harry had. Tell Laura that Christopher, most of all, would be appalled at his mother's behavior. Where was the gall Cora had mustered at the Fall Festival? Instead, she just shook her head in small bursts at Luke then dropped her eyes to her lap.

"And what kind of man," Laura snapped, pointing a manicured finger at Luke, "has the indecency to show his face in our home when we gather to remember our son? You aren't half the man Christopher was."

Her words pierced Cora like a fiery hot poker, leaving her stunned. Luke's tender, pained eyes begged her to say something. Anything. But the deafening tone returned, making it hard to think. Cora felt so removed, as though she were watching the painful scene play out on a screen rather than right in front of her. How did she defend without also risking severing the only family ties she had to Christopher?

"Excuse me, Mrs. Bradford." Ina's frail voice piped up, pulling Luke and Cora's attention. "I knew your son. And I believe you, in fact, are the only one here disgracing his memory. Christopher was kind and gentle. Your behavior tonight is neither. I also know this young man." She placed a firm hand on Luke's arm. "He is every bit as good and kind and honorable as your son was. There is no doubt in my mind that Christopher would quite approve of Luke."

Gratefulness welled up in Cora's heart at Ina's courage and fortitude. But it was quickly overshadowed by a sickening mix of embarrassment and shame that she could muster neither. A wave of heat rolled over Cora's whole body under the scrutiny of the room.

Laura, mouth pressed into a thin line, slowly lowered into her chair.

Luke reached over and held Ina's hand, still resting on his arm, then stood from the table and turned to Cora. "I think I should go."

"I'm coming with you," Ina said loudly from the other side of him. He helped her to her feet, and the two started for the door.

This was insane. Did Cora leave with them or stay and keep her obligation to Christopher's family? Panic raged and her chest tightened. All attention was now on her. She finally looked to Laura, whose smile was smug as she watched Luke and Ina leaving.

The sight set off a cataclysmic shift in Cora's heart. *What are you doing?* As though she'd just woken from the nightmare that was this dinner, the room stopped spinning. She jolted to her feet, her plate clanking against the table.

"Laura, you invited Luke here. Was that a test or something?" Confidence grew inside Cora with each word. "The best way I can honor Christopher's memory is to be happy and love again. He'd want that. You know it."

"Well, can you believe this, Susan?" Laura directed the question at Christopher's aunt across the table, who offered Cora a sympathetic smile.

The sound of the front door closing from the other room ignited the urgency stirring in Cora. "Harry, I'm sorry but I've got to go."

"Of course." He stood and followed her through the living room then opened the front door for her. "I never dreamed she'd behave this badly. It's been difficult for her, seeing you move on, but that's no excuse. I'm so sorry."

Cora's heart skipped at the sight of Luke helping Ina into the front seat of the truck. It was a miracle they'd not yet left. She turned and searched Harry's familiar gray eyes. "Christopher got so much from you. Most of all your kindness. Thank you for everything. It'll be okay."

"I hope so." One corner of his mouth turned up just like Christopher's used to.

Their likeness to one another used to haunt Cora, but at that moment it brought her a hopeful comfort. The heels of her boots pounded the walkway as she sprinted toward Luke, who rounded the front of the truck toward the driver's side. She already had one reason to hate this day. Maybe God would spare her another.

"Cora, don't." Luke held out a hand as she caught up to him at the truck. Far off in the distance, a flash of lightning illuminated a mountain ridge, mirroring the brewing storm deep inside him.

"Luke, I'm sorry." She reached out for his arm, but he pulled away.

"I came here for you, you know. Even though Harry and I both had reservations, I still came to support you. Both Ina and I did." Over his shoulder, he found Ina watching them intently. Cora had put her through this nightmare, too. His jaw clenched. "And you just sat there and let that woman make me look like some jerk."

"I just couldn't get my thoughts straight. But—"

"But what? I know today is hard. You should know by now that I fully respect what you've been through. I've been patient and understanding, even when you're having a bad day and take it out on me. But this is too much, Cora. Something's got to give here." He gestured back and forth between the two of them. "There's got to be a give and take."

Thunder rumbled overhead. Cora turned away from a foreboding wind that whipped around them. When she looked back at Luke, her eyes were charged with the same anger he'd seen earlier. "Give and take? You mean like giving me the impression you were around for good only to take it away without so much as a warning?"

Luke's head swam. It was impossible to follow her. "What are you talking about?"

"I know about the big assignment from your editor in New York. All that talk about being there for me, and you were planning to leave." She wiped at a tear that rolled down her face.

Luke shook off the twinge of sympathy pinching at him and reached for the truck's door handle as frustration took over. Just like the mess with Dennison, he was being blamed for something he didn't do. Feeling helpless even to defend himself picked a still-healing wound.

A single raindrop landed on his head as he pulled the door open. "I don't know where you're getting your information, but you need to get your facts straight before making accusations."

"Luke, please. You aren't going to leave me here, are you?" She folded her arms around her body and looked to the sky as rain began to fall lightly.

"Why don't you get a ride from your pal Laura?" He climbed into the truck and slammed the door shut, his gut wrenching at his own harsh words. But the palpable hurt stiffened his resolve, and he turned the key in the ignition, yanking on the gear shift. As they pulled away from the curb, he watched Cora, standing in the rain, growing smaller and smaller behind them.

"You're really going to leave her there?" Ina waved a handkerchief at him.

Luke took it and wiped his face, eyes glued to the road. If he looked back at Cora again, his resolve would melt away completely. This was already going to be a painful ride home. His heart couldn't take what would surely be even worse—her riding in silence behind him. "I'm sure she'll be fine."

But would he? He'd never had a broken heart. If this was what it felt like, a whirlpool of disappointment and emptiness and regret, it'd be his first and his last. He wasn't cut out for loving someone who didn't love him back.

CHAPTER Twenty-Three

Distant sirens rang through the night sky that poured with stinging rain. Cora stood at the side of the road, staring at the truck smashed against a black shadow of a tree. A muddy pile of rocks littered the road. She blinked through the frigid water that poured down her face, a pounding panic shaking her from head to toe.

She peered through the dark passenger window. A flash of lightning illuminated the silhouette of a man slumped over the steering wheel. Her breathing labored between short sobs. Cora reached out, her hand trembling so violently she could barely grip the door handle. When she pulled, the entire vehicle shifted. Her shriek matched the screeching steel as shivers shot up her spine.

"Luke?" The desperate question rasped out in a cracked whisper.

Nothing. Only the hiss of steam or smoke, she couldn't tell which, coming from the mangled truck's hood filled the air.

Oh, dear God, please, not again.

Unable to touch his still body, Cora backed away from the truck on wobbly legs. Her feet stumbled from the smooth pavement to uneven, soggy ground. A familiar high-pitched level tone filled her ears. The blinding soundtrack to the ongoing horror of her life.

She startled and fought against hands that took hold of her arms from somewhere in the deepening darkness. The truck, and Luke, faded from her vision until everything went black.

"Cora, dear, please wake up."

A sharp breath stung her aching throat. Cora blinked through blurred vision and worked to sit up. Something soft dabbed at her wet eyes and face, blotting out the daylight too.

"There now, it's all right." It was Ina's tender, shaky voice. "It was just a bad dream. You're okay."

Cora took the handkerchief handed to her and wiped her nose. She peeled back the hair stuck to her damp forehead and looked around her bright, tidy, cheery living room. It was everything she was not.

"The accident again?" Ina's bony hand was cold on Cora's.

"Yes, but..." Cora reached for her water bottle sitting on the coffee table and stole a sip in an attempt to keep the threatening tears at bay. "But it was Luke."

At the mention of his name, Cora folded, overcome by an avalanche of sobs. As if losing Luke in real life wasn't enough, her torturous dreams emphasized the loss in the cruelest way possible. Her worst fear imagined, played out like an immersive production she had no option to refuse.

Ina's hand rubbed along her back as Cora rocked back and forth. Wave after wave came relentlessly, taking a little more of her breath and strength with each pounding hit.

The accident.
Christopher.
The hospital.
The cemetery.
The empty house.
The solitude.
The loneliness.
A stagnant career.
A hopeless future.
Luke.

There really was no such thing as a fresh start after so much hurt and grief. No second chance. No mercy she had prayed God would send her.

"I can't do this anymore." She straightened and searched Ina's withered face.

A trail of a tear on Ina's wrinkled cheek glimmered in the light. "Can't do what?"

Cora flung her arms around the cabin. "This! This life. This house. The memories. The sadness. It's too much."

Ina settled against the cushions, folding her hands in her dainty lap. "What is there to do, dear? The troubles you have will follow you no matter how far you run. Trust me, I know from experience."

Cora dropped her head into her hands and grunted. Truth was, she couldn't imagine leaving the cabin. But she couldn't go on like this, either. "I'm just so tired of being beaten up by the memories. The hurt is too heavy." She looked over her shoulder and searched Ina's kind eyes. "What if it never goes away?"

"It won't go away. Not entirely. It's a part of you, dear. You must decide that even a life that includes the hurt will be enough. Until then, it won't be. And you'll spend your life searching for something that doesn't exist."

Cora's throat scratched with another growl. Ina had come out of her grief already. Cora was trapped inside hers, imprisoned, but for something she'd done nothing to earn or deserve. She wiped hard under her eyes again and pushed to her feet. "You make it sound so easy."

Ina looked delicate and frail alone on the overstuffed couch. "Maybe not easy, but it is a simple truth. The Bible tells us that the light shines in the darkness, and the darkness cannot overcome it. God is fighting for your healing, child. Believe and have faith."

"I've been waiting for three years, and what have I gotten? A few good weeks and false hope that things were turning around." Her fingers flicked at a new tear betraying her boiling frustration. "How do I keep trusting when the darkness keeps pushing in?"

Ina tapped a finger against her lips. "You know, it's not surprising Luke replaced Christopher in your dream. But it was just one argument. You haven't lost him yet."

The image of Luke driving away last night, leaving her standing in the freezing rain, filled her mind. "It sure feels like I have."

Cora turned toward the kitchen, bumping into the walker sitting at the end of the couch. She moved it in front of Ina and left the room. It was Luke's night to fix dinner, but he wouldn't be walking through the door in his apron tonight. Despite Ina's loving presence, it was the first time since Luke had moved to the lake that Cora felt alone.

She stood in front of the open refrigerator, the cool air soothing her flushed face and neck. But there was nothing to soothe her soul. She'd reached her limit. Hope in a happy future was something she'd have to craft in her now ironic romance she would somehow have to miraculously finish writing with a broken heart.

Luke flipped down the truck's visor to block the bright morning sun as he drove down Main Street. He passed several men loading brown corn stalks into the back of a truck with Laurel Cove Public Works in dark green letters down the side. As the truck idled at the light, Luke leaned against his fist, arm propped up against the door frame. A festive new banner hung over the street, advertising the annual Laurel Cove Christmas Festival coming up in a few weeks. The town sure liked its festivals.

He usually enjoyed the upcoming holiday season. But after the blow up with Cora more than two weeks ago and no word from her since—not even for Thanksgiving—he wasn't in a very festive mood. So far, time wasn't healing the wound he'd endured that night.

Time also hadn't dwindled how often she invaded his thoughts. Every morning he woke with her on his mind. Every night, he stared at the ceiling, playing over the night when everything had fallen apart.

Why had she accused him of planning to leave? How could she sit idly by, letting him endure Laura's chastising? Those thoughts always teetered, however, back to concern. Were she and Ina doing all right? How was her writing coming along? And was Cora missing him, too?

A short honk pulled his eyes to his rearview mirror, then the green light ahead of him. He waved an apology to the driver behind him and eased his foot off the brake. A moment later, he pulled into an empty spot in front of Brewed.

His hands rested on the steering wheel at ten and two. Even if Cora did miss him, maybe their chance was gone. Her baggage, loaded down with grief and sadness that may haunt her forever, was too much for him to carry. He winced at the thought as he turned the truck off and pushed at his seat belt buckle.

That wasn't who Luke wanted to be. Especially for someone he loved. But it's who he'd been for his mother. His throat swelled and eyelids fell. There was nothing to be done about his past mistakes. New mistakes now loomed ahead of him like ghostly figures waiting to either be brought into focus or left undeveloped. It was up to him. But how?

He startled at a knock on his window. Jack peered in, face serious. Luke sighed heavily then stepped out of the truck. "Hey, man. Sorry."

"You all right? I waved at you, but you seemed pretty far off." Jack's hand was firm in Luke's. As they stepped up to the curb, Luke noticed a black book tucked under Jack's arm. The word BIBLE gleamed silver in the sunlight when they turned toward the door.

"Uh, yeah, I guess. I'll tell you about it inside."

Two cups of coffee and a plate of pancakes later, Luke rested his elbows against the table and watched a couple holding hands walk down the sidewalk across the street. It seemed he'd never have that. "We haven't spoken since."

A deep sigh from Jack pulled Luke back to his friend. "Man, Luke. I'm really sorry. Have you tried to reach out? Do you even want to?"

"No, I haven't. I spent the first few days so frustrated and hurt. Then after that, it felt like too much time had gone by. Since she hasn't reached out either, I just figure she doesn't want to talk."

Jack nodded. "But *you* want to, right? Talk?"

Luke's eyes fell to the table. The ache inside him was undeniable. "Yeah, I do."

"Then do it. Call her or go over there. Surely you've heard the saying that you only regret the things you don't do."

Jack's words struck a bitter chord. He already harbored enough regret over lost time and unclaimed opportunity with his mother.

His veins pulsed with a sudden urgency as he looked back to Jack. "I know you're right. But I don't want to live in the shadows of her grief forever. What if she can't get past this? And what if I don't have the patience and the grace to support her through everything she's been through?"

"Do you love her?"

Luke's heart leapt from within that undeniable ache. "Yeah, I do."

Jack picked up his Bible from the seat of the empty chair next to him. He flipped through it as though looking for something, then stopped and ran his finger across a page. "Love bears all things, believes all things, hopes all things, endures all things."

Luke considered the words. "What's that from?"

"First Corinthians, chapter thirteen. Folks refer to it as the love chapter. There's a lot more in there about what love is and isn't. But that particular part serves as a great reminder of what love is capable of." Jack spun the Bible around to face Luke and pushed it across the table.

Luke moved his sticky plate out of the way and scanned the words Jack had just read aloud. The verbs stuck out to him as though on fire. *Bears. Believes. Hopes. Endures.*

"Listen," Jack continued. "Loving Cora doesn't magically erase all past hurts or obstacles either of you brings to the relationship. But if you let it, love sure gives you more than a fighting chance."

Luke thought back over the weeks spent with Cora. He'd had a small glimpse of all the things the Bible said love could do, but then he'd given up when things truly got tough. Maybe Jack was right, and the first step was to reach out and see if love offered them a fighting chance. He couldn't live with the regret of not finding out.

The corners of Luke's mouth pulled as he closed the Bible and handed it back to Jack. "So, you just walk around with this in case someone needs an impromptu life lesson?"

Jack laughed heartily, taking it. "Yeah, it's kind of like my superhero weapon. Like Thor's hammer, only everyone's worthy of picking it up."

Luke joined him in laughing. His heart warmed, the comparison striking him as poignant.

"Nah." Jack set the Bible back down on the chair next to him. "I just came from Bible study. My brother and several other guys get together every week at the church. You should join us."

"I might just do that." Luke had never been a regular church goer. But until now, he also hadn't realized his need for imprinting such important truths on his heart. And if love did, indeed, give him a fighting chance with Cora, he wanted to be as prepared as possible to love her—and love her well—forever.

CHAPTER Twenty-Four

The tiniest of white flakes danced in a wild frenzy outside, shrouding the lake in a frosty curtain. Cora sighed, her breath fogging the window her desk backed up to. The first week of December was late for the first snowfall in these parts, but why'd it have to be today?

She picked up her phone and scrolled to her weather app. A bright yellow sun showed over 12:00PM. *Thank goodness.* By noon it'd be sunny and warm enough to keep anything from sticking to the ground. At least her run to town for groceries tomorrow wouldn't be in jeopardy. She slipped her phone into the deep pocket of her oversized sweater and returned her attention to the task at hand.

The blinking cursor on her laptop mocked her. One more challenge, distraction, or interruption and she was liable to throw in the towel on this book all together. What business did she have writing a convincing love story, anyway? The draft of the book her publisher was clamoring for was due to her editor in just over three weeks, and all she had to show for it was a handful of lackluster chapters.

She pecked out a new sentence, read over it, then pressed on the backspace key until it all disappeared. Beyond her closed bedroom door, the unmistakable banging of baking sheets sounded from the kitchen.

What now? She saved the file, though there wasn't anything new worth saving. In a few quick steps, she crossed her room and made for the stairs as a yawn pulled through her.

The last few weeks had been long and arduous. Cora had often been up before the sun to get in a few hours of writing before breakfast. She barely had enough time left to cook three meals, clean up, oversee Ina's baths, organize and distribute her medications, and keep up with errands in town. She had appreciated his help before, but with Luke no longer coming by, she realized just how much he'd made this arrangement possible.

And yet he hadn't called since that awful night at the Bradfords. Neither had she. Now, after all that silence, too much time had passed. If it wasn't for his glowing cabin windows she could see every night from her deck, she'd think he was already packed up and gone for his assignment.

"What are you doing?" Cora reached the kitchen to find Ina standing next to the open dishwasher with a glass mixing bowl in hand.

Ina startled, catching herself with her other hand on the edge of the counter. "Oh, dear. I didn't mean to disturb you. You get back up to writing now."

Cora took the bowl from Ina and placed it in a cabinet next to the refrigerator. She spotted Ina's walker parked on the far side of the kitchen table, well out of the woman's reach. Prickles surged through her. "I can't focus on writing when I'm worried about you doing things you shouldn't. You can help me by staying out of trouble."

"I'm not a child, you know." Ina's lips pursed and her chin tipped up before she turned sharply for the walker several feet behind her.

In her haste, Ina wobbled, with nothing to hold on to. Cora lunged just in time to thread her arms around Ina's waist and keep her from falling to the ground. An intense, stinging pain radiated through Cora's big toe as her foot slammed into the corner of the dishwasher door. "Oh, come on!"

The women hobbled over to the kitchen table together, and Cora eased Ina into a chair before falling into the one next to it. What else could go wrong? She kicked her slipper off and inspected her throbbing toe. When she found no blood and was able to wiggle it back and forth, she folded her arms across the table and laid her head down.

"I really was just trying to help." Ina's voice was small and meek.

Cora's heart sank. Ina didn't deserve her foul mood. "Of course. I know. I'm sorry I snapped. I'm just starting to question if I can really write this book."

"I wish you'd ask Luke for help. The two of you really need to work this whole thing out anyway. You haven't even mentioned him since that night."

"Why would he want to help me after the way I treated him?" She'd been hurt by Luke keeping his plans from her, but with each passing day, guilt over her own part in that fateful night weighed heavier and heavier on Cora.

Ina cleared her throat and pushed at the bridge of her glasses. "Maybe he'd want to help *me*."

The breath stilled in Cora's lungs. Another drop in her brimming bucket of guilt. She really had perfected making things all about her, hadn't she? Cora had made a promise when she invited Ina to come live with her. It wasn't fair that Ina's needs were not being properly attended to so that Cora could meet the other obligations she'd gotten herself into. Nor was it Ina's fault that Cora had ruined things with Luke.

"You're right. I'll reach out to him and see if we can work something out." She nuzzled her foot back into her slipper then reached for Ina's hand. Was Ina trembling more than usual? "I'm still very glad you're here."

"Thank you. I am, too. I just don't want to get in the way. I believe you need this book more than your readers do. You've got to get it done."

"Well, we'll see what we can do."

Cora helped Ina get settled in front of the television before climbing the stairs. Back in her room, she stood by the window and pulled her phone from her pocket. Before her nerve left her, she punched out a quick text to Luke and hit Send.

Outside, the sky was clear, and the sun sparkled against the frosted ground. A sense of destiny stirred inside Cora as Ina's words echoed in her mind. It was a lovely notion that she needed this book too. That maybe somehow getting through this story would teach her something or bring her out farther from these dark few years. But her heart just wasn't in it.

No, her heart still was fully focused on Luke Bassett.

The kayak crunched against the frozen grass as Luke let it drop at the water's edge. Maybe it was his thick Boston blood, but with the sun now shining and the water glassy, the cold weather was his favorite to ride in. Plus, a good long ride always helped to clear his mind.

He intertwined his fingers, making sure his gloves were tight, then pulled his knit hat down over his ears.

"Come on, buddy." Luke waved to a prancing Toby dressed in a puffy canine jacket under his life vest. More than ever, the dog had become his constant companion.

With one foot in the kayak, Luke's phone buzzed in the zipped pocket at his side. He'd better check it before they got going. One look at Cora's name glowing on the screen sent his heart racing. He ripped a glove off and navigated to the message.

CORA: HI. CAN WE TALK?

LUKE: SURE.

Luke watched for her reply then nearly dropped his phone when it rang in his hands. Toby barked and stood to all fours, gently rocking the boat under Luke's foot.

With his heart in his throat, he answered. "Hello?"

"Hi, Luke."

Her voice melted him. "Hi. How are you?"

"I'm okay, I guess. You?"

"Hanging in there." His breath puffed white clouds into the frigid air while he waited through a long moment of silence. "What did you want to talk about?"

"Well, it's been a long time and..." Her voice trailed off again.

One corner of his mouth pulled, sympathizing with her hesitancy. She'd beaten him to calling, which he'd planned to do after his ride. If she was feeling half as nervous as he was, he understood. "It's okay, Cora."

She drew in a sharp breath. "Ina asked me to call you. I'm having a hard time managing everything on my own while trying to write this book. Is there any way you'd consider coming over to sit with her during the day for a few hours so I can get some writing done? It's not going too well so far."

A pit opened up in Luke's stomach. That was why she was calling? She just needed his help? He jerked his head to call Toby out of the boat and stepped back onto the shoreline. Pacing, he searched for words amidst the stinging disappointment.

"Of course," she continued quickly, "if you'd be more comfortable having her at your house, I completely understand. I could bring her and pick her up whenever it's convenient for you. She really enjoys your company."

"No, no." Even though Luke's hopes were dashed for the moment, he wasn't about to give up the chance to at least be back in Cora's presence. Plus, he missed his amusing and eye-opening conversations with Ina. "I can come there. My days are pretty flexible. How about ten in the morning?"

"Sure. That's great. Then I can be done in time for you to get home for dinner."

His mouth twisted. He missed dinners with them the most. Still, he'd take what he could get. "That's fine."

"Okay, great. See you tomorrow." Relief oozed from her softened tone. "Thank you, Luke."

"Sure thing."

The call disconnected and Luke stared at the darkened screen before returning the phone to his pocket. He pulled his glove over his now ice-cold fingers.

"Come on, Toby." The dog bounded from behind a tree and leaped back into the kayak. Luke made short work of starting their ride, desperate for that head clearing and prayer more than ever.

Several strong strokes glided the kayak out of the cove and into open, calm water toward the center of the lake. He stilled the paddle and inhaled deeply. As if on cue, Toby's nose pointed skyward and twitched too. Luke's lungs stung as he tipped his head back and let his eyes ease shut. *God, am I crazy to keep hoping for more from Cora?*

With a long exhale, he lowered his head. His eyes landed on the small island in the distance, the tops of its trees dusted lightly in white. Pulled like a magnet to metal, Luke zeroed in on its shore and started paddling.

Several minutes later, Luke's arms and shoulders screamed at him as the kayak slid with ease up onto the shore of the island. He stepped out after Toby, tied the kayak up, and then took long strides toward the opening of the marked trail. He marveled at how the dog, ahead of him by several steps, seemed to know where to go as if he'd been to the island many times.

Luke's breath puffed ahead of him in short bursts as they reached the clearing where he and Cora had stood many weeks before. He pulled off a glove. The light layer of snow on the topmost stone brushed away easily. Luke traced Ina and Charles's initials with a finger then bowed his head and closed his eyes.

"God, I haven't been the most devoted or disciplined. I'm not even sure how to do this. But I want to do better. The people I've met here—Ina and Jack...and Cora—have made me realize how much I need you. I regret not being there for my mom. Please forgive me for not being the son I knew you were calling me to be."

Luke swallowed hard against the catch in his throat as Toby nudged his cold nose under Luke's hand at his side. "Yes, I'm thankful for you too, boy."

With his eyes closed again and head bowed, his prayer continued in his heart.

I believe you also brought me here for Cora. I don't know if we've totally screwed that up. But if you mean for us to be together, help me to make the most of this new opportunity with her. Please heal her heart.

He opened his eyes and ran his hand over the flat, smooth rock again. He finished aloud again, it feeling right to let his words float into the sky heavenward.

"Help us to see that our life together, even with its imperfections, can be enough. And help me, God, to let the love you've given me for Cora bear, believe, hope, and endure all things. Amen."

By the time Luke pushed off the shore and started his and Toby's journey back across the lake, his heart was lighter than it had been in months. As Cora's cabin came into view, a hopeful smile crept across his tight, cold face. He wasn't sure how, but he knew down deep that tomorrow marked a new beginning.

CHAPTER
Twenty-Five

From high above the town square, Cora could see for miles across the breathtaking mountains ridges. The cloudless, crisp blue sky popped against the bright orange and yellow and red-topped trees below. She closed her eyes and focused on letting her chest rise and fall. The happy sound of children laughing below pulled a smile across her face. This spot, high above the Fall Festival, was her absolute favorite.

A sudden violent wind blew in a fury. Her eyes slammed shut and both hands grabbed the thin bar holding her into the bucket seat of the Ferris wheel. When her eyes dared to open, the bright blue sky was transformed into a swirl of angry black clouds. Her ears filled with the pounding of her own heart and the rumble of thunder overhead. She had to get down.

Below her, however, cheery sunlight still shone over the happy scene of children and families playing around the festival grounds. A cry escaped her as another gust of frigid wind rocked the car, slamming her into the side. She clung to the rail, closing her eyes tightly.

What is happening?

"*Just let go, Cora.*"

Christopher?

Cora peeked her eyes open and turned her head cautiously without letting go of the side. Christopher sat calmly next to her, his smile relaxed. Behind him in the distance, lightning struck in a spidery display.

"*You can't join them down there unless you let go, honey.*"

Cora cut her eyes to the ground. Her heart jumped at the sight of Luke standing below with a huge white teddy bear tucked under his arm. The storm raging in the sky was no match for the sight of him. She grinned, carefully waving down to him.

"*What are you afraid of?*" *Christopher asked.*

"*Of losing him like I lost you.*" *Cora watched helplessly as lightning struck only a few yards from where Luke stood, somehow still bathed in sunlight.*

"*You can't protect him from everything, just like you couldn't save me.*"

Cora strained her voice over the groan of the storm. "*But at least I can choose to not put myself through the possibility of being hurt like that again.*"

Christopher tilted his head. "*At the expense of not being happy? That's an awfully steep price.*"

"*I've paid so much already.*" *Cora's throat stung, tight with tears that matched the intensity of the chaos around them.*

"*Love isn't an exhaustible currency. You've got plenty, and it's not like this is a gamble. He loves you, and you love him. Don't you?*"

The leaping in Cora's heart answered for her. "*Yes.*"

"*Then you'll always come out ahead.*"

Cora eased her grip on the rail and straightened in the seat. Below, Luke was now joined by a spry and youthful Ina. The smiles on both their faces radiated joy as they motioned for her to come down. The swirling sky above her stilled, the gray clouds fading like a fog that burned off in the warmth of the day.

Cora reached a hand to her cheek, warmed by the exposed sun. She turned to Christopher, who looked out over Laurel Cove. He was contented and relaxed.

"Will you come along?" Cora asked.

His kind eyes that she'd cherish forever found her. "No, honey. You and I, we've had our time. You've managed to hold on an extra three years. It's time to let go now. Fall, Cora. Fall in love again, and don't look back for me."

The words stole a beat from Cora's chest, but a lightness came over her too. "Thank you, Christopher. For loving me so much that I didn't know how to live without you for a long time. I'm going to try and love Luke as well as you loved me."

She reached out for Christopher's hand, letting go of the thin bar in front of her. For a brief moment, the sensation of falling came over her, sending her pulse racing. In a blink, she was standing before Luke, her feet planted firmly on the straw covering the festival grounds. His hand was the one she found and held tightly. She had let go and fallen right into the hands of the man she now loved.

One corner of Cora's mouth pulled as she closed the cover of her black journal and tucked it into her oversized purse lying on the passenger seat of her car. The dream she'd had last night was too good, and thankfully incredibly vivid, not to write down. It would no doubt be awesome inspiration as she continued writing the novel.

But with the dream, God had redeemed the torture she'd endured in countless nightmares. He'd also given her more than just writing fodder. She now had permission to let go of her past, and Christopher, in order to really live again. She would never not miss him, but she was free of the chains of her grief. Now, she just needed the courage to step out in faith and fix things with Luke.

Cora pulled the strap of her purse over her shoulder and stepped out of the car. She started the long walk from the back of the busy grocery store parking lot. Instantly, the radiant grin on Luke's face in the dream sprang to her mind and pulled a smile from her.

"Hi, Cora."

Cora turned to find Harry and Laura staring at her from under an open trunk hatch. Harry lifted a brown bag from the full buggy and set it inside the car.

Cora stepped back as Laura lunged for her, hands outstretched. "Oh, I'm so glad we've run into you. I'm not sure you received my text messages."

She had—and had left all of them unanswered. Cora nodded, lips pressed tight.

"Well, I don't blame you for not responding. My behavior that night was simply unacceptable, Cora. I was so *rude*." Laura wrung her gloved hands, sorrow etched into the lines of her face. "I know you can understand the terrible things grief can do to us, but it's no excuse. I hope you'll forgive me. Will you?"

A warmth settled in Cora's stiff posture, relaxing her enough to clear her head. Laura was right. If anyone understood the terrible things hurt and longing caused one to do, it was Cora. "Yes, I forgive you. But I'm not the only one who really deserves your apology."

Laura's gaze fell to her feet. Cora looked over at Harry, who winked at her as he placed a hand on his wife's shoulder. Slowly, the two women who shared the pain of losing a husband and a son connected again.

"Yes, I do owe Luke an apology." She and Harry exchanged a look, and Laura nodded softly. "Harry says he is a very nice man whom Christopher would quite approve of. I suppose I'd have known that for myself if I'd given him a chance."

Cora's dream flickered in her mind. "I do think Christopher would approve. Thank you."

The women embraced, and Cora reveled in the comfort. After promising to keep in touch more often, Cora finished the walk into the grocery store with a hopeful heart now also fueled by continuing redemption.

Her nerves had gotten the best of her that morning when Luke had come over to sit with Ina for the first time since their fight. Not only was she unsure what to say, she didn't want to spoil her post-dream mood with the temptation to ask him about his plans to leave. She'd scooted out before he'd had a chance to say more than hello.

This new hope, however, convinced her redemption would indeed continue. Even if she had to beg for it. And even if being with Luke meant long-distance love.

"She's the most stubborn woman I've ever met. And that includes me." Ina shook her head as she picked up a card from the deck sitting between her and Luke on the table.

"I can't argue with that." Luke studied the cards in his hand. Cora had left him reeling when she'd barely made eye contact with him before leaving for the grocery store over an hour ago. "I still don't understand how she got the idea I'm leaving Laurel Cove. Did she say anything to you?"

Luke took the card facing up then discarded a jack of spades. Ina immediately picked up the card and added it to her hand. "Well, the last thing I remember talking about before the dinner was your new assignment."

A furrow creased Luke's brow. "The online feature? That's not really an assignment, but what about it?"

"I simply told her you'd heard from your editor in New York and it sounded like everything was going to work out or something."

Luke's pulse quickened. He laid his hand of cards facedown on the kitchen table and studied Ina. "But you told her that it was an online article that's just going to use one of the calendar photos, right?"

She shrugged her dainty shoulders. "I'm not really sure we got that far. It's your turn."

Luke noticed her cards shake in her hand. She steadied them with her other hand but winced. "Are you okay?"

"Yes, I'm fine. Let's just play."

He rubbed a hand over his coarse cheek and leaned back in the chair, thinking over this new information. It was insane. Cora thought he was leaving based on one incomplete, although not entirely false, conversation. Ina had meant no harm, but the turmoil caused by a few left out details was dizzying. Just as quickly as this new information spun him for a loop, his head cleared. This also meant there was a simple explanation and maybe, just maybe, he and Cora stood a chance.

Luke leaned and pulled his phone out of his jeans pocket. This couldn't wait. He needed to at least make the first move.

"Hey, it's still your move," Ina protested, but set her cards down and rubbed up her arm.

"I just need a minute." He worked his thumbs across the screen.

LUKE: CAN YOU SPARE SOME TIME TO TALK BEFORE I LEAVE WHEN YOU GET BACK? THANKS.

CORA: ABSOLUTELY.

Her response came before he'd even set his phone back down on the table. Hope radiated from his toes to the top of his head.

"You look like the cat who caught the canary." Ina chuckled then pushed her glasses up on her small nose and stared at him, sober-faced, through the bottom of her lenses. "It's your turn. Play or forfeit."

"Oh, I'm playing." Luke picked up his hand then the queen of hearts she'd discarded. Then he fanned out his hand in front of her before sitting back with arms crossed over his chest. "I believe that is rummy."

Ina leaned over and studied the display of matching cards. "Well, I declare. It finally happened. Lucas Bassett, famous Pulitzer Prize winner, beat Ina McLean at rummy."

"Now, there's a headline." Luke shook with laughter.

Luke looked past Ina, who worked to gather the deck, through the living room and to the front door. He imagined Cora walking through, groceries in tow. A smile tugged. For all the things he'd prayed for just yesterday, God was already delivering hope in spades.

"I'm sorry we didn't quite have it ready earlier. It's been a zoo today."

"Oh, that's okay. I had some other errands to keep me busy. Thanks, Kathy." Cora set her wallet down on the counter as the pharmacist turned to retrieve Ina's prescriptions. Truth was, after getting Luke's text about needing to talk, she was anxious to get back.

A stack of calendars in a box on the other side of the register caught her eye. She picked one up and ran a finger along the title. It was printed in white block letters over a photo of the town square decorated with pumpkins and planters filled with colorful mums: "Laurel Cove in Pictures." Below that it read, "Photographs by World-Renowned Pulitzer Prize-Winning Photographer Luke Bassett." Pride welled up inside her. Even if he wasn't staying, at least he'd made a difference in not just her life but the town as well.

"Here you go." Kathy returned to the counter and placed two small white paper bags on the counter.

"Thanks. I'll take this too." She slid the calendar over toward the register.

Back in her car, she stole an extra minute to flip through the calendar. With it so cold outside, the groceries in the back would be fine. January's photo was a stunning shot of a leafless tree silhouetted in front of a purple evening sky with the outline of the town hall in the background. A few more flips and she awed at a cheerful photograph of farmers gathered at Brewed's counter for lunch. With each month, Luke's passion and talent was on display for her to marvel at.

When she turned the page to October, however, her breath caught. It was the lake. Their lake. There was no mistaking the rise and fall of the mountain range she'd traversed during countless panic attacks. The calm water mirrored autumn's most brilliant moment.

After studying the photo long and hard, Cora flipped through the last pages before turning it over in her hands. Below several logos of local businesses, a professional headshot of Luke's smiling face stared back at her from the back cover. She scanned the short bio to the right of his picture. Her heart thundered as she read the final line.

Mr. Bassett now resides full time in Laurel Cove.

After reading it over multiple times, Cora flung the calendar onto the seat next to her. By the time she pulled out of the parking spot and turned left onto the highway at the end of Main Street, her thundering heart was replaced with a skin-tingling excitement. There must have been a terrible misunderstanding. He wasn't leaving. In fact, it looked as though Luke was very much here for good. She couldn't get to him fast enough.

"Oh, come on. Even I knew that one." Ina scrunched her nose at a trivia show contestant who'd just been disqualified by an offensive buzzer.

Luke chuckled, set aside the book he'd been pretending to read, and stood from the couch. He couldn't sit still with the energy bouncing around inside him. The floorboards creaked in front of the window as he paced, watching for Cora's car.

The familiar vibrating of an incoming phone call jostled in his pocket. He came to a stop in the middle of the window when a local number he didn't recognize showed on the glowing screen. "Hello?"

"Luke?"

"Yes, this is Luke."

"This is Laura Bradford."

He went stiff as a board, defenses instantly on alert. What in the world did she, of all people, want? "What can I do for you?"

"You don't owe me this, but I hope you'll give me a moment of your time."

Frankly, he wanted to put Laura and the whole awful evening behind him for good. With no sign of Cora's car outside, he drew in a deep breath and remembered his prayer to bear all things. "Yes, of course."

"My behavior at the dinner for Christopher was abhorrent. I did indeed invite you to our home, though I never entertained the notion that Cora would actually bring you. I was unfairly testing her devotion to our son." A soft but long sigh followed a brief moment of silence. "But you took the brunt of my anger of having to live life without Christopher. Just when I think it's getting easier, the grief rears its ugly head. I lost myself. I hope you'll forgive my actions."

Luke wasn't sure what had prompted the change of heart in Laura, but he had no desire to waste energy on holding a grudge. *God, help me show her grace.* "Thank you, Mrs. Bradford. I forgive you. And I'm sorry for your loss."

"Oh, thank you, Luke. I can't tell you how much this means to me. And to Harry. I do hope you won't hold this against him. He seems to really like you."

Respect for the man tugged at Luke's heart. What an interesting and unexpected blessing to have Christopher's father in his life. "I like him, too. Listen, I do appreciate your call, but I hope you'll also reach out to Cora. I'm sure she was very hurt that night, too."

A short laugh flitted through the phone. "You two are peas in a pod, watching out for one another. She said the same thing about me calling you when I ran into her outside the grocery store earlier."

A commotion behind Luke whipped him around. Ina lay slumped on the floor in front of her armchair, the side table turned over next to her. "Laura, I've got to go."

In just a few steps Luke was by Ina's side. Her face was ashen, beads of sweat pearling across her forehead. Luke patted her face. "Ina! Ina, can you hear me?"

No response. Panic welled up in Luke as he sat back on his heels and dialed 911. After relaying the situation and giving Cora's address, he laid the phone face up on the floor and listened as the dispatcher talked him through administering CPR.

Lord, save her.

The prayer came as repetitively as the compressions Luke managed to the rhythm of the woman's voice counting through the phone. What felt like an eternity later, a hand rested on Luke's shoulder, and a man in a dark-blue uniform took his place. Another man set a large red bag on top of the coffee table and began retrieving instruments, sending Luke's phone tumbling to the floor.

He ended the call with the dispatcher and wobbled to his feet. Cold air prickled his damp forehead and neck as he stepped through the open front door onto the porch. Without pausing, he broke into a sprint to the end of Cora's driveway. He wanted to be the first thing she saw before turning down the driveway and finding the startling lights of the ambulance.

His labored breath and the electricity of adrenaline pulled his hands to his hips. He bent at the waist, focusing on filling his lungs. When he straightened, he spotted Cora's car coming down the narrow lake road. He trotted toward her and put a palm up as the car slowed, her quizzical expression coming into view.

A lump swelled in Luke's throat. This wasn't going to be easy. *Lord, equip me to endure another hard thing with Cora. Save Ina and give us all strength for whatever comes.*

CHAPTER Twenty-Six

Nothing could have prepared Cora for the scene before her. Luke's somber expression. An ambulance rumbling in her driveway, the red lights causing dread to rise inside her with every flash. Those lights, they entranced her. Luring her back in time.

Cora jumped at Luke's touch against her arm.

"They're ready to pull out." He reached for her elbow and gently turned her toward his truck. "I'll drive us. Do you need to get anything else from inside?"

"No. I carry it all with me." Cora patted the side of her purse. She climbed into Luke's truck, and it was as though time stilled. The familiar sound of the gravel crunching under rotating tires faded into white noise.

Cora wasn't sure how much time had passed when her eyes focused on the shadow of one of the paramedics through the back window of the ambulance. They followed behind, just like before, on the two-lane highway to town.

Forcing herself to pull her thoughts away from the worst-case scenario happening beyond those doors, Cora turned to Luke. "You said it just came out of the blue?"

She watched his jaw flex and unflex repeatedly. "I did notice her trembling more than usual when we played cards earlier. And she rubbed at her arm as though it bothered her. But I didn't think much of it. I should have."

"There's no way you could have known." Cora placed a hand on his arm.

His concerned eyes found her. "I was so scared, Cora."

Emotion threatened to overcome her, tightening her chest and pricking the back of her throat. But truth was, relief was there, too. "Is it awful that I'm grateful it was you and not me?"

Luke's thin smile brightened his eyes enough to stir Cora. "No, it's not awful. I had the same thought. I'm glad they were loading her into the ambulance by the time you got out of your car. It's a blessing you didn't have to see her inside the house if..."

His voice trailed off, but Cora's mind finished the same thought she'd already had. A rush of tingles covered Cora's body. She willed a deep breath to calm her. "Well, we're not going to think about that. We're going to pray God heals her and we can bring her back home soon."

"That's right."

"This is like déjà vu." Cora forced a laugh as Luke steered the truck into the hospital's parking lot at the same time as the ambulance pulled up to the emergency entrance.

"Yeah, and not the good kind."

Before Cora knew it, Luke had stepped out and trotted around the front of the truck to open her door. His hand slid naturally into hers as they headed for the automatic sliding doors. After checking in at the front desk, they took seats in the same waiting room they'd occupied just weeks before.

She watched Luke keep his eyes glued to the doors where nurses periodically stepped out to give families news of their loved ones. Even in this moment of distress, she was taken by how handsome he was. But his strong jaw was no match for his loyalty. His soft, caramel-colored eyes no match for his kind heart.

"I'm so glad you're here."

"Me too." He shifted in his chair to face her and took her hand. "Cora, I wanted to talk today because I realized why you thought I was leaving. Ina told me that she—"

"I know, Luke." Cora held her hand up. "I also know that you're not leaving."

"You do?" The surprise on his face surpassed the concern for a moment.

Cora spotted a box of Laurel Cove calendars just like the one at the pharmacy, sitting on a table between rows of waiting room chairs. She grabbed one and handed it to Luke, the back cover facing up, as she retook her seat.

With a finger on his bio, she let him read. "Call it my author deductive reasoning, but you can't very well be planning to leave if you've declared residency here."

His eyes brimmed with hope and expectancy. "How could I leave?"

There was no better feeling than being the one Luke looked at that way. Still, regret pinched at her. "Luke, I really am sorry I didn't stick up for you right away at the Bradfords'. There's no excuse. How can I make it up to you?"

A heat rose quickly to her cheeks when Luke cocked his head and arched his eyebrows. But when he stroked a thumb across the back of her hand, she thought she'd come undone.

"Ms. Bradford?" A red-headed nurse stepped into the waiting area. "The doctor would like to see you both now."

As they followed the nurse through the double doors next to the check-in desk, Cora held tightly to Luke's hand. She would never *not* hate hospitals. But if she had to be in one, Luke was the one she wanted with her. Always and forever.

"Mrs. McLean suffered a stroke."

Luke sighed, Dr. Howard's words slamming like a heavy door. At least it was the same doctor who had cared for Ina several weeks ago.

Cora lowered her hand from in front of her mouth. "How bad was it? Is she ok?"

The doctor studied Ina's chart in his hands, lips pressing together tightly. Luke's heart raced. It wasn't a good sign.

Dr. Howard let out an audible sigh and removed his glasses. "It's hard to say. Right now, she's heavily sedated, so we'll have to wait and see. I don't want to give you false hope. At Mrs. McLean's advanced age, the chances are not good that she'll recover."

Luke wrapped an arm around Cora's shoulder. She turned into him, tears already falling. "Thank you, doctor. What can we do now?"

"She's stable. You can go in and sit with her if you'd like. The next few hours are critical. We'll keep a close eye on her."

Dr. Howard patted Luke's shoulder then tucked Ina's chart under his arm and headed down the hall. Luke pulled Cora into a tight hug. As if knowing Ina's condition weren't hard enough, Luke's heart broke for Cora's worry and sadness.

"Do you want to go in?" he asked softly.

She stepped away and wiped at her tear-stained face. "Yeah."

Luke pushed through the heavy door, and they both stepped into the dark room. It wasn't like last time. Ina's feisty Southern voice didn't greet them. There were no stubborn protests about going home. Instead, Ina had never looked smaller or more frail lying in the reclined bed. Tubes ran from her arms to bags of medicine hanging from poles by the bedside. Machines blinked and beeped with various vital signs.

Cora gingerly picked up one of Ina's hands and stroked it. "Oh, Ina."

Luke stood at Cora's side. There were no words to soothe or fix. He bit against his quivering lip, thinking back to the frantic moments before the paramedics arrived. He could understand the helplessness Cora must have felt at the accident with Christopher. Wanting to do more but having no real control.

After several minutes without speaking, Luke and Cora settled into the chairs against the wall at the end of the bed. Maybe they couldn't do anything, but they could simply be there for Ina. It was something.

"You know," Cora whispered, voice strained, "Ina became my family when I had none."

Luke swallowed hard. "I know she did."

He took the hand Cora held out to him. She squeezed tightly. "But so did you, Luke."

Luke blinked back tears that suddenly threatened to fall. He inhaled sharply and looked back to Ina, his chuckle filling the room. "That's pretty much her fault. Not all of her advice was solid. Like not kissing you." He rolled his eyes at Cora, who managed a giggle. "And she might have single-handedly created the chaos about you thinking I was leaving."

Cora wrinkled her nose and twisted her mouth. "Uh, yeah, I guess so."

"But," Luke continued, studying Cora's slender fingers intertwined with his, "she also taught me what love really looks like. That it's messy and imperfect and worth fighting for. I'll be grateful for that as long as I live."

Cora's features softened, head tilting toward him. Her blue eyes and full lips reflected his whole life from inside the dimly lit room. Her forehead was warm against Luke's mouth as he pressed a kiss against it. She nestled against his shoulder, and they both watched Ina for a long moment.

After a while, Cora's chest rose and fell with even breaths. Luke glanced down and found her eyes closed. Just as he leaned his head back against the wall, a high-pitched alarm sounded from the machine next to Ina's bed. Cora startled awake and they were both on their feet in a heartbeat. In another moment, the room filled with several nurses followed by Dr. Howard.

All the air left Luke as he and Cora were ushered out of the room. He took her hand and led her to the window at the end of the sterile hallway. "I'm no good at this, but I think we should pray."

She nodded shortly, wiping at fresh tears.

He took both of Cora's hands in his and closed his eyes. In this moment, he was certain God didn't care for the right words, so he trusted whatever came to his mind.

"God, we need you. Please be with Ina. Be with the doctor and nurses." He swallowed past a lump as his voice cracked. In the moment, a mix of sadness and peace flooded over him. "God, if this is Ina's time to be with you and with Charles, take her quickly. Give us the peace and faith to know you are in control. If these are Ina's last moments, we thank you for our grief, because it means she was a blessing to us."

Dr. Howard stepped from the doorway of Ina's room, now quiet. His face was somber as he approached them.

And Luke knew. His prayer had been answered. God had taken Ina swiftly and peacefully into his arms. A single tear fell down Luke's cheek as Cora folded into his arms, soft cries shuddering against his chest.

In the sacred, holy moment, Luke grieved again for his mother and the time lost. He grieved with Cora and Harry and Laura for Christopher. He grieved for Ina, who'd become his family too.

But in the midst of his sadness, he was indeed blessed. Blessed by knowing people who were worth grieving. And blessed beyond measure by the woman he held in his arms. Suddenly, his forever was wrapped up in her and in the promise of love's fighting chance.

Chapter Twenty-Seven

The funny thing about ships sitting at the bottom of the ocean was that they straddled existence and non-existence. Wreckage lay dormant, the almost undetectable movement of the dark water like the subtle breath of a sleeping giant. A shadowed, ghostly apparition of life that once was. There was a peace in the silent grave that wouldn't stop existing just because it was often forgotten.

Far up on the surface, waves ebbed and flowed with the rhythm of life. Sometimes, when the waves gently rolled, one was left to contemplate the ghosts resting below and the lives they'd lived. Other times, winds rushed violently and stirred up storms that pulled attention away from anything other than survival.

And sometimes, in order to survive, one had to let the current lead them away from where the wreckage lay below. To calmer water. To where friendly winds blew. To solid ground. Where living could continue beyond survival and thrive.

The glorious ship the wreckage once was became the thing of legends. It was remembered and celebrated in its prime. Its tattered sails, broken masts, and cracked hulls were restored. With each memory remembered and told, it rose to the surface, whole again. Forever a part of those still living.

Cora opened her eyes as Luke's truck rolled to a stop, the sensation of floating along calm waters having soothed her on the short ride through the cemetery. She squinted, thankful for the cheery sun after two weeks of heavy snow. As hard as the day was, gloomy weather would have made saying her final goodbyes to Ina even more difficult. The funeral may have been delayed due to the severe weather, but God had gifted them this perfect sunny day to honor their friend.

"Which way?" Luke asked.

"Left, then the first right at the top of the hill."

He had been so wonderful since Ina had passed away. They'd shared in their grief for her. It unexpectedly comforted Cora and helped her realize that grieving alone all those years hadn't done her any good. Luke had checked in on her, helped make arrangements, and even continued praying with her. Not just for Ina but for their budding relationship. Even amidst a new grief, she hadn't felt this hopeful in a long time.

In fact, despite the fresh hurt, Cora had managed to finish writing her novel—maybe her favorite to date—in record time. Fully inspired, she'd written furiously day and night. Just that morning, she'd turned in the first draft to her editor well ahead of schedule.

"Right here. This is good." Cora was surprised by the smile that crept across her face as the truck eased to another slow stop a few moments later.

Hand in hand, the frosty ground crackling beneath their feet, Cora and Luke made their way to a spot under a large arching oak. Its leafless branches invited the bright sun onto the white marble headstones in front of them.

It was time to formally introduce her new love to her first loves.

"This is Christopher." Cora waved her hand toward the white headstone marked with his name. Luke's heart soared when her bright blue eyes sparkled up at him in the sun. "And this, Christopher, is Luke."

Her gloved hand squeezed around his. Luke stood taller, full of both pride and reverence.

"And this..." Cora spoke softly and motioned to the matching headstone next to Christopher's. "This is Everly Faith."

Luke's breath stole from his lungs as he read the epitaph to himself.

EVERLY FAITH BRADFORD
Born into the arms of Jesus
November 14...

His eyes fell shut before he could finish. He didn't need to read the year; his heart knew. Suddenly, Luke understood the full weight of Cora's grief. She'd not only lost a husband that day, she'd lost a child. He had so many questions, but could only manage to gaze at her—the tears that choked him preventing any words.

She dabbed at the corner of both eyes with Ina's handkerchief she'd carried to the intimate funeral. "I was just over three months along. We hadn't even told anyone. Christopher had wanted to sit with it, just the two of us, for a while longer. The accident sent me into early labor, and she couldn't be saved."

Luke swallowed hard. "I'm so sorry, Cora."

It was unfathomable that she'd suffered this immense loss for so long—alone.

Her eyes fell to her hands, which twisted the white linen handkerchief. "There's more. I also can't have any more children. I know that might change things for you."

When Cora's shoulders began to shake with soft cries, Luke wrapped his arms around her. Knowing the terrible amount of loss the accident had caused set off an avalanche of gratefulness for her recovery.

At the same time, an unexpected and strange joy surged. If she worried what he'd think about her inability to bear children, it meant that in her future, he was there.

He looked down and tilted her chin upward until her brilliant eyes met his. His thumb brushed away a tear before he leaned down and pressed his lips to hers. "You, and you alone, are enough for me. Now and forever."

"I love you, Luke."

With those simple words, Luke came alive for the first time in places he hadn't known were dormant. He breathed out. "I love you, too."

Her chest heaved as he embraced her tightly and kissed her deeply. Forever, the people Cora had loved and lost would be woven into the tapestry of their life together. She'd take them with her along the way, and he'd be all the luckier for it. Though, what more luck did he need than being loved by Cora Braford?

By the time the kayak slid up onto the smooth pebbles of the small island's shore, Cora could barely feel the tips of her fingers. With two feet on the ground, she jumped up and down to get her blood flowing while Luke tied a line from the kayak to a nearby tree.

"How did I let you talk me into this?" She swatted his arm as they turned and headed for the opening in the woods to the trail.

"Oh, come on. You said yourself you needed to get out after last week's snow."

"I didn't mean get out *in* it, exactly." He was lucky he looked so cute in his hiking boots, utility jacket, and moleskin hat with fur lined earflaps. If she didn't know any better, she'd say he was a local through and through.

They'd been inseparable since Ina's funeral. Luke brought Toby to her place and cooked dinner every night. She'd taken him to the Laurel Cove Christmas Festival. And he'd helped her decorate her Christmas tree last night, just in time for Christmas Eve. It was the first one she'd put up since the accident.

"You know," Cora said, taking Luke's hand to steady herself over a few craggy tree roots over the steep trail, "I don't even want anything for Christmas. I've already got everything I want."

"Is that so?" Luke chuckled as they came to the clearing at the top of the island. Snow covered the grass in a smooth white blanket.

At the stack of rocks, Cora dusted the snow off the top and rested her hand against Ina and Charles's initials. "I sure miss her."

"Me, too." Luke stepped up beside her and handed her a large smooth gray stone. "I actually wanted to bring you out here for a reason. I think it's time you and I start our own stack."

Cora nestled the heavy rock in the crook of her arm and studied the letters etched into it.

CB + EFB + EB + IM
Never Forgotten

Christopher Bradford. Everly Faith Bradford. Ellie Bassett. Ina McLean. All of the people they loved most were there. She cut her quickly filling eyes to Luke. "I can't believe you did this."

"It only seems fitting that our life together starts with their memories." He took the rock from her and laid it on the ground next to Ina and Charles's tall stack. "And what about me? Can I ask for something for Christmas?"

The way his eyes twinkled quickened Cora's pulse. "Uh, sure."

He pulled another large smooth rock, this one a light brown, from his bag and handed it to her. "Why don't you put this one down."

Cora carefully knelt and placed the rock on top of the first one. She ran her fingers over the markings as she read them aloud. "LB + CB, Engaged December 24..."

Cora's voice trailed off as her heart skipped a beat and she pushed to her feet swiftly. A gasp escaped when she turned and found Luke down on one knee. In his hand, he held out a gorgeous vintage diamond ring that sparkled in the sunlight.

"I am not a man without regrets. If you'll let me, though, I'll spend the rest of my life being a husband with no regrets. Somehow, I think I loved you the day you yelled at me on your porch in your pajamas."

Cora laughed through tears.

Luke's upturned mouth twitched, and he wiped a tear that had begun to fall down his cheek. "Every day since, I've loved you more and more. Ina helped me see it. Maybe it's why she gave me this ring. It's the same one Charles gave to her right here at this spot the day they made a lifelong commitment to each other. I can't promise you a life together will always be easy. But I can promise you it will be enough. *You* will always be enough."

He covered his mouth with a fist and looked away. Cora's heart swelled at his emotion. She put a hand on her hip. "So, what exactly is it you want for Christmas?"

Luke's sweet caramel eyes beamed at her. "Cora Bradford, will you be my wife?"

"Yes, Luke Bassett, I will." With that, she threw her arms around his neck and kissed him.

How did she get so lucky to be loved so well by not one but two amazing men? God's timing *was* perfect, even for complete healing. She'd give anything to have not lost

Christopher, but there was sweet blessing and redemption in her new forever love.

"I can't believe how well the ring fits," Luke said as he shoved a few handfuls of newspaper under the logs he'd just stacked in Cora's fireplace.

A slight chill covered her after their ride back across the lake, but nothing but warmth radiated from her full heart. Cora held her hand out in front of her and admired the ring. It felt like one last gift from Ina, and a part of her Cora could carry with her forever.

Luke sat back from the fireplace, mouth pulled to one side. "The fire isn't catching great. Do you have any more newspaper?"

She looked around the cabin, not sure where any more would be. Then she remembered a bundle of old newspapers in the coat closet she kept for just this reason. "I think I've got some, yeah."

At the coat closet off the living room, Cora pulled the string and the dark space glowed. She knelt and pushed a few things around, accidentally jostling the box of recovered items from the accident. It toppled to the side, its lid coming lose. With a sigh, Cora leaned in farther to retrieve something that clanked against the floor and rolled to the back. As soon as her fingers wrapped around the smooth, cool glass, she knew exactly what it was.

She stood and stared at the familiar label, a huge grin spreading across her face.

RACHEL: NICE PHOTO. SHE LOOKS LOVELY. AND YOU LOOK HAPPY.

LUKE: I REALLY AM.

RACHEL: ME MARRIED AND YOU ENGAGED. WHO WOULD HAVE GUESSED?

LUKE: I KNOW. MOM WOULDN'T BELIEVE IT.

RACHEL: I WISH SHE WAS HERE.

LUKE: ME, TOO. GOT TO RUN. CALL YOU SOON.

Luke smiled at his sister's reaction to his news. Maybe she and Harley would make the trip to Laurel Cove for his and Cora's wedding. *Man, how things change.* He slid his phone into his back pocket as Cora returned from across the room.

"Here you go."

"Great, this should do it." Luke took the small stack of paper from Cora and quirked his mouth up at her. "What's that funny look for?"

"Oh, nothing." She shrugged her shoulders, but the smirk on her face said otherwise.

He stood, hearty flames now engulfing the logs, and joined her on the couch. She avoided eye contact with him, but the smirk remained. "No, what gives? Something's up."

"Oh, I just found the perfect Christmas gift for you."

Luke laughed and eyed her cautiously. "Just now? In the closet?"

"Yep."

"Well, you can't tease me. Give it to me now." He poked her side, inciting a fit of giggles.

"Okay, okay! You're as bad as a child." She scooted away and shifted to face him on the couch. Her hand reached behind her, but she paused, holding something behind her back. "Before I give this to you, I want to say something serious."

"All right." Her full lips enticed him with a tender smile.

"I didn't realize until just now that I still had this. It's from the day of the accident."

Luke's face fell, the seriousness of the moment suddenly very palpable. His instinct told him he'd want to remember whatever was about to happen.

She studied him a long moment before continuing. "And really, it's not from me. I think it's more from Christopher. I know he'd want you to have it."

Luke watched as Cora took from behind her back a small glass jar. Immediately, excitement and awe swirled inside him. He knew that jar. It was the strawberry jalapeno jelly he'd been searching for since he arrived in Laurel Cove. "How did you know? Where did you get that?"

"This was Christopher's favorite too."

Bewilderment took over Luke, swirling inside him like a blustery winter snow. "What? You're kidding."

"No. In fact, the day of the accident, we were running late heading home because he insisted on driving out to the one farmer's stand that still carried it. He'd heard the family who made it was going out of business, and he wanted to stock up."

Luke read over the simple label for Three Stars Farm. It looked exactly how he remembered it, with a simple black silhouette of three stars arched above the words. "This is incredible."

"That's why you couldn't find it. And when I realized you were looking for the exact same one, I guess I wasn't ready to tell you about the amazing coincidence." Cora scooted close enough to him that their knees touched. "But now, it just makes me happy. Like you were meant to be here all along, part of some amazing story God created just for us. Way better than any best-selling story I could ever write."

"Thank you so much."

Luke's hand rubbed along her soft cheek and found the back of her neck. He leaned in and let their lips come together in a tender kiss.

He still had so much to learn about love. But if what Jack said was true, about true love giving folks a fighting chance, he didn't have anything to worry about. In his heart, Luke was certain. They'd already won.

ACKNOWLEDGEMENTS

First and foremost, I have to give praise and glory to God for his faithfulness. For a few years, I wasn't sure when I would write again. Life happened and other priorities shifted to the front, leaving me little time to write. But God...

God placed this story on my heart in a way that made me anxious to tell it. It poured out of me—fast. In a blink of an eye, these characters came to life in such a vivid way that I've never experienced. I *felt* their grief. There's no doubt in my mind God will use this story to touch the lives of those hurting from loss. That will be my prayer. I'm so humbled and grateful to be a vessel for the important message of hope and love's healing hand.

Eric, my husband and best friend, your enthusiasm for this story makes me both laugh and shake my head in disbelief. I can't tell you how truly fun it was to go off on brainstorm tangents with you. Your ideas are all over these pages. It's been a joy working with you in this little corner of my world. Thank you for your unfailing support.

Emma, my sweet girl, you won't ever know how much I appreciate the countless cups of coffee you brought me while writing. I also want you to know I see a unique creativity in you that I'm sure God has big plans for. You're amazing.

Finally, to my critique partners, Toni and Jen, thank you for your hours of attention to this story. Your ideas and feedback not only helped polish the book but also taught me so much about writing and storytelling.

ABOUT THE AUTHOR

TERESA TYSINGER is an author of charming Southern contemporary romance inspired by grace. She writes on the fringes of being a wife, mom, and full-time communications and public relations professional. Teresa is a proud member of American Christian Fiction Writers, the Association for Women in Communications, as well as the Religion Communicators Council. She loves coffee, traveling, and cries at just about anything. After living a decade in North Carolina, Teresa now resides in Texas with her husband, daughter, and dog.

CONNECT WITH TERESA

www.TeresaTysinger.com
www.facebook.com/teresatysingerauthor
www.twitter.com/teresa_tysinger
www.instagram.com/teresatysinger_author
www.pinterest.com/teresatysinger

ALSO IN THE LAUREL COVE ROMANCE SERIES

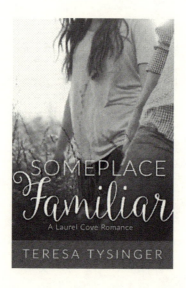

Can Livy and Jack survive the destructive pain of their pasts and ultimately discover God's grace waiting to renovate their hearts?

Available in Paperback
and eBook on Amazon

What people are saying about *Someplace Familiar*

"Teresa Tysinger's debut novel is a smashing hit from page one. This is a well-written, heart wrenching and gut pulling story that readers will absolutely love, leaving them lingering on thoughts of hardships and love."
Sydney, *Singing Librarian Books*

"Bottom Line: The setting is gorgeous and vivid, quaint and quirky. The characters are fun and relatable, the kind of people you'd want to be friends with. The romance is smokin' hot (honestly, keep a freezer handy) but laced with mutual respect for each other and for God's guardrails."
Carrie, *Reading Is My Superpower*

"A stunning debut! It isn't often an author can pull off a novel of such depth and beauty (and some fun flirtations!), but Teresa Tysinger has done it."
Mikal Dawn, author of *Emerald City Romance Series*

COMING SOON FROM TERESA TYSINGER

OCTOBER 20, 2020:
*Somehow, This Christmas:
A Laurel Cove Novella*
in the *Something Borrowed:
Christmas Weddings Collection*

2021:
The two final stories in the
Laurel Cove Romance Series!

GET A *FREE* ROMANCE COLLECTION!

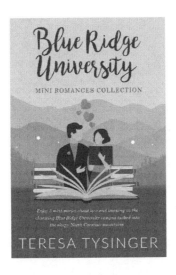

The *Blue Ridge University Mini Romance Collection* includes three mini stories (each about the length of a book chapter) set on the beautiful campus of the fictional Blue Ridge University tucked into the charming mountains of North Carolina.

As my gift to you, it's yours for FREE when you sign up for my newsletter, which I call *The Little Blue Cottage*. You not only sign up for news about my books, chats with other Christian authors, and giveaway announcements, you also join a community of readers and writers just like you!

Get your FREE copy of the *Blue Ridge University Mini Romance Collection* by subscribing at TeresaTysinger.com/home/newsletter/

Made in the USA
Columbia, SC
18 November 2020